Stained Glass . . .

He lay on his back, surrounded by a pool of what had to be blood. At the moment, it was no more than a tarry stain. A lone fly buzzed around him. My knees went weak, and I sank to the floor. I didn't need to go any closer, because there was no doubt in my mind that he was dead. That gray color didn't belong to a living person. Besides, the cause of death was obvious: a large shard of glass protruding from his chest.

This was my second . . . no, third dead body. How was it that I had made it through more than forty years without even a hint of violence in my life, and now within the space of a couple of months I had encountered three corpses? What had I done to deserve this?

Berkley Prime Crime titles by Sarah Atwell

THROUGH A GLASS, DEADLY
PANE OF DEATH

Pane of Death

Sarah Atwell

BERKLEY PRIME CRIME, NEW YORK

THE BERKLEY PUBLISHING GROUP
Published by the Penguin Group
Penguin Group (USA) Inc.
375 Hudson Street, New York, New York 10014, USA
Penguin Group (Canada), 90 Eglinton Avenue East, Suite 700, Toronto, Ontario M4P 2Y3, Canada
(a division of Pearson Penguin Canada Inc.)
Penguin Books Ltd., 80 Strand, London WC2R 0RL, England
Penguin Group Ireland, 25 St. Stephen's Green, Dublin 2, Ireland (a division of Penguin Books Ltd.)
Penguin Group (Australia), 250 Camberwell Road, Camberwell, Victoria 3124, Australia
(a division of Pearson Australia Group Pty. Ltd.)
Penguin Books India Pvt. Ltd., 11 Community Centre, Panchsheel Park, New Delhi—110 017, India
Penguin Group (NZ), 67 Apollo Drive, Rosedale, North Shore 0632, New Zealand
(a division of Pearson New Zealand Ltd.)
Penguin Books (South Africa) (Pty.) Ltd., 24 Sturdee Avenue, Rosebank, Johannesburg 2196,
South Africa

Penguin Books Ltd., Registered Offices: 80 Strand, London WC2R 0RL, England

This is a work of fiction. Names, characters, places, and incidents either are the product of the author's imagination or are used fictitiously, and any resemblance to actual persons, living or dead, business establishments, events, or locales is entirely coincidental. The publisher does not have any control over and does not assume any responsibility for author or third-party websites or their content.

PUBLISHER'S NOTE: The recipes contained in this book are to be followed exactly as written. The publisher is not responsible for your specific health or allergy needs that may require medical supervision. The publisher is not responsible for any adverse reactions to the recipes contained in this book.

PANE OF DEATH

A Berkley Prime Crime Book / published by arrangement with the author

PRINTING HISTORY
Berkley Prime Crime mass-market edition / November 2008

Copyright © 2008 by Penguin Group (USA) Inc.
Interior text design by Kristin del Rosario.

ISBN: 978-0-425-22501-1

BERKLEY® PRIME CRIME
Berkley Prime Crime Books are published by The Berkley Publishing Group,
a division of Penguin Group (USA) Inc.,
375 Hudson Street, New York, New York 10014.
BERKLEY PRIME CRIME and the BERKLEY PRIME CRIME design
are trademarks of Penguin Group (USA) Inc.

PRINTED IN THE UNITED STATES OF AMERICA

10 9 8 7 6 5 4 3 2 1

Acknowledgments

Nobile claret opus, sed opus quod nobile claret
Clarificet mentes, ut eant per lumina vera
Ad verum lumen . . .

—Abbot Suger of Saint-Denis,
De Administratione

Writing this book was a real treat for me, because I could revisit my days as a medieval art historian and talk about stained glass. In fact, I named a character after the college professor who first introduced me to the glories of medieval glass, although I doubt he ever thought I'd use what I learned from him in this particular way.

Many thanks to my agent, Jacky Sach, who made this possible, and to my editor, Shannon Jamieson Vazquez, who always manages to ask the right questions to make the book better. All writers should be so lucky.

Once again I have to thank Elise Stone, who helped me to scout appropriate houses in Tucson, and her merry band of local assistants who answer all my dumb questions about Arizona (and if I have moved any mountains around, that's my fault, not theirs). Thanks also to Lorraine Bartlett and my blog buddies on Writers Plot; to Carol Kersbergen, who I swear is promoting my books to all of Philadelphia; and to the ever-supportive Sisters in Crime (including the Guppies).

And I can't forget to mention those fans who wrote and asked, what's going to happen next?

Chapter 1

❀

I surveyed the glass studio with pleasure. Another good day, after a whole string of them. My pieces were all cooperating, and I had a good supply on hand to stock my shop Shards. And those were just the bread-and-butter items, the ones that sold well to the walk-in tourists who wanted an upscale souvenir of Tucson to take home and admire during their cold East Coast winters. But even better, I was happy with the more challenging individual pieces I was trying out—the ones with unknown commercial value but which gave me a great sense of personal achievement. After ten years of blowing glass, I had finally reached a peak of some sort, and I intended to enjoy every minute of it.

I took one last glance at the studio: tools clean and back in their places, glass furnaces shut, glory holes turned off, annealer turned on. I had no classes to teach for a couple of days, and I could look forward to some uninterrupted work time. Life was good. Glassblowing was my second career, and I still felt passionate about it—and lucky to be able to do it full-time. When I'd thrown over a steady (and well-paying) job as a New York stockbroker, there had been plenty of people who told me I was crazy. When I had moved as far away from them as possible, they had written me off. But I was happy with what I had created in Tucson: a successful shop and studio, with ideal living quarters close by. I still loved working with hot glass, and much to my surprise, I had found I liked teaching others to do it as well. And the beginner's classes were fun—people came into them wide-eyed and cautious, and most often emerged proud and eager for more.

Why was it that when things go well, I start worrying? Everything was great: My glassblowing classes were consistently filled; the shop was showing a nice profit; I had a new employee, Allison McBride, helping out my long-term salesperson Nessa Spencer to cover additional hours; I was seeing a lot more of my brother Cameron, since he was courting Allison; and my formerly bleak love life was blossoming nicely, since my ex Matt and I had recently gotten back together, sort of. So what did I have to worry about?

I turned off the lights in the studio and went through the connecting door to the shop, where Nessa was ringing up purchases—quite a few, apparently—for a couple of tourists. As I walked in she caught my eye and nodded toward the front of the shop. I followed her look and saw Madelyn Sheffield holding a large plate up to the light. I suppressed a grimace and headed over to greet her.

Maddy was not one of my favorite people. In a parallel universe we could have been friends, since we had a lot in common: We both worked with glass, we both had shops in Tucson's Warehouse District, we both taught classes. But the long and the short of it was, I couldn't stand the woman. I considered myself a craftsperson; Maddy thought she was an Artist, with a capital A. She worked with flat glass, making pretty stained-glass window ornaments, ersatz Tiffany lamps, and that ilk. Okay, I'm a snob: I think that working with hot glass takes a lot more skill and dedication than cutting out charming little pieces of colored glass and sticking them together. Maybe I was a wee bit jealous, since she sold a lot of pieces—easier for tourists to pack?—but I thought her product was merely pretty, and far from inspired. Looking at her careful manicure, I had to wonder how she managed to make anything at all.

I waited until she had returned the piece she had been examining to the shelf before greeting her. "Hi, Maddy. What brings you to this end of the street?"

Maddy pirouetted gracefully, her filmy clothes swirling. I felt clunky beside her in my sweaty cotton tee and jeans, but swirly wouldn't work with blazing furnaces. Besides, I outweighed her by a good twenty pounds. On me, those fabrics would look like limp rags. But the outfit worked for her, and it bolstered her artsy image. "Oh, Em, there you are! I wanted to speak with you about something important!"

Maddy seemed to speak with whispery exclamation points at all times. I had no idea what she could want. If she was trying to recruit me to work on some arts festival, or if she wanted to display her little pieces in my shop, she'd get a fast "no" from me. No way. But since she was a colleague of sorts and it was a small community, I had to be polite. "Okay," I said cautiously, "what's up?"

Her carefully made-up eyes darted around the shop, and she leaned toward me to say in a conspiratorial whisper, "I don't want to talk about it here. Can we go somewhere? Private?"

This was odd, coming from her. I considered the possibilities. I live over the shop, but I didn't want to bring her into my personal space. Although I indulged myself with a brief image of my two dogs gnawing at her ankles—not that they'd ever do that. Fred, my wirehaired dachshund, and Gloria, my English bulldog, were always polite to strangers. I checked the time—barely five o'clock, so the local eateries wouldn't be too busy yet. I would have suggested Elena's, the restaurant nearby that was a favorite haunt of local artisans after hours, but I'd never seen Maddy there, and I wasn't about to be the one to introduce it to her. I had an awful vision of Maddy pitching a line of adorable stained-glass bar fixtures to Elena, and shuddered. "How about El Saguaro down the street? We should be able to get a booth this time of day."

"All right. But right now!"

Nessa had finished up with the customers, sending them on their way with their wares carefully wrapped. She eyed me expectantly, with a wicked gleam in her eye: She knew how I felt about Maddy. "Nessa, can you cover? I'll be back before six." I hoped.

"Certainly, Em. It's been quiet today. If you're not back by then, I can close up. Oh, Allison said she'd be in late tomorrow—she has to register for one of her second-semester classes, and the professor wanted to talk to her. She should be here by ten."

"Not a problem. I can come down early." Shortly after arriving from Ireland as a teenager for a summer almost two decades ago, Allison had married a smooth-talking guy who turned out to be trouble—and after years of suffering under his oppressive thumb, she'd finally summoned up the courage to leave him and was now taking the opportunity to explore a lot of new things, including classes at the university. She worked part-time in my shop, and Nessa and I helped her juggle her working schedule to accommodate classes. It was a pleasure to watch her bloom.

I turned to Maddy. "Okay, let's go."

As we walked the short blocks to El Saguaro, Maddy prattled on about this and that. Since she had requested this meeting, I wasn't about to work to make conversation. I nodded to a few familiar faces along the way, and checked out shop windows. It was time to shift items in my own display again, and I was looking for ideas. At the restaurant I led the way, plunging into the interior, then waiting a moment until my eyes adjusted to the dark. As I had hoped, it was fairly empty, so I headed for a corner booth and settled in. A young waiter approached quickly. "I'll have a beer—Corona. What about you, Maddy?"

"Oh, just an iced tea would be fine for me. Please." She simpered at the waiter, who blushed. *Why did that work?* I wondered, not for the first time. If I tried it, someone would probably offer me an antacid.

The waiter nodded and quickly reappeared with our drinks, which he deposited on the table with a flourish, earning another smile from Maddy. He went away happy. I turned to face Maddy. "Okay, why all the secrecy? What's this about?"

Maddy took her time adding sugar to her tea, squeezing lemon into it, stirring it. I was getting ready to throw something at her when she finally spoke. "Em, I need your help."

I tried not to let my surprise show. This was certainly unusual—not the request, maybe, but the fact that she'd admitted needing something from me. "Okay, I'm listening."

She sighed. "It's complicated. Well, let me say for a start that I've been offered this absolutely tremendous opportunity—a commission, I guess you'd say—to do something unprecedented and spectacular. It could make my name in artistic circles. I mean, Em, this is big, really big." Her eyes darted around the dark interior, as if looking for eavesdroppers.

I was becoming more and more mystified. I wasn't sure what would be considered "big" in the stained-glass world, and I couldn't for the life of me see where Maddy, with her mediocre talent, might fit into it. "Go on."

She leaned forward, her hands clasped on the table. "Em, can I trust you?"

"Yes." *Cut to the chase already, lady.* "I won't say anything to anyone else, if you don't want me to."

"Good. Thank you. It's like this, you see . . . You've heard of Peter Ferguson?"

I had to stop and think for a moment. "You mean, the software guy?"

"Yes, that's right. What do you know about him?"

Where was she headed with this? "Genius programmer, pretty good entrepreneur." My brother Cam, a software engineer in San Diego, had mentioned Ferguson to me on more than one occasion—and it was tough to miss the profiles that appeared in *Newsweek* and on CNN and most other public sources. "Didn't he just retire?"

"I don't know if 'retire' is the right word. He decided he'd accomplished all he set out to do, so he sold the rights to the programs and shut down. And he's bought a house in Tucson!" She looked at me to see if I was properly impressed.

I wasn't, particularly. There are plenty of rich folk in Tucson, and I rarely if ever crossed paths with them. What did one more matter? "So?"

Another quick look around. A few more people had drifted in, but there was no one sitting near us. "He's remodeling this wonderful house on the east side of the city, near the national park, you know? And he's asked me to help him with part of the design."

Now I really was stumped. Maddy made glass fripperies. What did she know about architectural design? "That's nice," I said noncommittally.

She must have picked up on my skepticism. "No, not

with the actual remodeling. But"—her voice dropped even lower, so that I had to strain to hear her—"he's got this fabulous collection of glass panels, and he wants me to help him showcase them."

Ah, now I could see the light at the end of the tunnel. Interesting—I had never heard Ferguson's name mentioned in connection with glass art, but he certainly had the money to acquire whatever his heart desired, if the news reports of the sale of PrismCo were anywhere near true. Why he had chosen Maddy of all people to help him with setting up a display boggled me, but it was none of my business. Or was it? After all, she had asked me to help her with something. It was about time I found out what that "something" was.

"Maddy, what do you need me for?"

She gave me a calculating glance—trying to figure out which story to give me, or maybe how gullible I was. "Em, let me be frank. What Peter envisions"—I noted the use of his first name—"is a free-flowing space that integrates the stark scenery of the Arizona desert with the lush color of centuries worth of glass. He aims for nothing less than to capture the light of the present and filter it through the 'lights' of the ages." She stopped to gauge the effect of her statement.

I wanted to gag—she sounded like the worst combination of a florid art history text and a Tucson tourism brochure. If Peter talked like this, they were a match made in heaven. And I still didn't see where I fit. "Okay, he wants to install his art panels to take advantage of Arizona light. Got it. Not a bad idea. But what do you need me for?"

A brief flash of pain crossed over Maddy's face. "Em," she said carefully, "this is a really important commission, and I want to be sure I get it right. I could use an outside eye, just now and then. And he's already said he wants glass lighting fixtures to coordinate with his pieces, and I told him I knew just the person to do it."

Ah. The bait. Making pretty lamp shades for the big cheese, while Maddy got all the glory. There must be more to it than that. "I assume he'll pay for this?"

"Of course he will." She mentioned a figure; I swallowed hard. For that amount of money, I might even make glass Mickey Mouses. Mice. Whatever.

But I'd still be stuck working with Miss Maddy, and it would probably eat up a lot of my time—time that might be better spent working on my own pieces. On the other hand, if the publicity was good . . . "There will be some press coverage, I assume?"

Did she look relieved? "Of course. I'm sorry, I thought you would assume that. Your name would definitely be associated with this project, and it will be highly visible, I assure you—in the right circles."

It was tempting, particularly those dollar signs, but I still wasn't convinced. "Maddy, before I sign on for anything, I want to talk to the guy, get his take on what he wants, scope out how much work this would take. I don't know if I want to get involved if it's going to eat up huge chunks of my time." Or if he wanted me to turn out dreck.

She stared into space, as if thinking. It must have been painful, based on her expression. Finally she answered. "I think that could be arranged. Are you free tomorrow?"

Now it was my turn to be surprised. "He's in town now?" I hadn't seen any mention in the press, but then, I didn't have a lot of time to read the papers, much less watch the local news.

Maddy nodded solemnly. "Don't say anything—he's trying to keep a low profile. He comes and goes, since the house isn't quite livable yet, but he wants it finished within a few months. And he's very hands-on. He wants to know what's going into the house, down to the smallest detail."

That could spell trouble, I reflected. If—and it was still

a big if—I agreed to do this, I would insist on artistic control of my own products. No way was I going to turn out crap just to make Peter Ferguson happy, especially if it was going to get any publicity. But I decided to reserve judgment until I had met and talked to the man.

Whoa, Em. How cool is this? A one-on-one with a national figure, one who had more money than God, or at least the Vatican. Something to talk about, whether or not I took the job. Sure, I'd be happy to meet the guy, at least this once.

"I think I can clear my schedule for tomorrow, Maddy. What time?"

"Shall we say morning? Ideally you'll have to see the place at different times of day, so you can see how the light falls, but I want you to have an idea of the space. And talk to Peter, of course. Let me tell you, he has a good eye. Oh, and I should drive. I don't know if you could get in."

I was afraid she would ask me to wear a blindfold next. All this cloak-and-dagger stuff seemed kind of silly to me—we've had celebrities and millionaires in Tucson for quite awhile, and they always kept a low profile.

"One condition, Maddy: I get to tell my brother Cam." When she started to protest, I went on. "He's completely trustworthy. And if he learns that I've met with Peter Ferguson without telling him, there'll be hell to pay, and I've got to live with him the rest of my life. Deal?"

"Deal," Maddy said reluctantly. "But no one else—not your shop people or your customers. Agreed?"

"Agreed." I figured there was no point in telling her about Matt, who just happened to be Tucson's chief of police, if she didn't already know. And since I wasn't even sure I'd be going through with this, I didn't need to fill him in yet.

"Good." She was definitely relieved now. "I'll swing by about ten, all right?" She raised her glass. "To a rewarding collaboration."

Chapter 2

❖

Maddy and I parted ways outside El Saguaro, after she had generously picked up the tab. I walked back slowly, turning over what she had said. Something still didn't feel right. Why would a computer mogul worth millions pick artsy dabbler Madelyn Sheffield to execute an important commission? How had they even crossed paths? I'd have to ask—if I decided to get involved at all.

Still, if I was honest with myself, I was excited about the prospect of meeting someone of Peter Ferguson's reputation, up close and personal. I didn't hang out with a lot of celebrities, so it would be a new experience. That still didn't mean I would agree to Maddy's proposition. I took my work seriously, and I wouldn't compromise it just for the glamor of the gig. After all, what good was terrific publicity if the product was trash?

As I approached my shop I could see that the interior lights were off, so Nessa had closed up and gone home, as she'd said she might. That was fine with me: She knew the business as well as I did, and there was no point wasting time on a slow day. Besides, I was itching to go home and call Cam to fill him in on my prospective brush with computer stardom.

I climbed the exterior staircase to my apartment above the shop. I had purchased the building more than ten years earlier, before the Tucson arts scene had taken off. It had been a risky investment at the time, but now I could pat myself on the back for a brilliant business decision. Right. At the time I had been scared to death, and the decrepit building was the only place I could afford that had both viable work and sales space as well as living space. I had done most of the rehab of the former factory by myself, and I was happy with the results.

As I unlocked my door, my doggie welcoming committee surged forward to greet me: Fred, who took his role as alpha male seriously, and Gloria, who was willing to wait for her share of affection while Fred ran in circles around my ankles. He tried to boss her, she mothered him, and I adored them both.

"Hey, guys, you ready for a walk?" Tails wagged in unison. I grabbed two leads, picked them up, and headed back downstairs. We spent a productive fifteen minutes investigating all the new smells around the trash cans in the alley behind the shop. I dutifully picked up the doggie by-products in plastic bags, deposited them in the trash, and then hoisted the pups one under each arm and carried them up the stairs.

"Food time." More excited dashing in circles. I scooped out some wet food and laid it down. Finally, duty done, I went to the phone to call my brother.

My brother is the dearest person in the world to me. Our parents are both dead, but they had never been warm and fuzzy types, and as a result Cam and I had formed a tight bond. Eight years younger than I, Cam had been a quiet, studious boy, and had suffered the usual slights that nerds seem to attract. I had done all that I could to encourage him in his academic interests, and when, like so many of his species, he had discovered the wonderful world of computers, I had heaved a sigh of relief. He had been moderately successful with the environmental analyses that his California company was renowned for; and he was still unattached, even though he was a sweet and considerate man. At least, *I* thought so, but I have to admit I'm slightly biased. I had just begun to worry about him when he fell head over heels for Allison McBride on short acquaintance. I had no problem with that, since I admired Allison and considered her a friend. But rather than latch on to him, Allison was taking time to find out who she really was, which frustrated my brother no end. I was caught in the middle: I applauded her choice, but I ached for Cam. Still, I held on to the hope that things would work out for them in the long run.

I hit his speed-dial button. He answered on the second ring. "Cameron Dowell."

"Hey, brother of mine—why so formal?"

"Oh, hi, Em—I didn't look at the ID. I was working on a piece of code and I guess my head is in work mode. To what do I owe the honor of this call?"

"Hey, I call you regularly, don't I?" I struggled to remember the last time and gave up. "Anyway, I've got something really neat to tell you. Only you can't tell anyone else."

"Okay. Besides, I talk to about three humans a week, and I don't think they know what a conversation is. What's up?"

"Peter Ferguson is living in Tucson and I'm going to meet him tomorrow."

Cam's silence went on so long I was beginning to wonder if he'd passed out.

"You there?"

"What? Oh, sure. Hey, that's really interesting. The whole cyber community has been wondering what happened to him. After he bailed out of PrismCo he sort of disappeared. So he's in Tucson? For keeps?"

"I think so. Apparently he's building a house, or fixing one up—that's why I'm going over there." Funny, I had expected more enthusiasm from my brother. "You don't sound very excited. Is there something I should know?"

More silence. Then Cam said slowly, "I'm not sure. How much do you know about him?"

"Not much. I know the name, and the name PrismCo. He founded the company, right?"

"Yeah. He was a real pioneer, and he had . . . has a very creative mind. But . . ."

His reluctance was driving me crazy. "But what? Come on, spill it."

"There were some bad feelings when he left PrismCo. Like he took his profits out, and the company just imploded. It's not really clear whether his leaving was cause or effect, but there were some unhappy people. What's he want you to do for him?"

"Actually, it was Madelyn Sheffield who brought me in. You remember her? She does stained-glass, um, art."

"Spacy blonde with ruffles? I think so. I didn't think you two were buddies."

I snorted. "We're not. But she came to me and asked me to help. I haven't said yes, but I'll admit I'm curious to meet the man. I can still back out, if something smells."

"If you want my opinion, make sure you get paid up front."

That piqued my curiosity. "Why? Does this guy have a reputation for stiffing people?"

"I'd hate to go that far, but there's something not right there. What does he want you to do?"

"Maddy tells me he collects stained-glass pieces, and he wants to showcase them in his house. She wants help with the lighting, or so she says. I get the feeling she's scared to death of blowing the job and wants some backup. I said I'd talk to the man, look at the place. I haven't committed to anything yet."

"Well, that sounds tame enough. Have fun. You can fill me in over the weekend."

"You're coming back again?"

"Why, you tired of me?"

"No, of course not, idiot. Does Allison know?"

"Yes."

I waited for him to elaborate, but he didn't. "Okay, I'll look forward to seeing you. The usual time?"

"I think so—Friday dinner, latish. Okay?"

"Better than okay. Then I can dish about the mysterious Peter Ferguson. But I'm teaching Saturday afternoon, remember. The usual beginners class, and some of my advanced students wanted some furnace time, and probably some hand-holding to go with it, so I'll probably be down in the studio most of the day."

"Not a problem. I'll find something to keep me busy. See you Friday, then."

After we hung up, I wondered how things with Allison were going. We had an unspoken pact not to talk about it, period. I had given my blessing early on, and now all I could do was wait and see what happened. Allison was thriving; Cam was chafing with impatience. But there was nothing I could do about it. I couldn't even provide wise counsel, since my own romantic life was a mess, or at least had been.

When I first arrived in Tucson, I'd devoted 110 percent of my energy to getting the business started. When I came up for air, Police Chief Matt Lundgren had drifted into my life, through a friend of a friend. We had enjoyed an intense few months of a relationship, and then his so-called ex-wife had appeared out of nowhere, and I had run in the other direction and plunged back into my work. That had been status quo until the past summer, when Matt and I had been thrown back together by an investigation. Luckily the almost-ex was now completely ex, and we were back together again, a bit older and wiser, and more careful. I wasn't sure where I wanted us to go, and we were taking it slowly. But all in all, I had no advice to dispense; I was as clueless as Cam when it came to relationships.

As promised, I was downstairs in the shop early the next morning to open up for the day. I looked up at nine forty-five to see Allison arrive.

"Good morning, Em," she said cheerfully, hanging up her jacket.

"Same to you. I thought you'd be later than this. Your meeting go okay?"

"Grand. The professor's a lovely man, just wanted to know would I be up to the reading."

Allison was taking literature classes, satiating a long-suppressed hunger. "That's good. So your schedule is set, now?"

"That it is. I'll let Nessa know when she arrives. You're dressed nicely—have you plans?"

The fact that she noticed that I had put on something special for my audience with the great Peter Ferguson made me wonder how bad I usually looked. "I'm meeting a possible client. You'll be all right here on your own?"

"Of course."

I hesitated before saying, "I talked to Cam last night." I watched for her reaction.

Allison dimpled. "As did I. He'll be here tomorrow, right?" Then she laughed. "Em, don't look so worried. We'll sort things out in good time. Just let me enjoy my freedom for a bit."

"That's what I keep telling him, but I think he saves all his patience for computer codes."

Maddy chose that moment to make her entrance. She seemed fidgety. "Ready, Em? Oh, good morning, uh, Allison, is it?" Maddy's eyes darted to me, asking if I'd spilled the beans already.

"Yes, I'm ready. Allison, I should be back by lunchtime." I looked to Maddy for corroboration, but she shrugged. "Or later."

"Don't worry, Em—I'm sure I can manage. Madelyn, lovely to see you again."

I suppressed a smile. Maddy was too oblivious to catch the sarcasm in Allison's voice. As we approached Maddy's car I asked, "Where are we going?"

"I told you—east, out past South Houghton Road." Her curt response discouraged further questions.

I settled back in my seat and watched the scenery— being chauffeured was a luxury I seldom enjoyed. Tucson boasts several pockets of exclusive and prestigious homes, primarily in the Catalina Foothills to the north, with incredible views—and price tags in the millions. Of course, such houses were in high demand, and empty lots had filled up rapidly in the ten years I'd lived in the area. I was surprised that somebody with Peter Ferguson's reputation—and money—hadn't opted for the obvious location but had instead gone for a different but no less expensive enclave on another side of the city. Still, the views of Saguaro National Park should be impressive from there, and privacy was guaranteed. In any case, the people I hung out with were more like me—hardworking tradespeople who didn't have a lot of money to spare, and I'd never had the privilege of visiting one of the spectacular homes. I was looking forward to the treat.

As we approached I could understand Ferguson's decision to locate there. We reached the foothills and began climbing. Apart from the security that the neighborhood offered, the vistas sprawling below seemed to roll on forever, and most of the homes took full advantage of that. In fact, in concept it seemed almost a waste to interpose ornate glass barriers, no matter how rare and valuable. I was getting more and more curious about what approach our reclusive genius planned to take.

It was hard to see many of the houses, carefully concealed behind walls or deliberately chosen plantings, or just set far back from the roads. There were few other cars. Finally Maddy pulled up at the entrance to a long driveway and leaned out of the car to push a button on a discreet security box I hadn't even noticed. When someone responded, she said, "Peter? We're here." Then she shut the window and began moving forward. I wondered about the absence of fencing, but realized how out of place that would look here.

"What was that about? It's not as though there's a gate or a pack of dogs. Or is there? A pack, I mean?"

Maddy glanced quickly at me, then away. "There's a security system. If it's breached, alarms go off."

I stared at her. "Is that really necessary? I mean, he hasn't even moved in yet. Most homeowners around here settle for a house alarm and leave it at that."

"Peter's concerned about his collection. He just wants to be careful." She didn't volunteer anything further.

I studied the house as we neared it. Like so many of the homes in this exclusive neighborhood, it was a sprawling stucco affair, a curious blend of medieval castle and humble pueblo, stretched along the contour of the hill like a tawny sleeping cougar. Since we were approaching from below, I could see that most of this side—the one with the view—

was made up of floor-to-ceiling windows. For a moment I thought irreverently how glad I was that I didn't have to pay for heating or cooling a place like this: That cost was probably bigger than my entire household budget—for the decade.

Maddy pulled into a paved parking area around the side and shut off her engine. She turned to look at me critically, and I almost expected her to tell me to stand up straight and mind my manners. "Let me do the talking. If you have any questions you can ask me later. I just want you to get a sense of the layout, so you know what you're working with."

I bit back a snarky reply. What did she think I was—the hired help? "Okay," I said, my voice tight. She gave me another look. Was she really nervous about having me here? Why?

We approached the front door, flanked by another low-key but complicated-looking security panel. Apparently Maddy knew it had been disarmed, because she went straight to the door and opened it. A rush of cool air poured out at us, and I was immediately sucked into the building by the promise of the view. Maddy looked annoyed as she pushed by me and called out, "Peter?"

A deep masculine voice called out, "In the living room. Come on through."

I was torn. Part of me wanted to meet this titan of the cyberworld; another part of me wanted to stand in the broad foyer and take in the striking architecture of the place. The designer had kept pesky things like walls to a minimum, the better to give access to the views from almost anywhere you stood. My first dazed impression was of acres of granite and polished wood, gleaming tile and rough adobe. The interior was both quiet and noisy, the many surfaces catching even the smallest sounds and echoing them back. The palette was monochrome, but the wash of color outside the windows—the vivid blue skies, the dusty greens of the native plants—more than compensated. I had to admit that I was impressed.

Maddy tugged at my arm impatiently, and reluctantly I turned to follow her as she led me to where Peter Ferguson waited.

Chapter 3

✿

Maddy headed toward the source of the voice. "Peter!" she said as she entered the living room, with me trailing like a U-Haul. She stopped abruptly, and I almost bumped into her, since I was too busy taking in the details of the house to pay attention.

"Hi, Maddy. And you must be Emmeline Dowell."

I stepped out from behind Maddy, then stopped dead, struck dumb.

I've been around a lot of computer nerds in my life, starting with Cam's high school and college buddies. Heck, I've always preferred geeks to studs—they're usually more interesting to talk to, once you get past their initial social ineptitude. And they're smart and often creative people.

Peter Ferguson was no nerd. Not even close. I took a moment to gather my scattered wits while making mental readjustments. It occurred to me that while I had read the occasional article or headline about the mysterious Mister Ferguson, I couldn't recall ever seeing a picture of the man. If I had been expecting a pasty-pale, scrawny guy with thick glasses, I was so far wrong it was laughable. The man in front of me was well over six feet tall, rail thin. Middle-aged, yes—he had to be a few years older than my forty-something. But no glasses—his brown eyes, laugh lines at the corners, were clearly amused. His pewter gray hair was cut short, but not short enough to suppress the curl, and I thought I caught the glint of an earring in one ear. His clothes were simple—button-down shirt with sleeves rolled up and collar open, well-worn jeans, sandals. Although it couldn't have taken more than a second or two for me to process this information, I realized he was waiting for a response from me with a smile lurking at one corner of his generous mouth.

Without thinking about it, I stepped forward and held out my hand. "Yes, I'm Emmeline Dowell. Em. I make hot glass, and Maddy said she needed some help." I was very proud to have remembered my own name.

I could almost hear steam hissing from Maddy's ears, but I really didn't care. Peter took my offered hand, shook it briefly, and said, "Welcome, Em. I've seen some of your work downtown. Nice." He let go of my hand, and I had to remind myself to do something with it.

"Thank you," I said demurely. I am not a demure person, but my mental data banks were working too slowly for anything more complicated. I wondered briefly if he ran into this reaction often; his expression was faintly amused, but not unfriendly. And, I realized, I was absurdly happy that he had seen and liked my work.

It was only then that I realized there was another man in the room. He was shorter, rounder, and definitely sleeker than Peter. He stepped forward and extended his hand as well. "I'm Ian Gemberling. Peter's bought some of his collection from me." He turned toward Maddy and nodded. "Madelyn, nice to see you again."

Maddy nodded, her back stiff. "Ian."

There was a moment of awkward silence, then Ian said, "Well, I must be going. Peter, thanks for showing me the place, and let me know if I can help with anything. Good to meet you, Em."

"I'll see you out," Peter said, and the two men left us alone. I seized the opportunity to check out the spectacular view again. Nice to know what a few million could get you in this neighborhood. I tore myself away from the vista when Peter returned.

"Peter!" Maddy's voice was sharp, and I almost expected her to stamp her little foot and throw a tantrum.

Peter took his own sweet time in turning to her. "Yes, Maddy?" he drawled.

"I wanted to show Em what you're thinking of for the glass panels, and you can tell her what you have in mind for the coordinating pieces." *And then she can vanish in a puff of smoke, because I don't want to share you with anyone.* Maddy didn't voice this last part, but I could almost hear her thinking it. Fair enough—I wasn't in the market. I had Matt, didn't I? Sort of? But it was hard to stand in the same room with Peter Ferguson and not admire the gorgeous package. A girl can look, right?

Maddy was apparently still talking. "Have the rest of the pieces arrived yet?"

"Some, not all. I wanted to be sure the security was set up before I brought them in. But I need to see them in situ before we make any plans." He turned back to me. "How much has Maddy told you about what I'm doing here?"

I took a deep breath to calm myself. "She said you wanted to use this place to give your glassworks the best setting possible. Although I must admit it seems a shame to pay for all this gorgeous view and then cover it up again." I stopped, appalled. I was already criticizing the man, and I'd barely met him.

"A fair judgment," he replied, undisturbed. "I've been waiting to see how the house shapes up, and how the glass panels look, before making any final decisions about placement. I'm glad you'll be a part of it. But you're not a native Tucsonan, are you?"

I shook my head. "No, East Coast born and bred. I've lived out here about ten years now."

"Ah. I thought I caught the accent. I'm from North Jersey myself. But it's been a few years since I spent any time there—work took me to California."

"And now Arizona. Why here?"

He shrugged. "A number of reasons. I wanted space, and light. Particularly light. And I wanted a change."

I wasn't sure if his last statement was addressed to us or to himself, but his tone was final, and it would be presumptuous of me to pursue the thread any further. After all, it really wasn't my business. I was here to provide glass, no more. If I wanted to; if he wanted me to. I realized that I wanted to. Whether he did, I wasn't so sure about yet. And from the expression on Maddy's face, I got the impression she wished I was about fifty miles off the New Jersey coast, and a hundred feet down.

Peter unslouched himself from the wall where he had been leaning. "I'm forgetting my manners. Can I get you two something to drink before we look around?"

"An iced tea, if you have it," Maddy simpered.

"Of course. I knew you'd be coming. And for you, Em?"

"That's fine for me." I didn't care what we were drinking. I wanted to look at the stained glass.

"I'll be just a moment. Feel free to look around." He disappeared through an open archway behind him.

As soon as he was out of earshot, Maddy turned to me and hissed, "I told you to keep your mouth shut."

"I couldn't be rude to the man, could I?" I replied, keeping my tone mild. My, she was touchy about Peter. "Isn't he used to talking to the little people?"

"Don't be snide, Em. This is a business arrangement, nothing more. You deal with him through me, or I'll find someone else for the fixtures."

I thought about my options. Maddy was a pain in the butt under the best of circumstances, and apparently she thought she had some claim to Peter—and would defend it tooth and nail. At this point I could decide that putting up with her wasn't worth the effort, and I could walk away, no harm, no foul. On the other hand, I was curious now: Peter seemed serious about his plans, had given them some thought. From what I'd just seen, I was pretty sure that he wasn't just looking to impress people with the money he'd thrown around acquiring a tidy little art collection. I found I really wanted to know what he planned to do with it. Which meant I had to make nice with Maddy. I could do that, couldn't I?

I held up my hands. "Message received, Maddy. You can take the lead. I'm just here to see the place, and the glass panels."

Maddy searched my face to make sure I was sincere, and I gave her my best wide-eyed innocent look. Before she could say anything more, Peter emerged from the kitchen, juggling three mismatched glasses. "This is the best I could do. I'm not set up for entertaining yet." He handed me a glass.

"Not a problem . . . Peter." I took it from him, our fingers brushing.

"Then let's drink to a happy partnership, and I'll give you the nickel tour."

We carried our drinks with us as Peter led us through the spaces of his house. They were too open to be legitimately called rooms, at least on the ground floor; we didn't visit the upper levels, although after listening to him for a while I had a sneaking suspicion that Peter would steal any corner he could for his beloved glass. Maddy burbled on, dropping arcane terms in a vain effort to impress her . . . what? Employer, lover? I couldn't quite figure out their relationship. For that matter, I couldn't figure out why there was one at all. *Stop it, Em. It's none of your business.*

To distract myself, I studied the existing lighting fixtures. While they were no doubt high-end and expensive, they were boring. Designed to be invisible. But at least they were inoffensive. Why would Peter want to replace them, if the focus of each room was to be on the glass panels? He had been fairly quiet, letting us absorb the spaces and understand the place. He had chosen this house well for his purposes: The sheets of plain glass faced in different directions, depending on the siting of the room, so there would be light catching the glass somewhere at any time of day. I found myself wondering how the rooms would be used.

As usual, I spoke before thinking. "How do you see these rooms, Peter? You are planning for furniture and stuff like that, right? Where do you expect to sit, and what do you plan to do?" Maddy glared at me again, but I thought it was a legitimate question, given our roles here.

His mouth twitched again. Did I amuse him? "If you're wondering, yes, I do have furniture, and I expect this to be a home, not an art gallery. But the furniture will complement the windows, not vice versa. I wanted to keep the place bare and clean for now—makes it easier to visualize the glass."

"We don't have to worry about teenage kids bouncing basketballs or anything, do we?" Was I actually prying? Was there a wife and kids waiting in the wings somewhere?

This time he smiled openly. "Nothing like that. I'm designing this space for my own enjoyment."

I noted that he hadn't elaborated about wife, kiddies, or even dogs, for that matter. Again, none of my business. But it was a large place for one man to ramble around admiring the pretty colors. Lonely.

His voice startled me out of my reflections. "I've uncrated one panel, to get a feel for it. Do you want to see it?"

"Ooh, Peter, which one? The Tiffany?" Maddy squealed.

"No, that's not here yet. Actually, I wanted to see how the Chagall looks."

I nodded. "Good choice—the color range should complement the desert palette. If it's anything like the Vence series, that is."

Maddy and Peter both turned to look at me, with very different expressions. Maddy managed to combine confused and furious; Peter looked inquisitive. He spoke first. "You've seen them?"

"Years ago. But if that's your model, I can see what you're going for—the simplicity of the chapel and the lushness of the glass." In fact, I realized I wasn't just sucking up—I did see it, in my mind's eye. My estimation of Peter's taste kicked up a notch.

Ever the polite host, he turned to Maddy. "Are you familiar with those panels, Maddy?"

"Not those particular ones," she said through clenched teeth. "Where is this window of yours?"

He smiled gently. "I saved it for last. This way."

We had almost come full circuit, back to where we had begun. At the end of the building off the main space there was a small room with windows on two sides; a third wall was lined with shelves, currently empty. A glass panel some six feet high was propped up against one of the dividers between the windows, its packing crate and padding lying on the floor.

Wow. I'd remembered right. The panel was clearly from the same period as the Vence windows, and shared the intense blues and yellows, as well as the sinuous lines. Behind it through the window the desert unfurled, a gold-brown expanse of sand that stretched to the next mountain range beyond. The sunlight poured through the window, casting pools of colored light on the pale stone floor; I could almost see it moving, like a liquid. For a moment I was speechless, awed by the rightness of the combination. And what I saw spawned a whole series of images, and I couldn't wait to see how the other panels he might have would fit. I knew exactly why he had started with this one.

I turned eagerly to Maddy, who looked bored. "This is fantastic! Maddy, what do you think? How would you tie this together with the windows in other rooms?"

Maddy looked at me to see if I was making fun of her. Deciding I wasn't, she ignored me but talked directly to Peter. "I love it, Peter! It's beautiful! This is going to be so exciting. I can't wait to see all the others. When will they all be here?"

"Sometime this week, Maddy. I've got some contractors coming in this week to talk about structural support—these things are heavy, and I want to make sure the frames can support them, since the house wasn't built for this kind of glass." Once again he turned to me. "Em, what would you suggest for lighting?"

I shook my head. "I'm nowhere near ready to think about that—I need to spend some more time with the pieces. And so should you—you need to see them at different times of day, under different conditions. It's not like going to the home store and picking out a lamp shade." I surprised myself with my own vehemence: I really did want to do it right.

Peter nodded, once. "Good point. And there's no rush. I want to get this right."

Was the man a mind reader?

Maddy apparently had had enough. "Well, Em, I think

we should be going, since there's not much more to see right now. Peter, let me know when the rest of the panels are here and uncrated. I'm looking forward to seeing them all." She stood waiting, and I realized I was supposed to move.

I turned to make my farewells, ignoring Maddy's glare. "Peter, it was a pleasure to meet you. And I second what Maddy says—if this window is any indication, the rest of the collection should be spectacular. Thanks for asking me to help."

He escorted us to the door, then leaned on the doorjamb watching as we pulled away—probably so he could arm the alarm system again. Maddy didn't say anything until we had reached the road. "I trust you've seen enough?"

I turned in my seat to look at her. "No, of course not. This is a custom job, and each room is going to be different, with different requirements."

"Fine. I'll take pictures." She gripped the steering wheel fiercely.

What was her problem? Did she think I was going to steal her glory? This was her commission, and I was only a bit player. Still, I had professional standards, and if I was going to create something that my name was attached to, I wanted to make it the best that my skills would allow. And it would be a privilege to work with these pieces—the likes of which I had only read about or seen in museums or churches. I could learn a lot from studying them up close.

Or was she afraid I was going to steal her man? From what I had observed, Peter didn't see himself in that role, but maybe Maddy had hopes.

But to keep close to the art, I had to keep Maddy happy. I sighed quietly. "How do you know Peter?"

"I've known him for years," she replied. She didn't add anything, and I wondered what the story was—and why she didn't want to share it.

I watched the scenery roll by as we headed back toward the city. "Who was that Gemberling guy?" I asked after a few moments, more to break the silence than because I was interested.

"Ian? He's an art dealer from Los Angeles. Peter has bought several pieces from him. You haven't heard of him?" She made it sound as though Ian Gemberling was a household name.

"No, can't say that I have. I don't pay a lot of attention to high-end dealers."

Maddy sniffed, then fell silent again. This lasted until we arrived back at my studio. She pulled up at the curb and stopped with a jerk. "Em, let's get this clear up front. This is *my* project. I'll let you know when and if I need anything from you."

My, she was being proprietary. "You know, we might want to work out a contract or something. We are going to get paid, aren't we?"

"Oh. Right. Let me put something together and I'll get back to you. Time plus material?"

This didn't seem to be the right time to argue with her, even though her terms were a bit insulting. "Let me think about it, and I'll look over what you come up with."

"Fine. I'll be in touch, Em. If you have any questions, give me a call." I waited for the rest of that statement—"not Peter." When she didn't add anything else, I opened the door and climbed out of the car, then watched her pull away, fast.

What was going on with her? Peter's collection promised to be better than I could have imagined—and it looked to me as though Maddy was completely clueless about what to do with it. But Peter did not appear to be a stupid man, and he had chosen her to work on this. Why?

One thing was abundantly clear: I wanted in. From what little I had seen and heard, this glass collection would be memorable, and it would be a privilege to work with it, even if that meant putting up with Maddy. Of course, spending time with Peter Ferguson would go a long way toward compensating for Maddy's snits. But I was there for the glass.

Wasn't I?

Chapter 4

❀

As I entered my shop, I checked my watch: not even noon. So much for hobnobbing with the rich and famous. I'd spent no more than an hour in Peter Ferguson's house. But I had come away with a lot to think about.

Allison looked up expectantly as I walked in.

"Hi, Allison—everything okay?" I asked. There were a couple of lookers in the shop, but they didn't appear serious.

"Fine, Em. Are you going to tell me about your excursion with Miss Madelyn?"

I shook my head. "Sorry, my lips are sealed, at least for the moment." I wondered briefly whether telling Cam would be the same as telling Allison, but I wasn't sure what their state of communication was at the moment, and I thought I should talk to Cam first. In any case, while I fully trusted Allison, who had long since demonstrated her ability to keep secrets, I thought I should stick to the letter of the agreement—at least until I had a contract in my hand.

Allison tipped her head at me but asked no more about it. "Shall I go to lunch, then? And can I bring you anything? Nessa said she'd be in about two."

"Sure—just grab me a sandwich and something to drink. I think I can handle things here."

Allison gathered up her bag and left in search of food. I put on a bright smile and approached the browsers. "Hi! Can I tell you anything about the pieces? I'm the glassmaker . . . ."

The afternoon passed surprisingly quickly. Even after ten years in business here, I sometimes had trouble gauging the traffic flow. Summers were slow, due to the blazing Arizona heat, and I tried to make as much inventory in the spring as I could. Business usually picked up nicely in the fall, but there was no holiday rush, which I might have expected if I had stayed back east. Tucson had been growing rapidly for years, and there were more and more families moving in, but that didn't mean they shopped in the trendy downtown district. I did more business with tourists, but they usually didn't plan on traveling for Christmas, so I didn't have to churn out a lot of volume. Things might have been different if I were selling through the Web, and I had considered it more than once, but I really didn't want to spent a lot of my time peering at a computer screen and filling orders. I was happier selling directly to the public, and working with a few galleries who knew me and my work. They had done right by me so far, and I saw no reason to change things.

When Allison returned, she and I traded off for a bit. I went upstairs to take the dogs out and gulp down my sandwich. After Nessa came in, I spent a little time cleaning up my place, something I avoided doing unless I knew I had company coming, which was almost never, except for Cam. I ran out to stock up on groceries and liquid refreshment, then took another shift in the shop. An ordinary day, but I had no complaints. In my spare moments, I puzzled over this morning's expedition. Why Maddy? Why me? What other treasures might there be in Peter's collection—and would I have a chance to see them? Why was Maddy acting so defensive? I wasn't about to poach on her territory. It was her commission and I respected that, as a professional colleague. Or did she have a thing going with Peter, and see me as a threat? I giggled at that idea. Whether or not I had any faith in her artistic abilities, I could not deny that she was more feminine and appealing than I had ever been or would be, and I was fine with that. Peter didn't seem to be married, and if she wanted to make a run at him, more power to her. I wasn't interested; I had Matt. Strong, dependable Matt. My interest in Peter was based purely on the collection he owned. *Keep trying, Em, and maybe you'll convince yourself*.

I left Nessa to close up at six, and went upstairs to throw together something for dinner. Let me make it perfectly clear: I am not a cook. I can keep myself alive, and I send up thankful prayers almost every day for the marvels of modern frozen food. I know my way around the microwave. What's more, I knew Cam really didn't care what I put in front of him. He was coming to Tucson to see me and Allison. In some order. I'd take him whichever way. But despite my lackadaisical culinary skills, once in a while I liked to make some "real" food for him, and that would probably eat up the time until he arrived. Taking stock of my options, I decided on my quick-and-dirty chili recipe. Some years earlier, knowing my attitude toward cooking, Cam had proudly presented me with a slow cooker for my birthday. Actually it had been an inspired idea: I could dump stuff in whenever I wanted, and go away and leave it for hours at a time. Over time I had evolved a flexible form of chili, which usually involved whatever meat I had on hand, plus some chopped onion and ancho peppers, which I had in abundant supply at all times. The longer it cooked, the better it got.

Since I knew it would take Cam a few hours to get to Tucson, I dumped the basic ingredients in the cooker and went on about my business. It was issuing good smells by the time Cam arrived. As usual, Fred and Gloria heard him before I did. He let himself in and allowed himself to be smothered with wet doggy love for a couple of minutes. I let the pups take first crack at him—I was the grown-up, so I could be patient. Finally he straightened up and I gave him the hug he deserved—and needed, by the look of him.

"Hey, brother of mine, you look beat. Traffic?"

He shook his head. "Not bad. I got a late start, and I had a lot to think about on the road."

"Well, let me feed you, and then you can crash or tell me all about it or whatever. You'll be here all weekend, right?"

"Sounds good. Yeah, but I probably have plans for to-morrow night."

Allison, I assumed. Although that "probably" mysti-fied me.

"Help yourself to something to drink. I personally am going to undertake the intimidating task of making rice in the microwave, and then we can eat."

"Far be it for me to interfere with such a delicate pro-cess."

Thank goodness we shared a gene for mild sarcasm.

In ten minutes I had steaming plates in front of both of us, with some bread from a nearby bakery, and cold beers all around. I waited a few minutes until he had forked up half the contents of his plate, then said, "So, what's going on?"

He avoided my eyes, chasing the last bite around his plate. Finally he said, "This back and forth stuff is getting old."

I assume he didn't mean coming to see me. "Allison?"

Still no eye contact. "She knows how I feel. Why can't she move to San Diego? Or I'll move here—I've told her that. I can get some kind of job, or telecommute. We can work it out."

Poor baby, he still didn't get it. "Cam, my sweet, innocent brother, you've got to be patient. This is the first time in her life she's been independent, and out from her jerk of a husband's shadow. She's enjoying it. That's not meant to hurt you, but she does need to grow. Heck, it's only been a couple of months. But pressuring her is only going to push her away."

"Yeah, yeah, I know—we've been over all this before. But how long is long enough?"

I shook my head. "I don't know, but don't give up. I know she cares about you." I stood up and collected the plates and deposited them in the sink. "Coffee? I picked up a pie at the bakery, if you want it. And there's ice cream."

"Sure," he said glumly. He sulked until I had put water on to boil and sliced pie onto plates—and added ice cream, of course. When I sat down again, he said, "So, how did your meeting with Ferguson go?"

"I wondered when you'd ask." In fact, he had been so uninterested in that event that I knew just how much he was hurting over Allison's resistance. "He's not at all what I expected."

Cam leaned back in his chair and finally looked at me, with a gleam of amusement. "You were expecting a geek?"

"Well, I don't think I ever saw a picture of him. I apologize: I assumed—wrong, as it turns out. He's really an interesting guy."

"Tell me again how the two of you connected."

I gave him the brief outline of Maddy's proposition, ending with a description of what I knew about the glass collection. "If the rest of it is anywhere near as good as the

Chagall I saw, this should be really something. I've got to say I envy him—he can create whatever kind of space he wants to show these off, and then he can live smack in the middle of them and enjoy them."

"Well, he's certainly got enough of that."

Was there a sharp note in Cam's voice? "Jealous?"

"No, it's not that. Look, I know some guys who have worked for him, and not everybody was happy about the way he folded up his company. He came out just fine, but some other people have had trouble landing new jobs, or ones as good. He got out at the right time."

I poked at my pie. "Are you saying that he did something wrong? Inside information? Or that he stiffed his employees?"

"I'm not sure. Maybe. Nobody's ever been able to make anything stick, but there are still some unhappy people around. But, to be fair, the computer industry is always like that, and there's always somebody whining about something."

I tried to match up shady dealings with the man who I'd seen this morning. He was smart enough, certainly. He was no naive data cruncher, out of touch with the world. Part of me wanted to believe that anyone who was as passionate about art, who really understood it, couldn't be dishonest. I certainly didn't want to think he'd used ill-gotten gains to assemble his fabulous collection.

"Em? Are you going to be working with him?"

"I don't know," I said slowly. "Maddy may be a problem—I'm still not sure why she wanted to include me, although I think she needs my help. Heck, *he* may not want me involved. But before I get in too deep, could you do a little snooping and tell me what you can find out about him?"

He brightened at that idea. "Sure, that's easy. Now?"

"Aren't you seeing Allison tonight?"

"Nah. She said something about meeting a bunch of people and planning for a study group or something. I'll catch up with her tomorrow."

Cam bounded out of his chair to unpack his laptop. I collected the dishes, smiling to myself. It took so little to make him happy—just give him a computer project to work on. Still, my request was more than just a diversion for Cam, who could handle this kind of thing blindfolded. I wanted to know more about Peter, because things just weren't adding up. He'd left behind a very successful business—under a cloud? He'd moved here to Tucson, where he didn't seem to know anyone—except Maddy (who in my opinion wasn't enough of a reason to cross state lines)? He was remodeling this huge and expensive showcase house—for sole occupancy? And, from what little I'd seen, he was too young and too smart to be content with doing nothing except admiring the pretty views for the next twenty or thirty years. *Stop it, Em,* I scolded myself. I had enough going on in my own life without getting involved in some kind of mess.

On the other hand, if Cam's report came up clean . . . I really wanted to know more about Peter.

As usual, it didn't take Cam long to troll through his online sources. I have great respect for computers and the Internet—I just don't want to know how to use them, beyond the basics. And, of course, I have Cam to do it for me. The best of both worlds. By the time I had made another pot of coffee, he was back at the table with a sheaf of paper, looking like an eager schoolboy. I set a mug of coffee in front of him and sat down across the table.

"What've you got?" I asked.

He looked puzzled. "Not a lot of negatives. More like a bunch of innuendos, if you know what I mean. What people don't say, or how they phrase their answers."

"You have to read between the lines?"

"I guess. Anyway, nothing illegal. Just a bunch of disgruntled people who think he should have kept the company going so they could keep their jobs."

"Is that unusual in your business?"

"Not really. Hey, you've read the papers—companies like this start up and fold all the time. Peter managed to ride out the dot-com bust pretty well, and it looks as though it was due to good management and a healthy cash balance more than luck—which is to his credit. He also had a strong product. Don't know how much of which he was directly responsible for—I know he's something of a legend for some of his early programs, but that was a while ago. The guy's what—fifty?"

Cam hadn't yet reached forty, so fifty probably seemed ancient to him—especially among programmers. "I'd guess. So if he had survived this long, why did he decide to fold?"

Cam shook his head. "I'm not sure. Could have been personality conflict, internally. There's one guy who's been the most vocal about the dissolution of the company. His name's Andrew Foster. He'd been there from the beginning, and he thought he didn't get a fair deal."

"Lawsuit?"

"No, nothing like that. Just a lot of complaining to the press, and then they stopped listening."

"So if he had had any real grounds, he would have sued?"

"Maybe. This is just a first pass—I can dig some more if you really want. How much do you need to know?"

I shrugged. "I'm not sure. I just don't want to waste my time with this commission if it isn't going to pan out. Hey, while you're at it, can you check out his collection of glass? What he's been buying and what he's paid for it?"

Cam grinned at me. "Thinking of padding your bill?"

"No, just curious. The art market always seems crazy to me anyway, but since he's got the bucks to play in it, I'd like to know what it's worth. And I think I met his dealer, or one of them—a guy named Ian Gemberling. Maybe that would be a good starting point."

"Not a problem." Cam finished his coffee and went back to his laptop. He returned more quickly this time. "There's not a lot of stuff online, and it looks like the big dealers and houses are pretty cagey about dollars, but I think it's safe to say that big-name glass panels go for mid to high six figures, maybe more. You know how much he's got?"

"Not yet. I've seen the house, and I think he's talking about maybe six rooms? I don't think he's going to mix and match pieces—more like one room, one window. Maybe. Maddy didn't seem very clear about it, or maybe she just didn't want to tell me. So let's say two or three million, if they're important pieces."

Cam whistled. "Must be nice. So, what's going on with this Maddy person?"

"I really don't know. We're in the same business, sort of, but if you want to know the truth, I think she's a light-weight turning out pretty tourist pieces. She seems to do well enough at it. But that doesn't explain where she met Peter, or why he thinks she's up to the job." I wondered if I'd ever find out—I was pretty sure Maddy wasn't going to fill me in.

"The rich aren't like you and me," Cam intoned.

"Yeah, they've got more money." I finished the quote for him. "Well, I'm willing to play along unless and until Maddy becomes too much of a pain in the butt. I don't need the business that much. Although it was fun meeting a real live titan of industry. Did you ever cross paths?"

"I wish," Cam answered. "I've looked at some of his code, and it's really elegant. There are a couple of things I'd love to ask him about. You don't think . . . ?" He looked hopeful.

"Not with Maddy standing guard at the gates. We'll

have to see." I caught a glimpse of my wall clock. "Shoot, it's getting late, and I've got a class to teach tomorrow. You want to walk the dogs, or shall I?"

"I'll do it—I need to stretch my legs after the drive."

"Thanks. I'll grab a shower. Breakfast?"

"Great."

He assembled leashes and headed out with the pups. I gathered up the papers he'd left scattered on the table, wondering idly what it would be like to spend as much money as you liked for a piece of art. What would I buy, if I had that chance? Something to think about.

Chapter 5

❁

Breakfast at my place is kind of a haphazard affair. Both Cam and I are morning people, so we mesh well there, but mostly we forage for whatever we can find to eat.

"What've you got on for today?" I asked, finishing my coffee. I knew I had a full day ahead of me.

He shrugged. "Allison and I are having dinner. She's off tomorrow, right?"

"Yup. I figured you'd be out tonight, so I'm meeting Matt." Since we had gotten back together, Matt and I were taking things slowly. Tonight we were going on a real date: Matt was taking me out to dinner. It was kind of nice, being courted. "Will you be out, uh, late?"

Cam tried to keep a straight face and failed. "Want a little privacy? We can go to Allison's place, although it's not quite as luxurious as these accommodations."

I looked for something to throw at him, but we'd eaten all the soft stuff. "Hey, I'm putting you up for free. I could go to Matt's place," I offered, with less than complete conviction. Matt still hadn't succeeded in exorcizing his ex-wife Lorena's presence from his house.

Cam sat back in his chair. "Isn't this ridiculous? You'd think we were kids. And backseats sure aren't big enough anymore."

"How did we manage to miss all that, back then?"

"I don't know. I can't make up my mind whether it's better or worse this way."

"I know what you mean." I wasn't as insecure as I had been at twenty-something, and I was certainly less easily embarrassed, but sometimes I wondered if I had missed the romantic boat, and I still wasn't sure how or why. But Matt and I had something good, and it would lead wherever it led. I was in no rush—or at least, not the way Cam was.

I stood up and dusted the crumbs from my lap. "I'll walk the doggies, and then I've got to get to work. Let me know if your plans change. Walkies, my loves?" Fred and Gloria had stationed themselves at my feet, hoping for a stray chunk of something yummy, but a walk was almost as good.

Dogs satisfied, I plunged into my day, and the next time I looked up it was after five. When my class was over, I cleaned up the studio and went back to the shop to catch up with Allison. Since she was with a customer, I wandered around my display area, repositioning articles on the shelves and making mental notes about what was selling well so I could make more. As I walked among the shelves, I couldn't help eavesdropping on Allison: She had picked up the language of glass quickly, and as a bonus, most patrons seemed intrigued by her soft Irish accent. She made a good salesperson, not that I wanted to keep her chained in my shop forever.

When she'd handed the customers their carefully wrapped package, she looked up to see me watching and smiled. "A nice sale, that one."

"And not the first. Business has really picked up lately, with both you and Nessa working up front. I hadn't realized how many people I lost when we were too busy."

"Ah, I'm happy to help."

"So, are you seeing Cam tonight?"

"I am. Em . . ." She hesitated, struggling for words. "You know I care for him, but he wants things to move so fast, and I'm not sure—"

I interrupted. "Don't worry about it. I already told him not to push. And I'm behind you all the way. You need to figure out what *you* want, and then you can think about what Cam wants."

"Thank you. I didn't want to make trouble between us all."

"No way. So, can you close up? I want to go get ready for my date of the week."

She almost giggled. "Ah, that's right—Matt's squiring you tonight. You go right on and pretty yourself. I can handle things here."

"You have a good evening too, and I'll see you when I see you."

I made my escape, went upstairs, fed and walked the dogs, showered—hey, glassmaking is hot work—and was just putting on the finishing touches—my earrings—when Matt arrived.

I opened the door for him. "Good evening, sir. My, you look spiffy."

He raised one eyebrow. "Spiffy? That's the best you can do? You, madame, look quite beguiling."

"Ooh, I don't think I've ever been beguiling before. Is that a good thing?"

"In my opinion, yes, most definitely. Are you ready? Because we have reservations."

"Oh my, a place that takes reservations. That *is* special."

I gathered up a light coat and my purse, and we sallied forth into the night.

"Matt, there's something I wanted to ask you about," I said, twirling the last of my wine in my glass. This was a really nice restaurant. Excellent food, happy patrons. And good company.

Matt leaned back and tilted his head at me. "That sounds ominous."

"No, not really. You see, I've been asked to work on a project, and I have a few questions. . . ."

"That you need to ask a policeman?" Matt straightened again, alert now.

"Nothing illegal. Look, none of this is official yet, but I wondered . . ." Why was I having such trouble putting my question into words? "Do you know Peter Ferguson?"

I'd managed to surprise him. "The computer guy? Is that what this is about?"

I nodded. "He asked a, uh, colleague of mine to oversee the installation of his glass collection at his house here in Tucson, and she asked me to help her out."

"So what's the problem?"

"For one thing, it's a very valuable collection. And I know he's security conscious—he's got the electronics in place at his house already, and he hasn't even moved in."

"You've been there?"

"Yes. Maddy took me over to check it out. She says she wants me to make glass components for the lighting, to co-ordinate with the collection pieces."

"Do I know Maddy?"

"Probably not. She's got a shop a couple of blocks from me—makes stained-glass thingies."

He looked at me critically. I seldom can slip anything

by Matt, but explaining why I didn't like Maddy would just complicate things right now. Luckily he didn't press. "All right," Matt said neutrally. "What is it you want from me?"

"Two things, I guess. One, can you tell me anything about the security in his neighborhood? Edge of the east side, overlooking the park. Two . . ." I paused, uncertain how to phrase this. "Is there anything I need to know about the guy?"

"As in, what? Is he mobbed up? Is he on the run from someone? That kind of thing?"

When he said it out loud, I realized how silly it sounded. "Maybe. I don't know. I'm just trying to make sure there aren't any problems on the horizon before I commit to doing anything. Right now I have no idea how much time this might take, but I don't want to waste it."

"Fair enough. Okay, the answer to the first question is that our taxpayers make sure that we keep a visible presence in that particular neighborhood, and we endeavor to keep them happy. And I understand some areas up there have hired supplemental security. I'd be willing to bet some of my force are picking up extra dollars doing that, on their own time. About the other, I can't say that I know much. You want me to run a criminal check, that kind of thing?"

I thought for a moment, realizing what an awkward position this put him in. "No, I guess not. I mean, he's a public figure, so if there was any dirt, like a criminal record, somebody would have found it by now. But if you hear anything out of the ordinary, would you let me know?"

"Of course. Are you going to meet the guy?"

"I already have, yesterday."

"Ah. What's he like? I only know what I've read in the papers."

"Not at all what I expected. Smart—I figured that. But from what little I've seen, he really cares about glass. It's not just, dare I say it, window dressing for somebody with a lot of money who wants to show off. Although apparently he does have lots of money. The collection could be worth millions."

"Interesting. Well, thanks for the heads-up—it's good to know he's in town. Now, can we talk about something more interesting? Like dessert?"

After dinner we drove back to my home. Matt pulled in behind the building, where I normally park. He turned to me. "May I see you to your door?"

"Certainly, kind sir. And may I offer you the proverbial nightcap?"

"I would be delighted to avail myself of your hospitality. Um, you said something about Cam visiting?"

"I did, but he claimed he was going to be out this evening, so we should have the place to ourselves."

"Excellent."

We climbed the stairs and enjoyed the dogs' welcome—they liked Matt, thank goodness.

"Would you mind giving them a quick walk around the block? That way I can slip into something more comfortable, and see if I can find that nightcap."

"I am at your service. But once around the block, right? My patience only stretches so far."

"Deal." I handed him the leashes. "Now, go!"

I watched as he disappeared into the darkness with Fred and Gloria, then turned back to my space. Matt was a good man, and in many ways we were well suited. But as I looked around my home, which I had found and bought and shaped into exactly what I wanted, I wondered if I could give it up—not that he had asked—or if I could see him somehow fitting into it—not that *I* had asked. Somehow I had always thought that by this point in my life I would know what I wanted, and now I was finding I had been wrong. *Enough, Em!* There was no urgency to make a decision right now, and I should just enjoy the moment and let the future take care of itself.

I could hear Matt's returning footsteps on the stairs, and I found myself smiling. The man really was in a hurry, so I headed for the bedroom and the filmy number I'd laid out, just in case.

Chapter 6

❀

Matt was gone by the time Cam let himself in late that night. I was too snug to bother looking at the clock. *Trouble in paradise?* I wondered as I drifted back to sleep.

I was not reassured by the sight of Cam's face at breakfast the next morning. "Problems?" I ventured, trying to be tactful—not easy, this early.

He shook his head. "I don't know. You remember that weird animal in *Doctor Doolittle* with the heads at both ends?"

"Yup. Why?"

"That's the way this feels. She says she loves me, but then she pushes me away. I don't know what to do."

"Wait. Be steadfast, brave, and true, and trust that it will all work out in the end."

He looked at me skeptically. "And how are things going with your warrior hero?"

"Just fine, thank you very much. Now can we talk about

something that doesn't involve our messy romantic lives? You have any plans for the day?"

"We thought we'd go see the San Xavier Mission— Allison hasn't seen it yet. You?"

"I might do some more work in the studio. I'm playing with a new technique—well, new to me—where you take colored rods and fuse them around the bubble and stretch it out."

"You really like trying out new techniques, don't you?" Cam said, almost wistfully.

"Sure. Hey, remember, I haven't been doing this all that long, and I know I've still got lots to learn. Besides, it keeps things interesting. Don't you find the same thing with computer code?"

He shrugged. "Sometimes. More in the hardware than the software these days. Maybe Ferguson had the right idea, getting out now. He's still got time to do something else with his life, if he wants to."

"Are you thinking about becoming an art collector?" I tried to lighten Cam's uncharacteristic morose mood. I managed to draw a smile from him.

"I don't think so. But aren't there some dude ranches around here? Maybe I could become a wrangler. Just for a change of pace."

"But then you'd have to really work!"

We bantered happily until Cam adjourned to the shower. I was surprised when the phone rang—Cam was just about the only person who called on this line, besides Matt, occasionally. I was even more surprised when I answered and found it was Peter Ferguson.

"Am I calling at a bad time?"

How had he gotten my number? I hadn't given it to him. Oh, right—he's a computer genius, so he could probably find anything. "Oh, no, nothing like that. I was already up, and I was just getting ready to head down to the studio."

Em, you're babbling. "What can I do for you, Peter?"
*Please don't say you're firing me before you've even hired
me.* I was surprised by how much I cared.

"A couple more of the glass pieces have arrived, and I
wondered if you'd like to see them?"

No mention of Maddy. Should I bring her up? I decided
against it. I would much prefer some quality time with the
glass—not to mention Peter Ferguson—without her intru-
sive presence. "When did you have in mind?"

"Today, if you're not too busy."

The glass in my studio wasn't going anywhere, and
Nessa could cover the shop. "Fine. Say, one o'clock?"

"Excellent. You can find your way?"

"I think so. You might as well give me your phone number, just in case I get lost."

I scribbled down the number he gave me, and hung up. I
turned to find Cam looking at me with a wistful expression.
"What?" I demanded.

"That was Peter Ferguson?"

I nodded. "He wants me to look at some more of his
glass panels. No, you can't come. Maybe next time." *Good
heavens,* I thought, *would there be a next time?* "And he
didn't say anything about Maddy. I wonder what that's all
about."

"You sure that's all he wants?"

It took me a moment to figure out what he meant. "Cam!
It's nothing like that. He knows I share his appreciation of
these pieces, and I'm not sure Maddy feels the same way.
It's a privilege to get to see them."

"Uh-huh. Did I mention that Ferguson doesn't appear to
be married at the moment? Although he was, at least once,
according to what I saw yesterday."

"So what? This is not a romantic rendezvous. This is
business."

"Whatever you say."

I had to think Cam's hormones were running amok, and he was seeing things that didn't exist. Sure, Peter was an attractive man, but I wasn't in the market. I was taken. I was in a committed and stable relationship. Uh-huh.

I was ridiculously pleased with myself when I managed to find Peter's house on the first try, since I was not exactly familiar with the upscale neighborhood. I realized as I approached the driveway that I hadn't asked about whether I would have any trouble getting through the security. I stopped beside the box at the end of the driveway and stared at it, trying to recall which button Maddy had pushed, and then jumped when a voice said, "Drive on up." I had to wonder what kind of system kept constant watch. Or maybe Peter had been hovering, eagerly waiting my arrival. Sure. I drove up the drive without setting off any sirens or attracting slavering Dobermans. I wondered what else his security system included. Obviously someone like Peter Ferguson would have access to the most cutting-edge electronics, but I still wasn't sure how those would be used on a hillside lot without fencing. I parked where Maddy had parked earlier, and after smoothing the wrinkles out of my pants and pulling down my shirt, I approached the door. It opened before I could decipher the unobtrusive intercom system. There he was in front of me before I had time to prepare myself mentally—and he looked as good this time as he had the first time.

"Em, thanks for coming. I hope I haven't taken you away from anything important." Today Peter was wearing a different, darker pair of jeans and a terra cotta–colored long-sleeve T-shirt that highlighted the silver cast to his hair. He looked completely . . . ordinary. I had to remind myself again that this man could probably buy a small country if he wanted to.

"Do people often turn down your invitations?" I said, more tartly than I intended. I was nervous, although I wasn't sure why.

He chuckled. "Actually, I don't invite many people here, so it's not a statistically valid sample. Come on in."

Nothing had changed since my first visit—the place was still empty and gleaming. "Is Maddy coming?"

"Come on through to the kitchen," he said. "No, I didn't invite her. I wanted to talk to you."

Why did I feel like a schoolgirl called to the principal's office? "Should I be flattered or worried?"

The kitchen was much like the rest of the house—acres of gleaming brushed steel, granite countertop, cool tile floors. Since the kitchen was at the rear of the house, the windows were small and looked out on the rising hillside dotted with scruffy mesquite and assorted cacti.

"Is it too early for a beer?"

"Sure, fine." This was a social occasion?

He pulled a couple of bottles out of the mammoth refrigerator and offered me one. I took it and twisted off the top—no fragile flower, I. He raised his bottle to me, and we drank.

I had no idea what to say next, but he solved that problem for me. "You look like you think I'm going to bite. Relax."

"Sorry. I just don't understand why I'm here." *And Maddy isn't.*

"Listen, I've got a couple of folding chairs in the—heck, I don't know what to call it—the big room? Can we sit down?"

"Sure." I followed him back into the main space and had to fight to drag my eyes away from the amazing view. I was raised on the East Coast, and even after ten years in Tucson I still hadn't gotten over how spectacular it could be. He gestured toward a chair, and I sat; he pulled another chair closer, perpendicular to mine, and then he sat. He took another long swallow of beer before he started speaking.

"You've got to be wondering why I hired Madelyn Sheffield for this job."

I stared at him, trying to decide how to answer. I opted for the truth. "To be honest, I have. I don't know how you know her, but what I've seen of her work is, uh, nice, but not at all in this league." Mediocre, trite, silly—there were a lot of adjectives I could have picked, but I was trying to be polite. "And if we're putting all our cards on the table, I've also wondered just why I'm here."

He twirled the bottle between his hands. "You're an intelligent woman, and I figured you would have questions. I thought it would be simpler if I just explained up front, and you can decide whether you want to work with me. With the collection."

"Thank you, I think. I'm listening."

"Your assessment of Maddy's talents is accurate. To put it kindly, I think she's reached her full potential running a small shop in a tourist mecca. She makes a modest living."

"Okay," I said dubiously. Did he lump me in the same category?

Again, he read my mind. "She can't hold a candle to you. You're serious about your work, and you're turning out some interesting pieces. Along with the commercial ones. I know—you've got to make a living."

Was he going to offer to be my patron? Play Medici? This was becoming bizarre. "You were going to explain what Maddy is doing here."

He sighed. "Maddy is the daughter of my mother's college roommate. They were close then, and they stayed close, and I guess you could say that my mother has had a huge advantage in terms of bragging rights. She feels bad about that, from time to time, so when I started talking about installing this collection, she remembered little Madelyn, and she decided she could make up for a lot by involving her. God help me, I agreed to go along. I'd met Maddy occasionally over the years, but she didn't leave any lasting impression. When I met her again after my mother had cooked up this little scheme, I was less than thrilled, but I'd already agreed, and my mother wasn't about to let me off the hook. And Maddy was so pleased, I didn't have the heart to tell her I wanted to back out."

I was beginning to see a glimmer of logic here. "So that's where I come in? I'm supposed to provide the expertise or whatever that Maddy lacks?"

"That's what I hoped. If you're willing. When I realized that I was stuck with Maddy, I started looking for someone to back her up, and your name came up a couple of times. I saw some of your work, and I liked what I saw. Look, I know that installing the collection isn't exactly rocket science, and I'm taking care of all the structural considerations, but I've asked Maddy to work out placement, coordinating other lights in each room, that kind of thing. I'm sorry if I insulted you, but the only way I could think of to bring you in was to think up some portion of the project that I knew Maddy couldn't handle—the hot-glass work."

"Were you serious about that, or was it only a cover story?" I didn't know if I felt relieved or disappointed.

"I'm serious. It's not a major commission, because I want to keep things focused on the panels, not tarted up with a lot of unnecessary accessories, but I envision harmonizing the interior lighting with the main panels. I want it to be unobtrusive but complementary. I have the awful feeling that Maddy would want to churn out mock Tiffany shades with themes to match the artwork." He gave a theatrical shudder, then looked directly at me. "What are you thinking?"

I took a second to figure out exactly what I did think. "For a start, I'm glad you told me. This whole thing didn't make a lot of sense to me. Maddy was not a logical choice for this kind of project, and she doesn't like me much, so bringing me in made the whole package even stranger. Now I can understand it, and thanks for laying it out. Did you tell Maddy I came with the package?"

"Let's say I suggested it strongly. Why don't you get along?"

"For the reasons you already pointed out: I think she's a lightweight, and I care about what I'm doing. She thinks she's an artist. I don't buy it, not that I'd tell her to her face. We're part of the same local community, so I don't go looking for trouble. But I think I can say that working with her is not going to be a picnic. She's already tried to shut me out—she didn't want me coming back here again. She wants control of things." I hesitated for a moment before adding, "And I think that's one of my conditions. If you want me to stay on and babysit Maddy, I'll need to have equal access to the pieces, if I'm supposed to come up with something harmonious."

"I wouldn't expect anything less. Let me worry about Maddy. So you'll stay?"

Had he had any doubt? The siren song of the glass had lured me here—well, that and some ordinary curiosity about a man whose name appeared in headlines. So sue me, I'm human. But the glass was the deciding factor: I wanted to see those windows, not just once, but again and again, under different conditions. I wanted to *know* them, internalize them, learn from them, and see what I could take from them for my own art. "I will, under those conditions. You manage Maddy, and I'll see that she doesn't go overboard with cutesy."

"Thank you," he said simply. We sat in silence for several beats, and then he stood up abruptly. "Do you want to see what else I've uncrated?"

I stood too. "Absolutely."

As we walked back toward the front of the house, I asked, "You know, Maddy hasn't filled me in on the scope of the project. How many rooms are you talking about? Which artists?"

"Six rooms, all the ones overlooking the desert, on the ground floor. You've seen the Chagall already. I've got a magnificent French medieval panel, very rich colors. A Tiffany, of course. A Matisse, a William Morris, a Frank Lloyd Wright. Those are the major pieces. There are a number of smaller ones, but they'll be easier to distribute, and I'm playing around with some display ideas."

We were walking slowly now. "And what were you thinking about placement?"

"I'm still working that out. Chronological order seems rather trite, and I'm still getting used to the house, how the light falls. You know, several of these pieces I've seen only in dealers' showrooms, by artificial light. I need to see them by natural light. Wouldn't you agree?"

"Completely. You can rationalize all you want, but there is still a visceral, emotional response to any work of art, and the windows incorporate a whole other dimension."

We had reached the doorway of yet another room. "Of course—light." When we walked into the room, I came face-to-face with the medieval window, and it stopped me in my tracks.

In college, and after, I had done the European grand tour thing and had ogled my share of cathedrals along the way. I know what an extraordinary effect medieval architects and glass artisans had achieved combining their solid stone with the ephemeral screens of colored glass. But finding one in front of me, illuminated by the intense Arizona sunlight, was an entirely different experience. I waited until my head had stopped spinning and tried to look at it dispassionately. It wasn't easy.

I barely heard Peter's soft voice. "For bright is that which is brightly coupled with the bright/And which the new light pervades,/ Bright is the noble work."

"Abbot Suger," I breathed. "Oh, lord, don't tell me this came from St. Denis?"

Peter smiled. "The first true marriage of form and philosophy, the divine light of God's wisdom embodied in colored glass. Almost makes you want to believe, doesn't it?"

I crept closer, examining the individual pieces of glass, their color, their inherent flaws. There was so much I could learn here, so much I could use. . . . I realized neither of us had spoken for a few minutes, and reluctantly I pulled myself away. "I'm sorry, was I being rude?"

"I don't mind being upstaged by the glass. And I'd be disappointed if you didn't feel that way about them."

I felt a stab of pure joy. I had been handed a great gift, unlooked for: the chance to work with these panels. Maddy and her petty jealousies faded to nothingness. "Are the others here?"

"Pace yourself, Em. As I am doing. You know what I mean."

"I do. To look at them all at once would be sensory overload." I drew a deep breath and let it out slowly. "So, where do we go from here?"

We spent a half hour or so hammering out mundane details of compensation and scheduling. I almost felt guilty about taking money for this project, but I still needed to make a living, and Peter had money to spare. I managed to cut what I figured was a generous deal for myself, even knowing I could have asked for more. It didn't matter.

I drove away feeling drunk. Not from that single beer, hours earlier, but from the glory of the glass, and the pleasures it promised in the days and weeks to come.

When I got home, Cam was gone, on his way back to San Diego, but he'd left me a note and a brief report, on the kitchen table where I couldn't miss it. I took care of my doggie duties, managed to scrounge together a meal from leftovers, and sat down to see what Cam had found. I wasn't sure what I was looking for, but I didn't want to get involved in a sticky situation, whatever that might mean. Had Peter put together his collection with funds that he had amassed by stiffing his staff and colleagues? And how would I feel about that? I didn't know. And what kind of a person was Peter Ferguson? I didn't expect Cam to hand me a detailed psychological profile based on a couple of hours of Internet surfing, but I was curious about the public perception of the man. "Secretive genius" came through loud and clear, but was he honest? Was he a dilettante who would lose interest mid-project? These were things I had to know before I signed on. No matter how attractive the man himself was, or how much I yearned to be around the glass itself. I settled down to read.

Half an hour later I had found nothing that changed my original impression of the man. There was no suggestion of illegal activity attached to his business, save from the disgruntled Andrew Foster, who had made some wild public claims and then subsided. Cam had included a few printouts about art sales, but clearly he hadn't been sure what he was looking for, which made it hard for him to search. I could give him a few pointers about that, if I needed more details. Ian Gemberling, it turned out, owned an upscale gallery in Los Angeles, dealing in a variety of media. He was probably important enough that I should have heard of him, if I paid any attention to that kind of thing, which I didn't.

Not surprisingly, since he was a multimillionaire, Peter's private life had also percolated into the media. Only one wife, and they had divorced about two years earlier. Two children, college age. I studied the lone photo of the former wife. Jennifer Ferguson—she'd kept Peter's surname after the divorce. She was sleek and elegant, with

Chapter 7

❀

Much to my surprise, over the next few days Peter, Maddy, and I came up with a schedule that worked. Maddy did whatever she did, and I didn't ask about the details. She and I went out together to see Peter a couple of times over the following week or two, to see the new pieces as they were uncrated and to present Peter with the concepts we had come up with. Maddy's efforts were predictably trite, but I managed to steer her away from the worst of her ideas without ruffling her feathers too badly. I was proud of myself for my restraint.

Peter and I carefully did not mention that I had been making my own trips out to his place so that I could spend quality time with the glass. These excursions had fallen into a pattern. Peter would disable his electronic watchdogs, let me in, and offer me something cold to drink. I would accept. We would then drift to whatever room he had assigned the newly revealed piece to. We would spend some time in rapt silence, absorbing the artwork. Then slowly I would begin to offer comments, make suggestions. Only once did I think he had chosen the wrong setting, for a delicate William Morris panel that was overwhelmed by the blazing Arizona sun. I thought it would benefit from more subtle lighting, and Peter agreed quickly, proposing a more sheltered position.

We avoided talking about Maddy for the most part, which I took as tacit approval of how I had been handling our joint effort. In truth, there was little for Maddy to do, beyond installing the panels and working up a few designs for the minor windows in the room. This was clearly a charity gesture on Peter's part. I in fact had much more to do. He could have opted for high-tech but unobtrusive halogen spotlighting, or gone with muted sconces that all but receded into the walls, but he gave me my head and let me play with forms and colors, trying to create pieces that harmonized with the windows without stealing any of their thunder. It was an interesting challenge—and our discussions were equally interesting.

The single largest piece was to be a chandelier in what would become the dining room, eventually. Given the layout of the house, one saw the hanging fixture from the hallway before entering the room to confront the incredible Tiffany panel, a variation of *The River of Life*, that dominated the exterior wall. The fixture's position would showcase my art, but I wanted to stay miles away from any kitschy pseudo Tiffany dome—there were far too many cheap knockoffs on the market these days. We spent a couple of hours one afternoon debating about alternatives.

"I love the way you're injecting some humor here—the image of water juxtaposed to the Arizona desert," I said. "I'd like to play off that—the feeling of water. Cool, flowing, if you know what I mean, and I want to keep it simple, clean, but make sure that the colors in the glass are tied in with the ones in the window. Not easy."

"Because he used his own glass?"

"That's part of it." Tiffany had experimented with techniques for glassmaking, and they weren't always easy to recreate. "But what he did with the glass—heck, you know as well as I do—it's practically three-dimensional sculpture." I ran a reverent finger over a particular fragment in the window, whose surface irregularities mimicked rippling water. "And because of that, it's too thick to use for a fixture with much lower light levels. If I'm not careful, it will look muddy and chunky. But I can't just do it thinner, because then you lose the sculptural quality. So I'm playing with some ideas about layering the glass, to kind of fool the eye. As Tiffany did."

"Interesting approach," he said, nodding. "What about supports? Do you plan to go with the traditional leading?"

"I haven't decided. The window is part of the wall, the structure of a space, so it's appropriate that it be substantial, both visually and for strength. But the light fixture floats in space and has to be more ethereal. I don't want it to look like a piece of Victoriana that just wandered in."

"What's the alternative?"

"Frankly, I don't know yet. I'm still trying to get the glass part down, work out the curvature. It's a little out of my comfort zone, but I'm learning."

"You aren't going for anything showy? Like a Chihuly sea creature?"

I had to check to see if he was making fun of me. He was. "You know very well how ridiculous that would be, in this context."

"Em, I have every faith that you'll find a way to make this work."

"You know, there's one thing that's been troubling me: How do you plan to protect the glass?"

He cocked his head at me. "Do you mean security? You've seen my alarm systems."

"Yes, I know, and I assume you've got that covered. But I mean, physically. You're not from around here, right? I don't know what gun laws are like where you come from, but around here, there's not a lot of regulation, especially for rifles and shotguns."

"Where are you going with this, Em?"

"There are plenty of guns around, and your place is pretty exposed. What's to stop somebody with a grudge, or just a bellyful of tequila, from taking a few potshots at your windows?"

"Ah," he said, smiling. "I wouldn't have expected you to think of that, but it has crossed my mind. I will be installing bulletproof glass on the exterior. And before you ask, this will be done as unobtrusively as possible, following the lines of the leading. And it will also be vented—I understand conditions can be rather extreme around here. Does that satisfy you?"

"That's perfect. It's just that I'd hate to see anything bad happen to the pieces."

"I understand."

Our eyes met, and I wondered what I saw in his. He had always been professionally distant in our meetings, and our discussions had focused on practical issues. Save when he talked about his collection—then, I saw flashes of passion. But he was still an enigma. He never mentioned any other people, and there was no evidence of others in the house, apart from whoever had carried in the glass panels—too heavy for one person to manage. But there was a lurking sensuality in him that was intriguing, and I wondered more than once who was on the receiving end of that. Not me, nor did I invite it. I valued the careful friendship we had established, and we both respected the limits.

And then it ended, in the most final way.

He called a few days after our last meeting to say that the final panel had arrived, and would I like to see it? It was a

Frank Lloyd Wright, one of his Saguaro series, which made it a particularly apt inside joke. But I had a busy week planned, and much as I wanted to dash straight out there to see the latest treasure, I had to put him off for a couple of days. We set a date for Thursday, two days in the future, in the afternoon when the sun would be low in the sky. I felt a mixture of excitement and sadness: excitement because now the ensemble would be complete, and I would know the full scope of what I was working with; sadness because this would be the last surprise, the last opportunity to walk into a room to something wonderful and to know that I would have the luxury of coming to know it intimately.

When the day came, I made the now-familiar drive and arrived on time. By now I was used to passing through the exterior defenses without announcing myself, so I drove straight up the driveway and parked. When I walked to the door, it was closed, so I buzzed the intercom and got no response. That was odd—until now Peter had always been waiting for me. After trying again, I reached for the door handle, and to my surprise the door opened.

My sensible inner voice told me to stop right there. Peter was absolutely scrupulous about security and had always been at least within earshot when I arrived, with or without Maddy. Maybe he was doing something in another part of the house? I felt silly just standing there, fretting because the door was open and it made me nervous. I told the inner voice to shut up and stepped into the cool dark hallway, closing the door behind me. "Peter?" I called out. My voice echoed off the walls, but I could hear no one stirring. Even the air was still, as though no one had used it lately.

I moved farther into the house, calling out again. "Peter? Where are you?" Nothing.

I looked around me, and everything seemed normal. Of course, there was very little to disturb, since the house was still unfurnished. No lights on, but there was still plenty of daylight, so that didn't mean anything. But the alarm system was not armed. . . . Now I really was getting nervous.

I walked into what we had dubbed the Great Room, the largest one with the most spectacular views. And then I saw him.

He lay on his back, surrounded by a pool of what had to be blood, though at the moment it was no more than a tarry stain. A lone fly buzzed around it. My knees went weak, and I sank to the floor. I didn't need to go any closer, because there was no doubt in my mind that he was dead. That gray color didn't belong on a living person. Besides, the cause of death was obvious: a large shard of glass protruding from his chest.

This was my second . . . no, third dead body. How was it that I had made it through more than forty years without even a hint of violence in my life, and now within the space of a couple of months I had encountered three corpses? What had I done to deserve this?

But at least I knew what I had to do now. I fished in my bag for my cell phone and punched the speed-dial for Matt. He answered on the second ring, sounding distant and official. "Chief Lundgren."

I took a deep breath. "Matt, I'm at Peter Ferguson's. He's dead."

As chief of police, Matt had long since learned not to ask stupid questions. "You sure?"

"Yes, I'm sure he's dead," I said with some asperity. "The blood's been dry for a while." Actually I wasn't sure how long, since the dry Arizona air sucks moisture out of everything—fast. I knew when I had last talked to him, but after that, it could have been any time. "I haven't touched anything. At least not this time. Not even the body."

Matt sighed. "Okay, stay there. I'll get the team together." After an infinitesimal pause, he added, "Are you all right?"

"I guess. Better than Peter, anyway."

"We'll be there in fifteen. Sit tight." He rang off after getting the address from me.

I wished that I hadn't known how a murder investigation worked, but at least I had friends in the right places. Matt was on his way, and he would figure this out. I stuffed my phone back into my bag. The initial shock had worn off, and I began to look around from my spot on the floor. That was when I realized that the glass panel that should have been in the room was gone.

That got me to my feet. I pivoted slowly, checking the rest of the room. After all, Peter could have moved it for some reason. No, it was not in the room, and there was nowhere to hide anything that size. Nor was there any packing material in evidence.

At that point I turned without thinking and ran to the adjoining room. Same thing: no panel. It was as though it had never been there. I went from room to room, and the story was the same. Peter's collection was definitely not here.

Maybe he had sent them out for cleaning. Or framing. Or he had stuck them in some special vault while he finished construction on the house. No, that didn't make sense—he had asked me out specifically to see the last one today. So it should be here, and it wasn't. Stolen?

I shivered, despite the heat. Peter dead, the artworks missing. But making off with multiple panels of stained glass would not have been easy. You didn't just pick one up and walk out with it under your arm.

I made my way slowly back to the entrance hall in time to welcome the police, with Matt Lundgren leading the pack. And to my eternal shame, I flung myself into his arms and said to his broad and manly chest, "Oh, Matt, it's gone!" before dissolving into sobs.

Chapter 8

❀

Matt proceeded to demonstrate the aplomb that had facilitated his rise through the ranks of Tucson's police force: He straightened his shoulders, patted me on the back with one hand, and pointed toward the front room with the other. "In there, and be careful."

When his crew had moved on, he stopped patting my back and said, "You found him? You're sure he's gone?"

I gathered the shreds of my dignity and stepped back, wishing I had a handkerchief on me. "Yes, I found him." I sniffed. "But what I said was, 'It's gone.'"

Matt looked blankly at me. "It?"

"Yes. The glass collection. All of it. Gone. As in, not here."

"Robbery?" Matt did catch on fast.

"How should I know? The pieces were laid out in different rooms the last time I was here. Today I can't find any of them." I paused a moment to gather my wayward thoughts. "I told you I was working with Peter. I needed to see the glass pieces so I could design fixtures to go with them. I've been to the house"—I stopped to count mentally—"maybe six or seven times? Alone, I mean without Maddy, that is. I was here a couple of times with her too. We all were. Here, I mean." I took a deep breath to steady my nerves, as the reality of what had happened began to sink in. Peter was dead. *What a waste*.

"Chief?" One of the officers called from the front room.

"Be right there," Matt answered. Then he turned to me. "Are you all right, Em? Do you need to sit down or anything?"

"In case you hadn't noticed, there's not much to sit on here. But I'm fine, Matt, really."

I was worried that he was going to ask me to stay in the hall and wait like a good little girl while he did all the police stuff, but he didn't say anything, although he gave me a long, skeptical look, and when he strode toward the front room, I followed. Nothing had changed, except now a circle of men in uniforms were staring down at Peter's lifeless corpse.

"You didn't touch anything, Em?" Matt asked.

"Of course not. I've been through this before, remember? I know the routine. I walked into the room, I saw him lying there, and it was pretty plain that he was dead. I didn't need to touch him. But you know my fingerprints are going to be all over this place, and so will Madelyn Sheffield's. I can give you her number. I haven't been upstairs—all the pieces he planned to display were going to be installed downstairs. But I've been in all the rooms on this floor, including the kitchen and the powder room. Just to let you know."

"You say there are pieces of art missing. Can you describe them?"

"Of course I can, in detail. Well, except for the last one, the Frank Lloyd Wright." Which I never got to see.

I swallowed hard. "I'll give you a list, but I'm sure Peter has—had—an inventory somewhere around, and his insurance company must too."

"You want to give me the bare outlines?"

"Six panels ranging in size from about eight feet by five feet, to fifteen feet high—the big one was going to go in this room here. Colored glass, a lot of lead holding them together, so they're heavy. Big name artists—Tiffany, Chagall, Frank Lloyd Wright. One medieval piece, and some smaller items. And big bucks—I think Peter said the whole collection was insured for around three million, although that was replacement value. Not that they're replaceable."

The officers were beginning to look shell-shocked. Or maybe they just found it hard to believe that anyone would spend that much on a bunch of windows. But solving Peter's murder was the first order of business.

"When did you last see the pieces here, Em?" Matt pressed on.

"Uh, last weekend, I think, but I talked to him on Tuesday. He asked me to come out because he'd just unpacked the Wright and he wanted to let me take a look at it. I was busy, so I couldn't make it until today." I shivered. Peter was alive on Tuesday; Peter was not alive today. How had that happened?

My mind went wandering off somewhere, although I vaguely heard Matt issuing orders to his officers, and a couple of them scurried off to use cell phones in various corners. Then he turned to me and said, "You know the layout—why don't you show me around? Let's start with the kitchen, shall we?"

"This way." I led him to the kitchen, which still looked sterile and unlived-in. Not even a drinking glass marred the expanse of polished counter.

Matt made a quick scan of the place. "Nice. Expensive."

"No doubt. He could afford it."

I leaned against the granite edge of the central island; Matt leaned against a countertop opposite me. "Em, I'm sorry."

"Why?"

"That you're mixed up in another murder. Since you called it in, I figured it would save time to come myself."

"I'm glad you did." I had been relieved when I saw him coming through that door. We'd been through enough for me to know that he was a good cop, and a good man to have on my side. "Is this going to be difficult, since I'm the one who found him, and you and I have a . . . thing?"

His mouth twitched. "Is that what they call it these days, a 'thing'? But the answer is no. It's a murder investigation. I've got a good team. I'll give them free rein and see what they come up with. What do *you* think happened? He interrupted a robbery?"

"I find that hard to believe. He was careful about security, so if the alarm never went off, he must have let that person in. Maybe there's a surveillance tape of some sort?" I looked at him hopefully.

"We'll check that out. Wouldn't there be people coming and going? Workmen, friends, whatever?"

I shook my head. "Not that I ever saw. He lived here alone—at least, I think he lived here. It's pretty sparse, as you can see. He could have been staying at a local hotel. But anyway, he didn't have a lot of friends around here."

"Exes? Lady friends?"

"Not that I know about. Look, Matt, we didn't talk about that kind of personal stuff. I can tell you he was passionate about his collection, and he was easy to work with. He asked for my opinion, more than once, and he listened to it." I hesitated before adding, "Cam did say he'd been married at least once, but he wasn't now."

Matt cocked his head at me. "You had Cam check him out? Why?"

"Heck, I was curious. I wanted to know what I was getting into."

"Huh. Did Cam find out anything else interesting?"

"What would you consider interesting? I assume you'll do a full profile on him, now that he's a murder victim. You'll find out that there are people who weren't happy about how he handled his business dealings, although Cam didn't find anything illegal. Heck, you're probably better equipped to look into the legal side than Cam is."

"I'll want to talk to him."

"He'll be here this weekend."

Matt was silent for a moment. "What about this Madelyn person you mentioned?"

"She's how I got sucked into this. Well, sort of. Okay, let me explain. Peter told me that his mother knew Maddy's mother in college, and his mother wanted him to help her out, so he offered her this commission, but then he kind of insisted that I be included in the package—"

Matt help up a hand. "Whoa, slow down. Let's take this one step at a time. Peter hired Maddy for this project?"

I nodded.

"And how did you get involved?"

"How do I put this tactfully? Maddy's skills aren't really up to this kind of commission—she sells little glass suncatchers to tourists. This really was an act of charity, and Peter knew that. So he went looking for someone to back her up, and he came across me. He said he'd seen some of my work. He figured he could work me in without ticking off Maddy and make everybody happy."

"How was it going?" Matt asked.

I considered how to frame my answer. "We were managing. Maddy doesn't like me much, but we were muddling along. I think Peter was pleased with how the project was coming."

"You had an official agreement with him?"

"Peter and I had a contract, in writing—I made sure of that. I assume he had the same thing with Maddy. He was paying for materials up front in my case, and we agreed on a lump sum on completion."

"How much?"

I mentioned a number, and he whistled. "Nice piece of change. You thought it was fair?"

I nodded. "I did. I just estimated my time and added a fee. I probably could have charged him a lot more and he wouldn't have complained. To be honest, I would have paid him for the privilege of working with the pieces—they're gorgeous. You will find them, won't you?"

"I hope so. We may have to involve the FBI—that's more their area of expertise. But the murder is in our court."

"What happens now?"

"Forensics. You know that. What can you tell me about the murder weapon?"

"Well, assuming he wasn't strangled or poisoned first, you mean that shard of glass?"

Matt nodded. "Is that sharp enough to kill?"

"You're asking me? I'm flattered. But I would say yes, assuming the killer managed to slip it between his ribs at the right angle. Glass is sharp enough, but not particularly strong—it wouldn't go through bone, for example. And whoever used it would probably have some cuts on his hand, unless he wore heavy gloves. It might require some skill to find the right place—or a lot of luck—but it wouldn't require a lot of strength."

"Were there pieces of glass like that lying around the house?"

"You mean, was it just sitting there, handy, or would the killer have had to bring it with him? I'm pretty sure Maddy brought some samples of art glass around, to match colors to the panels—you really do have to see them in place to gauge the quality of the light and the true color, and she knew that much. And she might have brought bits and pieces, remnants of other projects, just to see how the colors worked. So, yes, it's very likely that there were pieces handy here. You'll probably find some others. And they'll have Maddy's prints on them, and mine, and maybe even Peter's, and whoever sold them, and so on."

"Lucky I've got your prints on file." Matt smiled. "You don't like Maddy much, do you?"

I debated about how to answer that. "Not really. Look, it's not a personal thing—she's not someone I would have chosen as a friend, but that's irrelevant. It's that she gives the local artisans a bad name. She does trite commercial work and then wants to be called an artist. I think that rubs a lot of us the wrong way."

"Were any of them jealous about this commission?"

I shook my head. "I don't know how much they know about it. Nothing before the fact. I think Peter was trying to avoid notice, so he didn't exactly put an ad in the local paper. Besides, I'm not sure anyone else in Tucson was qualified to do this kind of work. Though Maddy told everyone who would listen, once things started rolling. I know she managed to get an article into the arts section of the paper." In which I had been graciously given one line, at the end.

"What about you? Wouldn't this boost your career too?"

"Maybe. But Peter wanted to keep things private, and I respected that. We agreed to let Maddy be the front person, when and if it came to that."

"Do you have any idea about who to contact now?"

"You mean, about his death? Nope. As I said, Cam mentioned an ex-wife somewhere, and Peter has to have had lawyers, but I don't know who they might be, or even if they're local. He never mentioned anybody to me."

"You two didn't have a lawyer to draw up your contract?"

I stared at Matt for a moment. "It never occurred to me. I trusted Peter."

We were interrupted by an officer. "Chief, someone's coming up the drive."

"Do you know who it is?" Matt asked.

"No. Woman driving."

Matt looked at me. "Maddy?"

I shrugged. "Could be, although Peter didn't say anything about her being here today. But I talked to him a couple of days ago, and things might have changed."

As we emerged from the kitchen, we heard the front door open, then a shrill female voice, which rose steadily in pitch as the officers there tried to restrain Maddy. I was surprised that she managed to slip through them, but she stopped at the entryway to the Great Room when she caught sight of the body. "Oh, no! Peter?" she wailed.

She turned to appeal to the gathered officers, and then she spotted me and fury flooded her face. "You killed him!"

Chapter 9

❀

For a long moment, nobody moved, everyone watching the near-hysterical Maddy, as if trying to figure out which way to jump. Matt stiffened to a heightened alertness. Had there been a female officer present, she would have been the likeliest candidate to reach out to Maddy. As it was, I was the only other woman in the room, and I wasn't about to comfort someone who had just accused me of murder.

Maddy finally seemed to realize that her histrionics weren't having much effect, and worse, they were messing up her mascara. She managed to pull herself together and began carefully wiping the smudges from beneath her eyes. She quickly zeroed in on Matt as the man in charge, and turned to address him. "Aren't you going to arrest her, Officer?" I had to restrain myself from laughing out loud.

Matt responded gravely. "That's a rather serious accusation, miss . . . ?"

"Madelyn Sheffield, Officer. I've been working with . . .

Mr. Ferguson for several weeks now on an artistic commission, and this woman here has been helping me. But I've known Peter for years."

"I'm Chief Matthew Lundgren, Ms. Sheffield," Matt said gently. "What can you tell me about the victim?"

Maddy's expression altered subtly, and I wondered if she knew about my relationship with Matt. "Peter? He was a sweet, dear man, and a great patron of the arts. He had moved to Tucson only a few months ago, but already he had made his mark."

I wanted to gag. As far as I knew, Maddy was the only person in town who had enjoyed his patronage. Apart from me.

"Since you knew him well, perhaps you have some information about his possible next of kin?" Matt went on.

"Oh, dear, let me think. His mother, of course. Oh, heavens—she'll be devastated. She positively adored Peter. Who's going to tell her? I would volunteer, but I'm just so shattered myself. . . ." Tears threatened again.

"If you will provide me with her name and address, I'll see to it that it's taken care of. Is she infirm? Should someone be with her when she hears the news?"

Maddy had to drag herself out of her wallow of self-pity to consider the question. "Penelope? No, she's quite a strong woman—and if you're wondering if she's old and frail, she's a very spry seventy-five. In fact, she may be off on one of her cruises—I recall Peter mentioning something about that."

"When did you last see Mr. Ferguson?"

"Let me see . . . today is Thursday, so it must have been . . . Tuesday? I brought out some glass samples for him to look at."

"Could you describe the glass?"

"Various pieces. I really can't remember. Why? Does it matter?"

Matt ignored her question. "How many, do you recall?"

"Six or eight, I think. Why is this important?"

"Did you take them with you?"

"Yes, I did, as far as I recall. Chief Lundgren, what is this about? What can my glass samples have to do with Peter's death?"

"Peter Ferguson was stabbed with a shard of glass. Ms. Dowell has identified it as art glass, of the type you use."

Maddy stared at Matt as the color drained from her face. "A piece of *my* glass?" she whispered. Before Matt could answer, her complexion took on a greenish cast, and she turned and dashed toward the kitchen. Sounds of unladylike retching followed. Matt nodded to one of his men, who stationed himself just outside the entrance to the kitchen.

"Well, that's an interesting response." Actually I was annoyed with Maddy, who seemed determined to milk the situation for the maximum possible drama.

"Em," Matt began.

When I turned to look at him, I didn't like what I saw. "What?"

"The woman has suggested that you had something to do with this death."

"That's ridiculous," I sputtered. "You can't possibly believe that!"

"Whether or not I believe it, it's my responsibility to ask her why she believes that."

"I should hope so! She's crazy to even suggest such a thing."

"Em," Matt said with surprising patience, "you still don't get it. I have to take her accusation seriously, which means I have to treat you as a suspect. At the very least I have to hear her out—and you can't participate in that conversation, nor can I share the content with you. Not at this moment."

I couldn't believe what I was hearing. Matt and I were intimately involved, and we'd already been through one all-too-personal murder investigation together. Surely he couldn't think that I had anything to do with this? Luckily I managed to hold my tongue, at least long enough to put myself in his shoes. He was, after all, the chief of police, and he had obligations. He couldn't play favorites or bend the rules just because it was me and not some random street thug. I counted to twelve, and by then I was able to answer him in a steady voice.

"I understand. What would you like me to do now? Should I stay?"

He took his time in answering. "I think it would be best if I talked to Ms. Sheffield without you around." He looked quickly at his watch. "Could you meet me at the station at four?"

I started to say, "Why not at my place?" but then realized that would be stupid. Of course we had to keep this formal, out in the open. "That would be fine. So I'm free to go for now?"

"You are. I'll see you later, Em. You'll be all right getting home?"

I nodded and started for the door just as an ashen Maddy emerged from the kitchen. "You're letting her leave?" she shrilled.

Matt ignored her protest. "Ms. Sheffield, do you feel up to giving me a statement now? Since you appear to be one of the last people to see Mr. Ferguson alive, I'd appreciate it if you could help me put together a time line." He carefully grasped her elbow and guided her toward one of the side rooms. He had now won her full attention, and I was forgotten.

I made my way slowly to my car, parked where I had left it . . . was it only an hour or two before? Then Peter had been alive, at least in my mind; now the image of his

corpse was etched in my memory. I opened the car door
and slumped into the driver's seat, numb. Here I was,
linked to another body. And that put Matt in a difficult position. We had not broadcast our renewed relationship, but
neither had we made a point of hiding it. We were both single and well past the age of consent. But then, neither of us
had expected to find me entangled in another murder that
he would have to investigate. All of which meant that we
would have to put our personal issues on hold for a bit
while he sorted out this mess.

And what on earth had prompted Maddy's accusation?
Was it professional jealousy? I knew I was the better
craftsperson, but I wasn't sure she would acknowledge
that. I was sure she resented my presence on Peter's project, but my role had been his doing, not mine—although I
didn't know what story he had told her. Or was her animus
more personal? She *had* been proprietary about Peter,
though I hadn't seen any chemistry between them. If anything, Peter had treated her like a slightly annoying poodle
nipping at his heels, although he had always been scrupu-
lously polite. Heck, he and I had ignited more sparks than
that, not that either of us had ever followed up. But had
Maddy sensed that? Was she angry at her perceived rejec-
tion? Angry enough to accuse me of murder?

If I kept this up much longer I was going to give myself
a headache. I counseled myself to wait and see what Matt
had to say later. Surely he would poke holes in whatever
story she concocted, and we could get on with finding out
who had killed Peter and what had happened to the missing
glass panels.

In a daze I drove away from the hills and toward the
city. Part of me wanted to go curl up at home and mourn;
another part of me was busy sorting through my work
schedule, which now had some gaping holes in it—time I
had set aside for Peter's project, which would never happen

now. That hurt too—I had become invested in the artistic aspects, and I had been having fun playing with colors and forms. What a waste. But did I mourn Peter's death, or my lost time and effort?

Both, I decided. Peter had been an intriguing and enigmatic man, and I had been enjoying working with him. He had a sincere appreciation for art, but he didn't try to impress, and I believed that he'd honestly valued my opinions. And, selfishly, I had to admit that this project would have boosted my reputation, certainly locally, possibly nationally. All moot now, because someone had killed Peter Ferguson and stolen his collection. Or vice versa.

I arrived at my shop and parked behind it. When I turned the engine off, I sat for a moment, trying to figure out what to do. At least I should tell Nessa what had happened. Damn, the press would be all over this, since Peter was a celebrity, and if it got out that I had found the body, that would just double the attention. For myself, I should put away the pieces I had been working on for Peter, because it would hurt to see them in the studio—but at the same time, putting them away would be like driving one more nail into his coffin, erasing him, and I wasn't ready to do that either. Normally I would have started some work of my own, which I always found soothing, but I didn't have time if I was to meet Matt in a couple of hours. In the end I decided to stop into the shop and give Nessa the brief outline, and then go up to my home and regroup.

When I walked through the shop's front door, Nessa looked up and said quickly, "What's wrong?" She knew me well.

"Peter Ferguson's dead. Murdered." I was glad that I had shared the secret of my commission with Nessa, whom I knew to be unfailingly discreet. It saved me a lot of explanation now.

"Oh, Em, how awful! What happened?"

"I went out to meet him today, and I found him." I fought off the urge to cry: Once a day was more than enough. Once a year was, for that matter. "And then Matt showed up, and then Maddy, and Maddy accused me of killing Peter."

It was kind of amusing to watch the warring expressions on Nessa's face. Sympathy morphed into scorn with a dash of amusement. "Well, that's ridiculous. You wouldn't kill anyone."

"You know that, and I know that, and I hope Matt knows that, but he has to take it seriously. I'm going to give my statement at the station in an hour or two. Can you handle things here?"

"Of course I can. Why don't you go on upstairs and settle your nerves?"

I snorted: I didn't think I had nerves. "Thanks, Nessa. I probably won't be back before you close up, so I'll fill you in tomorrow."

"That's fine, dear. You go on now."

I went. Upstairs the dogs greeted me with enthusiasm, and it wasn't even feeding time. When I threw myself into a chair, they seemed to sense my mood and settled at my feet, watching me. "It's okay, pals. I'm just a little sad." Was that what I was feeling? Peter should be mourned, and I wasn't sure who else was going to do it. His mother, surely. His children, hopefully. He had been a figure of some national prominence, and no doubt there would be glowing obituaries in the papers.

And then I realized that if this was going to make the news, I should tell Cam first. I checked my watch: He should still be at work. I reached for the phone and hit his speed-dial number.

Luckily he was there. "Hi, Em. What's up? Change in plans?"

"You might say that." There was no pretty way of putting this. "Peter Ferguson's dead. I found the body."

Cam was stunned into silence for several seconds. "Oh, Em, that's terrible. What was it, an accident?"

"No, he was murdered."

"You're kidding."

"I wish I was. And, Cam, it gets worse. Maddy accused me of killing him. In front of Matt."

"Em, I'll be there tonight."

"No, Cam, you don't have to do that. You were going to be here tomorrow anyway."

"Em, I'm coming. Once this goes public—I take it that it hasn't yet?—then this is going to be a real mess, and you shouldn't have to go through it alone. I can be there by nine. Just sit tight, okay?"

"Okay. See you later." Much as I hated to admit it, I was glad that Cam would be there to back me up, since Matt couldn't. I checked the clock: time enough for a quick shower before I had to leave to talk to Matt. And a quick walk for the pups, since I had no idea how long I would be at the police station.

Chapter 10

❀

I arrived at the police station before four. "Hi, Mariana, how're the kids?" The desk sergeant and I had known each other ever since Matt and Me, Round One.

"Oh, hey, Em. They're great. So you're mixed up in this Ferguson murder?"

"I am. What're the odds? Pretty soon people will start avoiding me. Is Matt free?"

"Just wrapping something up. I'll let him know you're here."

I took a seat and stared into space for a while, and Matt emerged after about ten minutes.

"Sorry to keep you waiting, Em. Come with me." He waited for me to stand before leading me toward the back of the building. I noticed that he didn't touch me. He was going to do this by the book. He stopped in front of an open door and gestured toward a small interrogation room. "Please, sit down."

I sat. "Okay, Matt, how are we handling this?"

He already looked tired. "I think you understand the problem. The fact that you and I have a preexisting relationship makes things complicated. I have to conduct the investigation of Peter Ferguson's death in a transparent manner. He was a public figure, and there will be a lot of interest in this case."

From his tone I could tell that he was already distancing himself from me. Even though I knew it was appropriate, it still hurt a little. "Matt, I already figured that much out for myself. Just tell me what I need to do."

"Let's review your contacts with Peter Ferguson, starting from the beginning. And I will be recording this conversation, if you don't mind."

Why would I mind? I had nothing to hide. "That's not a problem. Let's see . . . the first I heard about Peter, apart from what I've read in magazines, was when Maddy came to my shop about three weeks ago. . . ." Once again I outlined the sequence of events that had led to my unlikely collaboration with Maddy, and my series of visits to the house in the hills—including those that Maddy had not been part of.

"How many times would you say you were at the house?" Matt asked.

"I could check my calendar. It's not like I dropped everything else to work on his stuff. I think I told you—I'd guess maybe six or seven times."

"How would you characterize your relationship with Peter Ferguson?"

"I found him charming, interesting, intelligent. He knew what he was talking about when it came to his glass collection. He was easy to talk to and a good listener. I enjoyed working with him." My dry statements did little to capture the man, but Matt wanted facts.

"Were you personally involved? Outside of your professional interactions?"

I was beginning to get annoyed at this line of questioning. "No, of course not. How can you ask that?" Matt gave a barely perceptible shake of his head, and I remembered that this was being recorded. "No. I might have called us friends, nothing more."

"Did he ever make advances to you?"

I stared at him. He really was pushing it. "No, he did not. He was never anything but polite and courteous, and completely professional in our dealings."

"Do you know how he knew Madelyn Sheffield?"

"Peter told me that his mother and hers were old friends from college. He had known Maddy casually for years."

"Do you know if they were ever involved in an intimate relationship?"

"How am I supposed to know that?" I exploded. "It would have been inappropriate for Peter to tell me anything like that, not to say ungentlemanly, and Maddy and I aren't close enough to share that kind of information. To the best of my knowledge, there is not now, nor has there ever been, an intimate relationship between Peter Ferguson and Madelyn Sheffield. And that's all I know." I sat back in my chair and glared at him. He had me talking like some character from a bad novel, and I resented the question and the intimation behind it. What was this all about? "Matt, why are you asking me this? What did Maddy tell you?"

"I can't discuss that with you."

"If she's making up lies, don't I have the right to know?"

"Em, I can't tell you what Maddy said. Period. I just want to get your statement on record." His eyes pleaded with me.

I decided to back off—on the record. I could ask him privately. If he was willing to talk to me.

"Seriously, I've told you everything I know. Peter and I had a business relationship. I went to his house today for a meeting we'd set up a couple of days ago, to see the last glass panel, and I found him dead. I called you to report it. Do you know when he died?"

"The forensic team is running tests, but the preliminary estimate is sometime between twelve and twenty-four hours. Where were you yesterday?"

"I was in the shop or the studio all day, with Allison or Nessa. Last night I was home alone, unless you count the dogs." Too bad they couldn't act as witnesses. "Are you saying I need an alibi?"

"I just want to know where you were," he said doggedly. "No phone calls or visitors?"

"No, Matt," I said with as much patience as I could muster, "I was at home, and I read a book. Would you like to know the plot? No one called. I walked the dogs for the last time around ten, but you know how few people there are around in my neighborhood at that time of night, so there probably aren't any witnesses. I went to bed. That's it."

"Thank you. That's all I need for now." He looked at the small camera in the corner and nodded, and I assumed that was his signal to stop recording.

"This is going to be difficult, isn't it?" I said slowly.

He nodded. "I think we shouldn't see each other—socially, I mean—until we get this cleared up."

"I agree. I don't want to make your job any harder. But what about the news? What about Maddy? Can you keep her from blabbing all over town?"

"What part of it? The murder, us, or the theft?"

I realized then that I had completely forgotten about the theft while I was dodging suggestions of canoodling with Peter. "Shoot—what are you saying publicly about the missing art? I mean, that's tied up with the murder, isn't it?"

"Possibly. I've already contacted the FBI, and I'll be talking with them tomorrow. We haven't released any details. The statement will be that Ferguson may have interrupted a burglary at his home and was killed by persons unknown. As for Maddy, I don't have a lot of control over her actions. I've cautioned her about making any public statements."

"Even if she wants to fling unfounded accusations around? What's her line—that I killed Peter out of jealousy? Spite? Because he liked her better than he liked me? How high school is that?"

"Em, you admit you were there alone with him, on more than one occasion. We have no evidence about what went on."

I stood up, furious. "Matthew Lundgren, how can you sit there and say something like that? What kind of a person do you think I am? You actually believe Maddy's stupid claims?"

"Em, sit down. I didn't say that. But I have to investigate all possibilities."

I started pacing. "All? Like Peter's unhappy former employees? Like his ex-wife? Like some unknown art thief? Why are you looking at me?" I wasn't being exactly fair to him, but being accused of murder tends to upset me. Or even being accused of cheating on the man I . . . felt something strong for, which might be love if given half a chance.

I stopped pacing for a moment to collect myself, then sat down again. I could be adult and dignified about this, if I tried really hard. "All right, then. We're putting our personal relationship on hold until you manage to solve this murder. I get it. I'm a suspect, but I will point out that there are a lot more out there. Am I free to go now?"

"Of course. I'm sorry, Em. I know this is difficult. It's hard for me too. I'll do everything I can to get this cleared up as soon as possible. Oh, and can you be available to talk about the artworks with the FBI?"

"Sure, I'll be happy to." I couldn't save Peter, but I sure as hell would do whatever I could to see that his art didn't fall into the clutches of some black-market collector and disappear forever. I hoped whoever had the panels was taking good care of them. They were tough yet fragile at the same time, and I would hate to see them damaged.

"Then I guess we're done here." Matt stood up. "Thank you for coming in. I'll be in touch with you tomorrow, once I know what the FBI needs."

"I should be at the studio all day. I'm not sure what my plans are for the weekend—Cam will be around. But I promise not to leave the state."

I left the station in a huff, and my mood did not improve when I got home. The shop was closed, and I didn't like to work in the studio at night, without natural light. I went upstairs, fed the dogs, walked them, fed myself, then tried to settle down with a book or a magazine or the television. Mostly I waited for Cam to arrive. While there was nothing he could do, it made me feel better to know that he would be around. Maybe I had actually gotten used to having Matt to lean on, and now he'd pulled the rug out from under me. I understood his need to put some distance between us during this investigation, but that didn't mean I liked it.

Cam arrived as promised just before nine. There was no way I was going to fling myself in the arms of another man that day—I'd exhausted my quota with Matt in the morning, and look what good that had done. But I gave him a hearty welcome, seconded by Fred and Gloria. When the hubbub had slowed, he looked at me. "You okay?"

"So far. I talked to Matt this afternoon. Officially, that is. Unofficially he can't talk to me, if you know what I mean."

"That sucks." He hesitated a moment. "Ferguson's death was on the news. I caught it on my car radio."

I sighed. "I figured it was coming, but I have no idea what

that's going to mean around here. Did they say anything
about how he died?"

"Not that I heard. Just, 'Noted computer mogul found
dead in his Tucson home.'"

"That's probably all they've got. Matt was going to try
to downplay the art theft angle. Oh, Cam, I'm glad you're
here!" I decided one hug wouldn't do too much harm. Cam
was good at hugging. When he let go, I said, "Can I get you
anything? Food, drink?"

"Sure. But let's sit down and we can talk while I sort out
the grub. Did you eat?"

"I think so."

He snorted, then went to the refrigerator and started for-
aging. I sat at the table and watched. "I don't know how
this is going to play out, but if Maddy has her way, she's
going to trumpet the idea that I killed him in a fit of jealous
rage or something. She hasn't shared her strategy with me,
but she came upon the scene shrieking murder and pointing the finger at me."

"Why you ever agreed to work with her in the first place
is beyond me. She's a flake, and that's putting it kindly."

"Because I wanted to work with the glass, or at least I did
once I saw it. Before that, curiosity. I was fully prepared to
say no, but once I'd met the man, I liked him. And the glass
was magnificent. So I figured I could put up with Maddy."

"You didn't kill him, did you?" Cam ducked as I threw a
magazine at him.

"Not you too. No, I did not kill Peter Ferguson. No, I do
not know who did. No, I do not have an alibi for the time in
question, or at least not all of it. No, I did not steal his glass
panels—although, come to think of it, in my case that
would be a much better motive than unrequited lust. I liked
Peter, but I really loved his glass."

"Are the two connected? The theft and the murder?"

"No one's saying right now, but it's early days yet."

Cam set a plate with a sandwich in front of me. I poked at it. "What's this?"

"Tuna fish on whole wheat, heavy on the mayo. Has it really been that long since you've seen food that doesn't come with instructions?"

"I didn't know I had any tuna," I grumbled.

"It comes in those little cans—the ones that aren't dog food."

We ate in companionable silence for a few minutes, the dogs posted at our feet, waiting eagerly for any fallout. There wasn't any.

When he was done, Cam stretched out his legs under the table and leaned back. "So, now what?"

"I keep asking that," I said, picking up crumbs and eating them. I guess I *was* hungry. "Matt can't talk about it, and Maddy's going to talk too much. Oh, and I'll probably have to have a chat with the FBI tomorrow. I wonder . . ."

"What?"

"I know the missing pieces, probably better than Maddy. I know that tracing them is the FBI's territory, but I don't know how much they know about glass, and I know quite a lot. Would it hurt to put out a few feelers, see if anyone I know knows anything? If you see what I mean?"

"It could blow up in your face, Em—might look like you're trying to fence the stuff."

I hadn't considered that. "You have a point. How about this: You do your behind-the-scenes computer magic, and I can tell you if you're on the right track?"

"What am I looking for?"

"I don't know—yet. How much do you know about art theft?"

"Me? I write computer programs for ecological forecasts. Why would I know anything about art?"

"Well, pal, I think you're going to learn." I thought for a moment and realized I had my priorities wrong. "Cam, maybe while you're doing your computer magic, you can find out a bit more about Peter? I mean, I know you mentioned his business associates and a former wife, but I'd love to know a few more details about them. I mean, somebody killed him, and I don't want to be the only suspect."

"I'm on it, Em."

Chapter 11

❁

Matt called late that night to say that the FBI was sending someone the next morning and could we get together? While he phrased it politely, I took it to mean my presence was required. I sighed: I wasn't sure when I would get any work done in the studio, and I hated to fall behind. Thank goodness I didn't have a class scheduled until Saturday afternoon, and double thanks that I now had both Nessa and Allison to cover the shop. I could only be in one place at a time, and now I was supposed to be in three.

The next morning I dragged myself out of bed to find that Cam had turned on my television. "What are you doing?" I said on my way to the coffeepot.

"I figured we'd better know what the local news had to say about Peter's death. He was a figure of national importance. And besides, this is the second body you've found this year, which has got to be interesting to someone."

Actually Peter's was the third body, but it wasn't worth arguing about. "Oh, damn and blast. I hadn't even thought

about that. I hope Nessa and Allison are smarter than I am
about it." Much as I hated to admit it, Cam had a point.
Tucson news stations paid a lot of attention to local events
and surprisingly little to whatever went on outside city limits. This would definitely be their kind of story. "So,
what've the talking heads had to say so far?"

"Not too much. I'll bet Matt has been trying to keep it
hush-hush, which must drive them nuts. Anyway, the party
line seems to be 'computer mogul found slain in expensive
home, probably interrupted a robbery.'"

"They didn't mention what was taken?"

"Not that I've heard. Is that good or bad?"

I shrugged. "I really don't know. It's not like eight-foot
panels of antique glass are going to show up in local pawn-
shops, so the public doesn't have to watch for them, exactly."

Cam nudged me and pointed to the screen again. The
newscaster had been replaced by canned footage of Peter
from various events, and then a woman whom I recognized from Cam's printouts as Jennifer the ex appeared and
spoke. "Peter's death is a tragic loss to the computer community, and his children and I are devastated. I will assist
local officials in any way I can to see that Peter's killer is
brought to justice."

I caught a glimpse of Matt standing behind her, stone-
faced. I knew he hated public appearances like this, but Peter was a bona fide celebrity and there was no way around
it. Interesting that Jennifer had rushed to Tucson from
wherever she had been so quickly. I wondered what she
would bring to the table, if anything. She certainly looked
the part of the grieving widow, without a hair out of place.

"She sure got here fast," I said to Cam as I spooned cac-
tus jelly on an English muffin. "Wonder if it's concern about
poor Peter, the father of her children, or for his will?"

"Em, you need an attitude adjustment. Can't you see she's
suffering?" He smiled. "But from what I've read, she's been

very happy to use Peter's money to buy her way into the right circles. Lots of high-profile charity work. She likes the limelight."

Unlike Peter. "Well, I'm still glad they didn't say anything about the art. Did anyone mention me?"

Cam shook his head. "Not that I saw. Just 'police discovered the body of,' et cetera."

Maybe Matt had managed to keep me out of it, for which I would be eternally grateful. One murder associated with me, people could forget; two murders, and they'd begin to wonder if I was safe to be around. Not good for business. "Well, I've got to head out for the police station. You have plans?"

"Not yet, but I'm sure I'll figure out something. Unless you want me to come along?"

"No, I think I'd do better on my own. But keep an eye on the news if you can."

"Will do."

An hour later I presented myself at the police station, this time to a desk sergeant whom I didn't recognize. Matt came out to collect me, then escorted me to the same room we had used before. It was empty.

I took a chair. "You going to offer me coffee? And where's your FBI buddy?"

"You know how bad the coffee is here. And the agent should be here any minute—coming in from DC. Why don't we wait, and then we can do the social thing all at once."

I shrugged. This was his party. "Anything new? Like you've solved the murder?"

He looked pained. "Em, it's been less than twenty-four hours since we found the body."

"Yes, and isn't it true that if you don't solve it in twenty-four hours, the odds go way down? You have any suspects?" *Other than me, of course.*

He shook his head but didn't answer me directly. "You

know what I said yesterday. As long as you are under suspicion, I can't share that kind of information with you."

That still rankled. "Then maybe I can just spitball here, and you can nod now and then. From what Cam has told me, there were some unhappy people when Peter folded up his business. Are you looking at them?"

"Em," he protested.

I pressed on relentlessly. I wanted to get myself off that short list ASAP. "What about his ex? His children? Does he have a will, and who benefits? Have you found his lawyer yet? Contacted the insurance people?"

"Stop." Now I'd made him angry. "Em, I am not going to do this. If it weren't for your familiarity with the missing pieces and the whole setup at Ferguson's place, you wouldn't be here at all."

"Well, thank you for that, at least." Actually I was happily surprised that he recognized that personal knowledge of the missing art trumped written descriptions and fuzzy photographs by a long shot. "I'll be glad to help. If that's what you're asking."

He sighed. "Yes, Em, I would appreciate your input regarding certain aspects of this case. I acknowledge your professional expertise. But I cannot—I *will not* share information with you about Peter Ferguson's murder and our investigation. Is that clear?" He shut up and glared at me.

"Crystal clear, Chief Lundgren." I knew he was right, but that didn't make me feel any better. But I wasn't about to admit that he was right, so I clammed up too. We sat there in stony silence, waiting, until the phone rang.

Matt picked it up. "She's here? I'll be right out." Then he looked at me. "Okay, the FBI has arrived. Will you please try to stick to the art angle?"

"Don't worry, I'll be good. I'm sorry, Matt—I don't want to screw this up for you. And you know I want to see the murder solved and make sure the glass is recovered."

He gave me a long look, then left. I could see his point vis-à-vis the FBI. They could grab the art theft case from us and keep us out of the loop, or they could welcome our help with open arms. I was hoping for the latter. At least this would be interesting.

Matt returned with the visiting agent two minutes later; I could hear their conversation from down the hall, accompanied by the brisk rat-tat of heels. I watched eagerly as the dark-haired agent strode into the room, trailing Matt in her wake. Tall, slightly younger than me, and very much in command. She held out her hand.

"Hi, I'm Special Agent Natalie Karamanlis. And you are?"

I had to stand up to lean across the table and shake. Strong grip. No nonsense about this woman. "I'm Em Dowell. I found the body."

At that Natalie smiled. "Aha. Well, then, let's sit down and get this going." She waited until Matt, looking a bit bewildered at having been upstaged, took a seat.

"Okay, let me explain what I do and tell you why I'm here. You know about the FBI Art Theft Program?"

We both must have looked blank, because she nodded once and kept right on going. "Not many people do—the Art Crime Team has only been around officially since late 2004. Even though international art theft may run as high as six billion dollars a year." She waited while we gave proper thought to that information, which I admit shocked me. Why had nobody been paying attention? "So, there are twelve of us on the team, and we manage the National Stolen Art File, otherwise known as the NSAF, which is a computerized index. I'm assigned to this region. We go after anything that is uniquely identifiable and has historical or artistic significance. Which covers just about everything. You with me so far?"

"And how much do you get back?" I drawled.

"Not enough. Maybe ten percent? But we're working on it. And that's why I'm excited to be here. These are big pieces, and we should have good descriptions of them, and the theft just happened, so we should have a good shot at getting them back."

"Hear, hear!" I said firmly. Matt looked at me as though I had lost my mind.

Natalie, on the other hand, rewarded me with a thumbs-up. "Let me tell you right off, I read the file on you—both of you, as it turns out."

That probably explained the smile.

"So, now you've stumbled over another body?"

"Agent Karamanlis, my understanding was that the murder investigation was to be handled out of this office, and you're here to address the art theft," Matt said stiffly. I could tell that his ego was taking a few hits.

"Call me Nat—saves time. And you can't mean to tell me that you think these two events are unrelated?"

"We haven't determined that yet," Matt replied.

"Oh, come on, loosen up, Chief Lundgren. I don't want to steal your glory. I just think it would be easier to put all our cards on the table and not worry about who knows what. Don't you agree, Em?" she said, glancing at me.

Her use of not only my first name but also my nickname did not escape me, but I decided I didn't mind. "That I do, Nat. And I do think the murder and the theft have to be connected. You have any ideas?"

Matt glared at me; I glared back. She had asked me, hadn't she? And then I noticed that Nat was watching the two of us with an amused expression.

"You two have a history, huh?"

Matt tried to look outraged, but I grinned at her. "You *are* good, lady. I'm going to enjoy working with you."

"Em!" Matt protested. "Can we keep this professional?"

I ignored him and addressed Nat. "He wants me to stay

out of this because I'm supposed to be a suspect. My so-called colleague Madelyn Sheffield accused me of killing Peter."

"Did you?"

"No way."

"All right, then. Let's get down to business. What do you know so far? Oh, and I read the summary you sent me, Chief, so you don't need to repeat all the basics. I'll ask if I need clarification."

Matt was looking more and more frustrated, and I couldn't blame him, since Nat had taken over the discussion—politely, but quite firmly. He began, "Peter Ferguson was stabbed in the chest with a shard of glass sometime Wednesday and bled to death. He also sustained a blow to the back of the head, but it wasn't fatal. Em found him Thursday afternoon, and the ME estimated he'd been dead twelve to twenty-four hours by then. Em had gone to the house to look at some of his glass art. She's the one who told us that the glass pieces were missing."

Nat nodded and made a note on a pad. "Can you narrow down the time of death?"

Matt shook his head. "This is Arizona. There was a lot of blood, but the air is so dry around here that it dried very quickly, which tends to skew estimates."

"Okay—I didn't know that. Em, you and this"—she checked her notes quickly—"Madelyn Sheffield were working with Ferguson on installing the pieces?"

"Yes. He wanted to take advantage of the local light to show them at their best."

"You have a list of the works that have gone missing?"

"Only in my head. I assume he had documentation for them somewhere, but there was no reason for him to share that with me. I'm sure you've gotten in touch with his insurance company. Oh, and if you're wondering, they were definitely authentic."

Matt interrupted. "Excuse me, uh, Nat, but won't the insurance company have detailed descriptions?"

Nat sighed. "They will, but it's really hard to translate a visual medium into words, you know? Same with photographs. Ferguson did all the right things, provided lots of pictures, but it's not a perfect system. Now, Em here saw the pieces up close, and she's an artist herself, right? So what she has to say will add to our description of the pieces. That's why I want her included in this discussion."

I beamed at her. *Take that, Matt.* The FBI wanted my opinion, and I was going to make sure they got it.

"Okay, moving on." Nat sat back in her chair and looked back and forth at us. "Why isn't Madelyn here today?"

Matt and I exchanged a glance, which Nat did not fail to notice. Matt answered first. "Madelyn accused Em of killing Ferguson. I thought it best not to bring them in together. I'm sure you can talk to her on your own."

"Uh-huh. That the whole story?" Nat addressed me.

"Not really," I replied. "I know the collection far better than Maddy does."

"Funny—I did some internet searching before I left DC. I found an article from the Tucson paper about Ferguson and his art collection. But it was all about Ms. Sheffield—I think you got a single line at the bottom." She pushed a xerox copy of a newspaper article across the table toward me.

I glanced at it briefly, but I had seen it before. "I'm not surprised. Maddy is all about show, not substance. She was using this to boost her business."

"You don't like her much, do you?"

I figured I might as well be honest. "No, I don't. I think she's an opportunist, which wouldn't bother me if she backed it up with talent. I mean, we *are* both in business here, and publicity doesn't hurt. But she is not a good artisan." I thought I was remarkably restrained in my assessment.

"So why did Ferguson pick her for this?"

"Personal history. He wanted me on board as backup because he knew her weaknesses."

"He told you that?" When I nodded, she added, "So Maddy might have an axe to grind, eh?"

"Excuse me, but what does this have to do with the missing artworks?" Matt broke in.

Nat flashed him a smile. "Just trying to get the lay of the land. Ferguson moves to Tucson and buys a big expensive place so he can set up his glass collection. He's been here a couple of months and somebody kills him, and somebody makes off with the collection. Interesting. Who did he know around here? Did he socialize much?"

"Not to my knowledge," Matt said.

I interrupted. "He seemed to be more or less camping out in the house. There was almost no furniture. He said he wanted to get a feel for the place, get the glass situated, before he cluttered it up. I never saw anyone else out there, not even contractors or carpenters or whatever. Oh, I did see one of the dealers he used there once—Ian Gemberling. But I got the feeling Peter was pretty much a hermit, although he had a phone and his computer hooked up. And a sophisticated security system."

Nat made a note. "Matt, you checked out the security system?"

"Of course. No breach, so he must have known whoever it was, and let him in."

"Him?" Nat's eyes twinkled.

"I apologize—the gender-neutral perpetrator or perpetrators," Matt corrected himself.

"Gotta stamp out sexism where we can. Right, Em?"

"Matt's pretty well trained, Nat." I grinned at her. "But you have to know that it wouldn't be easy for a woman to move that glass alone, certainly not without damaging it. I'd guess it would take a strong man, probably more than one person."

"Fair enough." Nat leaned back in her chair and studied the ceiling.

Matt and I exchanged glances again, and then Matt spoke. "Where do we go from here?"

Nat's gaze returned to level. "We'll crank up the standard art-theft procedure."

"Which is?" I asked.

"First we get the missing stuff into the NSAF, which goes back to 1997. That gives us a framework—a detailed description—to work with and to distribute. There's a record sheet to be filled out—type of object, material, size, any special features, and, of course, photographs and sketches, when they're available. You have any of those details, Em?"

I shook my head. "Not really. But Peter must have had something, or his attorney, or his art dealer, or the insurance company."

"We're looking into that. Matt, I assume you're pursuing the usual forensics, alarm system, autopsy, witnesses, yada yada?"

"Of course," Matt said stiffly. Poor baby—he wasn't reacting well to Nat's disarmingly breezy approach. I for one thought it was a pleasant change from my last interaction with the FBI.

"And we'll pool our information, of course. In fact, here's my first peace offering: our file on Peter Ferguson." She laid a manila folder on the table: It was at least an inch thick.

Matt reached for it. "You've been keeping tabs on him? Why?"

"Our department hasn't, but we all share internally. I can even call for backup from the local office, if I need it." She looked really excited about that idea, and I wondered just how long she had been doing this. She couldn't be older than thirty, thirty-five tops. "He was a public figure and a computer genius. We like to know what people like that are up to. Would've been a thicker file, if he'd taken his company public—then the SEC would have gotten involved. But you'd know that, wouldn't you, Em?"

I looked at her, startled. I realized that she was signaling, albeit subtly, that she knew that I had once registered as a stockbroker. Not surprising, since somewhere in Washington my fingerprints were on file. All that seemed like another lifetime. "Yes. But he kept it private, until he dissolved the company."

She nodded. "Interesting choice. He could have made a whole lot more money with an IPO."

"Looked to me like he did just fine as it was," I countered.

Matt apparently had gotten tired of taking the backseat, because he interrupted. "Nat, is there anything in his file that jumps out at you? That might have some bearing on his death?"

"Too early to say. He had enemies, and some made threats. You'll have to see if they were anywhere near Arizona at the right time—there's a list of names in the file. But I don't think this was about money. The question is, was he killed because of the collection, or was the theft a handy cover-up for the murder?"

I definitely had an opinion about that. "Nat, that collection was magnificent *and* worth a lot of money. Not to mention physically unwieldy. It seems absurd that somebody would walk in and kill Peter, then decide as an afterthought that he might as well take a couple of tons of art along with him."

"I agree with you, Em, or I wouldn't be here. Not that there's any shortage of people with a grudge against Peter. Maybe the art was taken as revenge by somebody who knew how Peter felt about it. Or by somebody who figured that Peter owed him in some way. I do think that Peter's death was incidental to the theft. He stumbled into it unexpectedly and he got killed. I mean, who would deliberately choose a piece of glass as a murder weapon? It was already there in the house, right? If you planned to kill someone, you'd come better prepared, wouldn't you?"

I nodded firmly. "Yes. And it's kind of an unpredictable way of killing anyone. You do have to be skilled enough or lucky enough to get it through the ribs. It would almost be easier to disembowel someone with glass, rather than stabbing him," I said.

We all fell silent, contemplating that unlovely picture.

"You have any ideas, Matt?" Nat finally asked.

Matt said slowly, "We think his former business partner may be in the area."

"Andrew Foster? The one who kept yammering to the press? Good work! Have you tracked him down?" Nat was almost bouncing in her chair with excitement.

Matt shot me a warning glance before going on. "Not yet. We found his flight coming in Wednesday morning, and he picked up a rental car at the airport, but no sign since."

"So you've lost sight of him? You think he's hiding?"

"I don't know, but we're looking for him," Matt replied.

I had to admit I was pissed that Matt hadn't mentioned that to me. I tried to reason with myself that Matt had every right not to share this information with me, but I still wasn't happy about it. What else hadn't he told me?

I think we both jumped when Nat stood up abruptly. "Chief, can you find somebody to take me out to the site? I want to take a look around, check out access, that kind of thing. Get some pictures."

Matt rose as well. "Of course. I can have an officer take you."

"It's still a crime scene, right? You have anybody stationed there?"

"Yes, I left a man out there. It's a rather high-price neighborhood, and the neighbors are bound to be a bit upset."

"No doubt. I'll need to talk to Ms. Sheffield as well, if you'll give me her info. Em, where will you be later this afternoon?"

"Uh, in my shop or at home. I live above the shop. You've got the address?"

"Yes, great. I'll probably want to talk with you again, once I've seen Ferguson's place for myself. Oh, you have pictures of the pieces?"

"Sure—I took quite a few, for my own purposes. But won't the insurance company have better ones?"

"Probably. But I want to see them in context. And maybe you could sketch out a floor plan, show me what was going where?"

"No problem."

"Great. See you later, then. Let's see about that ride, eh, Chief?"

I realized I had been dismissed. I glanced at Matt and he shrugged, so I gathered up my stuff and left. Actually, I wanted to think about just where this investigation—or maybe two investigations—was going. I was impressed by Agent Nat—she seemed smart and open at the same time. Of course, the fact that she believed I was blameless didn't hurt. I hoped she didn't trample all over Matt, but he was a big boy and he'd just have to handle it. Right now I needed to get back to the shop and get some work done.

I found I was looking forward to seeing Nat later.

Chapter 12

❊

I drove home on autopilot, trying to mentally re-arrange my calendar. Work on Peter's commission—gone. That left a chunk of time open for my own glassmaking, but I was still saddened by losing the opportunity to work with his wonderful glass pieces. Tomorrow was Saturday: busy morning for the shop, and I had a beginner's class in the afternoon. Cam would be around all weekend, but I had no idea what his plans were. Normally I would say that it was none of my business, but since Allison was working for me, I was stuck in the middle. I hoped they figured something out soon. My own relationship with Matt was on hold, at his request. I understood his reasons, since the last time we'd been involved in a murder investigation together, he'd bent quite a few rules to help me and his superiors hadn't been happy about it. It couldn't possibly have anything to do with Maddy's ridiculous accusation that I'd been carrying on with Peter. Matt knew me better than that. Didn't he?

I arrived at my building and parked in the alley, then

went around to the front door to catch up with whatever was going on in the shop. Nessa looked up when I came in, and the concern on her face warmed me. "Is everything all right, dear?"

"As good as it can be, all things considered. Why me? What's gone wrong with my karma? I never used to find bodies lying around."

"Just coincidence, I'm sure. But it's very sad about Mr. Ferguson, isn't it? He seemed like such a nice man."

That stopped me cold. "You met him?"

"Oh, yes. He came to the shop a time or two, and he was very charming. He bought a couple of your larger pieces. Actually, I didn't realize who he was until you started working with him, and I checked the credit card receipts."

Huh. So he really had checked me out, and he had even bought some of my work. I was flattered—and depressed all over again. He was still dead.

I went to the back of the studio and spent the rest of the day tending to the pesky details of inventory and supply orders. The next time I looked up, it was closing time; I went back to the shop to find Nessa clearing the cash register. "Any calls?"

"No, nothing. Were you expecting one?"

"The FBI agent who's working on Peter's case—she said something about getting together later today, but maybe she got hung up out at Peter's house. I'm sure she'll track me down one way or another."

"No doubt. She is, after all, an FBI agent."

I smiled at Nessa's quiet humor. "That she is. So what's the schedule for tomorrow? Who's opening?"

"Allison said that she'd be in early—she wanted to spend the afternoon with your brother."

"Well, that's good to hear. Has she said anything about . . . anything?" I didn't want to sound nosy, but I figured Nessa would have some clue about what Allison was thinking.

"Not in so many words. I know she's very excited about her classes at the university. You can almost see her opening up—it's a joy to watch."

About what I'd figured—and told Cam. "I want her to be happy. Problem is, I want Cam to be happy too, and I'm not sure they want the same things. Oh, well, it's not in my hands. If it's okay with you, I'll go on up and see what Cam's doing. I'll be in first thing in the morning."

"Good night, dear." Nessa went back to tallying the cash, and I made my way around to the side of the building and up the stairs.

Since the dogs did not swarm around my ankles the moment I opened the door, I deduced that Cam was there and had taken them out recently. "Hello?" I called out.

"In here," Cam replied, emerging from the back bedroom. "I wondered when you'd get back. How'd it go with Matt? Did he shine bright lights in your eyes and demand a confession?"

"No, nothing like that. But there's a new FBI agent on the case—a woman with the Art Theft Unit, or whatever they call it. She knows all the dirt about Matt and me, and the last murder. That makes me a little uncomfortable, but it saves explaining stuff."

"Is she any good?"

"I don't know yet. She said we should get together again today. When I left the police station she was headed out to the crime scene. You haven't taken any phone messages, have you?"

"Nope, nothing here. Anybody have any leads?"

I shook my head. "Not that they've shared with me. No, I'm wrong: Matt said he thought Peter's partner, Andrew Foster, might be in town. So, you have any plans? Should we go out and find some dinner?"

Before he could answer, there was a knocking at the door. Fred and Gloria raced to stand at attention in front of it. I followed less quickly and checked the peephole: Agent Natalie, carrying what looked like . . . pizza boxes! Hallelujah.

I opened the door and said, "Watch out for the dogs. But I think they're more interested in the pizza than in you."

Nat grinned. "Smart dogs. I've got a beagle who's a pepperoni junkie. Sorry to barge in, but it seemed simpler than calling. And I took a chance that you hadn't eaten."

For some reason, the line "beware Greeks bearing gifts" popped into my head. Smart move on her part, to catch us off guard. But we had nothing to hide, and the pizza smelled wonderful. I stepped back to let her in. "If I were a dog, I'd be rolling at your feet about now. I love to eat but I hate to cook. Come on in."

She walked into the space, the dogs at her heels—they weren't about to lose sight of those interesting-smelling boxes. "Nice place—an old factory?"

"It was, until I bought it about ten years ago. Here, put those on the table and I'll get plates and stuff. You want something to drink? I've got iced tea, or something stronger. Or are you on the job?"

"Hell, a beer won't hurt, if you've got it. So, this must be your brother, Cameron?"

"See, Cam, I told you she'd read the file. Yes, Nat, this is my brother. Say something nice to the agent, Cam."

"Em thinks I'm a social moron. Nice to meet you—Natalie, is it?"

"Nat, please. Natalie sounds like a second-grade teacher."

"And I'm Cam. Can I have one of those beers too, Em?"

"Coming up." I collected plates and napkins, snagged a trio of cold beers from the fridge, and dumped everything on my all-purpose table. "Let's eat." We devoted an intense few minutes to distributing and consuming our first pieces of pizza, then came up for air. "So, Nat, you saw the crime scene?"

She nodded, chewed, swallowed. "Interesting place. But a forensic nightmare."

"What do you mean?"

"You've seen it—next to no furniture. Every surface is either shiny-smooth, like in the kitchen, or so rough that it couldn't take fingerprints. And whoever was there cleaned up good. We've found prints for the people we already knew were there: Peter, you, Maddy. We're sorting through a few more for any construction or delivery guys, but it doesn't look promising." She took another piece of pizza and bit into it with a blissful look on her face.

I waited until she had swallowed again. "Why are you telling us this? Doesn't this compromise your investigation?"

"Matt says you're good people, and I really don't think you killed the guy. What did you have to gain?"

"Maddy seems to think I had a reason to kill him."

Nat snorted. "Right. You lusted after Mister Billionaire who had a taste for art, and then you whacked him. Did you?"

"Which? What? Lust or whack?"

"Let's start with lust. Were you doing Peter Ferguson?"

I didn't know whether to be furious or amused. "No! He was an interesting and attractive man, and I'll cop to thinking about it for about twelve seconds. But I wasn't about to screw up a lucrative and highly visible commission for a roll in the hay, even if he did have millions."

Nat nodded. "Good. That's what I told Matt."

"Wait a minute—you discussed this with Matt?"

"It's part of the investigation, and we have to evaluate Maddy's accusation."

I was getting antsy, so I stood up and stalked to the kitchen area, leaning against the kitchen counter.

Cam had been watching our dialogue as though it were a ping-pong game, but now he decided to step in. "Let me get this straight—you think Em is in the clear?"

Nat turned to him. "Cam, I'm neither naïve nor stupid. I

would not be sitting here saying the things I'm saying if I didn't think Em had nothing to do with this. Relax. I just want to kick things around with her—she knows the people involved, and the place. And I've got something in mind for you too, if you're interested."

I was getting more and more bewildered, and it wasn't just the half a bottle of beer I had consumed. I returned to the table and sat down. "Okay, you think I'm innocent, and thank you for that. Does Matt agree?"

"For the record, he's not saying. Off the record, probably. So what's the story with you two?"

"We were . . . involved for a while a couple of years ago, and then we broke it off. But we recently sort of got back together again."

"Makes it hard for him, doesn't it? But he'll work it out—he's a good cop."

"I hope so. This is complicated enough. Okay, Nat, what is it you want from me?"

"Like I said. I know a lot about art theft, but you know about Tucson and who's who here. Anybody around who would handle a crime like this?"

"I don't know whether to be flattered or insulted. Sure, I know the local craftspeople, but I can't think of anyone who could pull off a multimillion dollar art heist. And that includes me—I wouldn't know where to start."

She waved a dismissive hand. "I don't mean the theft itself—anyone can hire goons for the heavy lifting. I'm more interested in what whoever it was plans to do with the art. If it's not a local, who would notice somebody from out of town, somebody who didn't belong?"

I felt a spurt of impatience at her blithe ignorance. "We get a lot of people coming through Tucson, you know. It's a big and growing city. And I'm not exactly a great socializer—I spend most of my time in my studio or my shop, working. If I don't work, I don't have anything to sell. So I'm not spending a lot of time hanging out with high-end art thieves."

"Don't get your panties in a twist, Em. All I'm saying is that you have better contacts around here than I do. I would appreciate it if you would use the resources you possess to facilitate my investigation."

Was she making fun of me? I looked her in the eye, and then we broke out laughing simultaneously. "I would be delighted to be of service to your endeavor, should my meager resources prove valuable." So there.

"Thanks. Look, I can imagine that you all got off on the wrong foot with the FBI before, but I don't play things that way. And I take all the help I can get. I promise I'll keep you in the loop too."

I wondered briefly how Matt felt about this kind of information sharing, but I decided that it wasn't any of his business. And Nat was right. After last time, it was nice to be included—and trusted.

Chapter 13

❋

I grabbed another slice of pepperoni pizza, but before I tackled it, I said, "Okay, Matt's big hang-up at the moment is that he thinks he has to treat me like a suspect. I figure the best way to deal with that is to find a few more suspects, or better yet, the real killer. You agree?"

Nat's mouth was full, but she nodded vigorously. I seized the opportunity to go on. "So who's on the short list? Matt said Peter's former partner popped up in town and then disappeared, which looks a little fishy. And I notice that his lovely ex-wife arrived here in record time and made sure she got some face time on the news. Unless you seriously think this was the work of some impersonal art theft ring?"

Nat chewed, swallowed. For once I waited until she could speak. "Let's start with that last one. Such things do exist, but big glass pieces would not be their first choice for a target—too hard to handle. I kinda like the others."

"Okay, why? Talk me through it. I don't know much

about either of the people." Only what Cam had found, but she didn't need to know that.

"Let's start with Jennifer. She and Peter got married young, right out of college. They popped out a couple of kids who're now in college. They must have been married almost ten years when Peter hit the big time. Good market timing on his part, and a dose of luck."

Cam spoke for the first time in a while. "I remember when his products first hit the market. They were works of art in their own right. Simple, and there were very few glitches, by industry standards. And he never rushed their release. He made sure they worked the way they should from the beginning. I have to say that earned him a lot of respect in the industry, and among his consumers."

Nat nodded. "Right. He was the golden boy. He had strong products and he stood behind them. And it didn't hurt that he looked damn good on camera. Right, Em?"

"I'll have to agree there. He was not at all what I expected from a computer geek." Cam looked miffed, but I ignored him.

"So that's why it was such a surprise when he shut down PrismCo," Nat went on. "No warning. No apparent business reason—sales were strong, and he hadn't overextended the company, either in staff or financially. So why did he fold up his tents? Cam, you have any ideas?"

"Nope. I was as surprised as anybody. The announcement really was a shock, and people did a lot of poking around in his code, to see if maybe there was some bug nobody had noticed yet and he wanted to get out while the getting was good. But everything was clean. The whole thing became sort of an industry legend."

Nat nodded. "That matches what I heard. So why was Andrew Foster so pissed, Cam?"

"I really don't know. Sour grapes, sounds like. He had a cushy job, and then Peter dumped him, along with all the rest of the staff. With nice severance packages, I have to say. I know a couple of people on the receiving end. I doubt Foster suffered financially, so I have to think it was more personal than that."

"But was he mad enough to kill Ferguson? He's had plenty of time to cool down."

"I can't answer that," Cam said. "But I can't imagine he would have made all those very public complaints and then turned around and murdered the guy. He must have known he'd be one of the first people the police would look at. And why wait this long?"

"Cam, those are good points, and I don't have any answers. Maybe he's been nursing a grudge all this time. We're just kicking around ideas here, right? So what about the missus?"

I pounced on that one. "Why would she want him dead? They've been divorced for a while. How'd she do in the divorce settlement?"

"Just fine. Peter was generous, and he didn't put up a fight. She got a nice lump-sum settlement, and the kids got trust funds."

"So she wouldn't benefit from his death? I assume he left a will?"

"We're looking into that, but I think the short answer is no. She had already gotten as much as she was going to get. The kids might get something more in his will, but they weren't anywhere near Tucson when he died."

"Yeah, but couldn't just about anybody with money hire someone to do the deed?"

"It's possible, but then we come back to the art."

"True." I sat back and tried to fit the pieces together, with no luck.

Cam's voice startled me. "So, let me see if I've got this right. There's no financial motive for killing Peter Ferguson? Nobody benefits—former employees, ex-wife, kids?"

"That's the way it looks, Cam," Nat said. "That's one reason why I think the art is the key. I mean, think about it. The collection is too big, physically, to haul off on the spur of the moment, so this had to be planned. Maybe Peter was supposed to end up dead, maybe not. Maybe the motive was financial, or maybe it was revenge. But you can't tell me these are two random events that just happened to take place at the same time."

The pizza was soon no more than a greasy memory, and even the dogs had given up hoping and settled themselves down where they could watch us in case something else tasty showed up. I sat back in my chair, finished my beer, and asked, "Okay, where do we go from here?"

Nat answered, with a wicked gleam in her eye, "I'm *so* glad you asked. Cam, are you in on this?"

Cam looked startled at being included at all. "Well, I'll do whatever I can to help Em, but I don't live around here, you know."

Nat favored him with a smile. "Yeah, I know—San Diego, right? But I'm sure you can wrap this up in no time, with your computer skills."

Watching her, I wondered if she was trying to butter Cam up—and if so, why. And then another thought struck me: Was she coming on to him? Oh, dear. I had no idea whether Cam's involvement with Allison was part of the "official" record—or whether that would matter to Nat, who seemed to make up her mind quickly and do exactly what she wanted. Cam was officially single and reasonably attractive—and he was also clueless enough not to notice if the FBI agent was hitting on him. Was I supposed to do something here?

While I waffled, Nat laid a hand on his arm. "Cam, I'm

asking you if you can help the FBI with some computer-related material pertinent to this art theft."

Cam's eyebrows shot up. "Can you do that? I mean, ask me, since I'm kind of involved already, with Em and all? And have you run this by Matt?"

"I trust you, and I've got a pretty good idea of your skills. You let me handle Matt Lundgren. Look, I could go through channels, use approved FBI staff and so on, but that will just slow things down, and stolen art moves quickly. Let me tell you, whoever has these pieces is not going to sit on them, because the longer they stay in one place, the more likely someone is to pick up the trail. Nope, if the person who took them is smart, he's got buyers lined up already. In fact, he probably had buyers lined up before he took them—wouldn't be the first time. Now he's just got to get them out of Tucson, fast."

"But who the heck would want to buy hot glass?" I knew it was a bad pun, but she knew what I meant.

"Collectors. You should know that, Em. People get obsessed by something, anything, and then they want more and more—bigger, better, rarer pieces. Peter Ferguson was a collector, and he had the bucks to indulge his passion and get exactly what he wanted. But sometimes even money isn't enough, and that's where the thieves come in. They target specific items or types of items, and they do their homework—they know what they're looking for, who has it, and who wants it. Thing is . . ." She paused, looking worried.

"What?"

"They usually keep their hands clean. That is, they don't kill. That's what's odd about this, unless Peter surprised somebody in the act. You said you had an appointment to meet him that day?"

"Yes, we had set it up a couple of days earlier, and I was

going to arrive at around three—I wanted to see the stuff by late-afternoon light. He was dead when I got there."

"Was he a heavy sleeper?"

My anger flared again. "How the hell should I know? I thought we'd gotten past that. We were not sleeping together. And if you think anyone could have sneaked into his house—through his fancy security—and crated up and moved six or more large and heavy glass panels without his waking up and noticing, you're not as smart as you think you are."

"Unruffle your feathers, Em—I didn't mean anything by it. And I agree with you. He had to be dead when this happened. But we still need to know why. Cam, that's where you come in."

"Me?" Cam was still lagging behind in the conversation.

"Yes, you." Nat reached into the bag she had brought with her and pulled out what I recognized as a laptop computer—a particularly sleek one.

Cam, however, took one look, and his face lit up. "Is that Peter Ferguson's laptop?"

Nat smiled. "Yup."

Cam reached out a reverent hand. "My God. Do you know what's on here?"

"Nope. I didn't want to mess with it. But I figured you'd know what to do with it."

Cam was cradling the object in his hands. He was speechless.

"Yo, Cam!" I said. "You still there?"

He looked at me with a vague smile. "Do you realize what this is? It's Peter Ferguson's computer," he said in a dreamy voice.

"Yeah, I got that part."

"Em, don't you see? This is like somebody handing

you the Holy Grail. This man was a genius with code. He wrote some of the most elegant programs in the business. It's a privilege to hold it. Who knows what's on this hard drive?"

Cam was enthralled; I was horrified. "Nat, why do you have this?"

"The FBI impounded the equipment, as part of our investigation. I didn't want to mess with it."

Cam nodded.

I still wasn't happy. "And why did you bring it here?"

"I need to know what's in that computer, and I want Cam to find out," Nat stated bluntly. "I'm assuming Ferguson knew all there is to know about computer security. I want you to get into it and tell me if there's anything on there about his collection—preferably something that gives us a motive for killing him."

Cam looked as though he'd received the greatest present in the world. "You want me to open this up?" Then his face clouded. "You mean, you trust me not to make a mess of it?"

Nat nodded. "I had you checked out—you're good. Maybe not quite in Ferguson's league, but I think you can handle it. Give it a shot. If you need some specialized equipment, the FBI'll foot the bill. Maybe we can even give you a consulting fee. But we need it yesterday."

"I'm . . . honored. Yes. Of course."

Cam didn't seem troubled by the revelation that the FBI had been investigating him. But they must have decided he was all right, and I guess I was in the clear too. *How nice to have a clean FBI record,* I thought wryly. "Is Matt okay with this?"

Nat tore her eyes away from my brother. "I pulled rank on Matt and claimed this was part of the theft investigation. I did promise to share whatever I found that might pertain to the murder, and I will. Now you—I want you to crank up your art contacts, see what you can find out."

"What are you going to be doing?" I said.

"Look, we're working together on this, Em. I'll see what buzz I can pick up through my FBI contacts, check out the ports—kind of from the outside looking in. You're the insider here, so you check out the people in Tucson. Let's hope we meet somewhere in the middle—wherever the glass is."

I wasn't convinced, but if this collaboration meant that I got to stay in the loop, it was fine by me. And I was sure I could come up with people to talk to in Tucson, other glass people. . . . "When? I've already got a busy day tomorrow, and a class I don't want to cancel." I wasn't sure I could reach all the people enrolled in the class, and I didn't want to piss them off by failing to show up. Whenever this was over, I still had a business to run.

"I can get on it right away," Cam piped up.

"Wonderful!" Nat beamed at him. "Why don't I swing by tomorrow afternoon and see what progress you've made?"

How convenient—just when I'd be tied up in a class. I was going to have to have a little chat with Cam about Natalie. To his credit, he looked far more interested in the computer, still in his hands, than in the living, breathing, and undeniably attractive FBI agent across from him.

"Works for me," he said.

I just shrugged. "What're you going to tell Matt?" I asked Nat. Poor Matt. Even though I was annoyed at him for shutting me out, I didn't want him to be blindsided.

"That I'm pursuing my own course of investigation, and I've brought in a couple of consultants. Is that acceptable? Or are you the type that has to share everything with your significant other?"

I wasn't sure that I'd define Matt quite that way, but I got her message. "As long as he still considers me a suspect, I don't think he'll even talk to me. So it's not a problem." Which was true, if galling.

She stood up. "Great. I'll see both of you tomorrow, then. Maybe you can point me to a good restaurant tomorrow night, and we can eat together? My treat. And who knows—we might even have something to celebrate."

"No problem."

I escorted her to the door. Out of Cam's earshot, I asked, "You sure you should be dragging civilians into this?"

Nat stopped. "Look, Em, one thing you've gotta know about me: I want results. Maybe I cut a few corners to get there, but I'm not about to break any laws. You and me, we want the same thing: to get those glass pieces back. The way I see it, you two are my best shot at that. If you think that messes up whatever you've got going with your cop friend, you'd better tell me now."

I shook my head. "I can't say how Matt's going to feel about you involving us, but that's not his decision—it's mine. And Cam's. I want to help, and Matt's doing his best to keep me out. So I guess I'm in. Cam makes his own decisions, and obviously he's thrilled to get a crack at the great Peter Ferguson's code. I probably couldn't pry him away from this if I wanted to."

"That's what I figured. Okay, then, see you tomorrow." She gave a mock salute and vanished down the stairs. I shut the door behind her and turned to face Cam, who hadn't moved, staring raptly at the laptop. It was as though he thought it would disappear if he looked away.

"Cam?"

Reluctantly he looked up at me. "What?"

I wasn't sure what I wanted to say. Should I warn him about Nat? Or was I imagining her interest in him? Or was the interest just a ploy to get him to do what she wanted? Too complicated for me. In the end, all I said was, "Can you handle this?"

He looked pained. "Of course I can, Em. What do you think I've been doing for the last ten years?"

I held up both hands. "No insult intended. It's just that most of the time there's not so much riding on your work—one man dead, millions of dollars' worth of art missing. Who knows what you're going to find once you access that thing?"

"Only one way to find out," he replied cheerfully.

Shoot—I realized his day tomorrow had just been co-opted by the FBI. "What about Allison?"

He looked at me as though I were speaking a foreign language. "Allison?"

"Yes, Cam, the woman you adore? Who's expecting to spend a chunk of the day with you tomorrow?"

"Oh, right. Well, she'll understand. But then I'll have to tell her what I'm doing. Can I do that? I mean, will Nat approve?"

Like I said, complicated. I hadn't taken that into account. But I knew Allison was trustworthy. "How about this? You can say that the FBI has asked you to help with the investigation. I'll back you up. You don't have to give her details."

"Good. Sure, that will work. She'll understand. And maybe I'll be done by Sunday."

"That fast?"

"Maybe. I won't know until I get into it, see what kind of encryption he was using, what protection. Heck, for all I know we'll find he used this to play games and did his real work somewhere else. Did you ever see what kind of equipment he had at his place?"

"Cam, I didn't spend much time there, remember? And we certainly weren't looking at his computer. No, I did not see anything. Though he could have had a luxurious hotel room somewhere, and kept the important stuff there." Yet somehow I doubted it. For one thing, I thought that Peter would not have wanted to leave his glass—if anything, he relished the time he spent alone with it. For another, he seemed to have been using the situation as a sort of spiritual retreat. This was a man who had money to burn, who could have afforded whatever luxury he wanted. But maybe that kind of abundance grew old after a while, and he wanted to purge himself. Not that I'd ever know what that was like—I was happy to be able to meet my mortgage payment every month. And to do what I loved. What had Peter loved? He'd walked away from the company he had founded, for reasons that still weren't clear. I could attest that he loved the pieces he had collected, but was that enough to satisfy him? I had seen no evidence of people in his life, and that made me sad. Not that I was anyone to talk.

This was getting me nowhere. It had been a long day, and tomorrow would be busy for both of us. "Cam, I need to get to bed. Put that thing"—I gestured toward the computer—"someplace safe. I'll walk the dogs and grab a shower. And maybe you should give Allison a call, tell her there's been a change in plans."

He nodded, his mind clearly somewhere else—no doubt running code in his head. "Sure, fine."

Nothing I could do about Cam. I collected the leashes, grabbed a jacket, and ferried Fred and Gloria down the stairs. In the cold night air, I followed the pups as they sniffed and squatted, wondering just what I had gotten myself into this time.

Chapter 14

❀

I was surprised that I slept at all, with so much bouncing around in my head. I managed to drag myself out of bed before the sun was fully up on Saturday morning. When I stumbled out into the kitchen area in search of caffeine, I found Cam sitting at my desk already at work. Cam has great contempt for my poor computer, but I'm no techie, and as long as it does what I ask—mainly, keep my business records in some sort of order and produce an invoice now and then—I'm not going to complain. He had banished my system to the back of the desk and had set up his own laptop, now bristling with additional cords, alongside Peter's.

With a cup of Cam's freshly brewed coffee in hand, I ambled over to him and peered over his shoulder. "How's it going?"

His eyes never left the monitor. "I don't know yet. It looks pretty straightforward, but I want to be careful to do this right."

"Can you get into his files or whatever?"

"Probably. I'll know more in a couple of hours. You going downstairs?"

"Yup. Should be a busy morning in the shop, and then I've got that class in the afternoon. Did you talk to Allison?"

I swear it took him a moment to recall who I was talking about. "Oh, yeah. I called her last night and said I'd be tied up today, and maybe we could get together tonight. I'll have to see how it goes."

If their relationship was going to last, Allison should know that nothing came between Cam and his beloved computer, and this was a special case. I sighed. "I'll try to explain it to her when I see her."

"She said she understood."

While I had my doubts about that, I'd wait and see what she really thought when I got to the shop. Right now I needed food. "Did you feed the dogs?" I asked.

"What? Oh, no, I guess I didn't. Sorry."

He really was absorbed if he could ignore the concerted attention of Fred and Gloria at his feet. "Apologize to them, not to me." I set about feeding everybody, got dressed, and then took them out for a walk. Despite the chill in the air, people were stirring early on this Saturday, and I waved at a few artisans I knew, most likely on their way to work.

After returning with the dogs, I made my way downstairs in time to meet Allison as she opened the front door. "Good morning," I said brightly.

She gave me a smile. "Good morning, Em. Lovely day, isn't it?"

Having dispensed with the trite formalities, I seized the opportunity to find out what was going on with her—and Cam. "You talked to Cam last night?"

She hung her jacket behind the counter before replying. "I did. He said he's working on something related to the Ferguson killing and couldn't talk about it."

"I'm sorry—I know you had plans. But it's true." I wondered why I was apologizing for Cam, but I knew how clueless he was about relationships. "Are you okay with that?"

She laughed. "What, that he finds his laptop more appealing than me? Em, don't trouble yourself. In truth, I'm happy to have a little breathing room. He can be a bit intense, don't you think?"

"Tell me about it." Was the bloom off the rose already? Well, I'd let the two of them work out . . . whatever. "Nessa's coming in at one, right? I'll hang around up here this morning, and then I've got the class later, so I'll have to set up for that. When are you going to get in some more furnace time?"

Allison was going through the start-up procedure for the register. "What? Oh, I hadn't thought—I've been so busy trying to sort out these university classes and all. It's like being let loose in a candy store, but it's been years since school and there's so much I don't know."

"Well, I for one think it's great. And you're lucky—you can take what you want and figure out what interests you."

The door opened with our first customer of the day, and we were off. The morning was busy with sales and lookers. Allison ran out for sandwiches at noon, and when Nessa arrived I headed for the studio to set up for my students.

In preparation, I checked the glass levels in my furnace, turned on the glory holes, and laid out the tools we would need. I emptied the annealer, where the last batch of pieces had cooled overnight, then turned it on—I would need to put the students' pieces in to cool overnight. I refilled a couple of the frit cans that were running low. And then the attendees started drifting in and I had no time to think. I had to keep an eagle eye on all the newbies to make sure they didn't burn themselves on something unexpectedly hot and didn't whack each other swinging a pipe around. Time flew.

It was after five when I waved good-bye to the last student and reversed the earlier process, turning off the glory holes, shutting the furnace door, and cleaning and stowing the tools. I gave a quick sweep to the concrete floor, checked the annealer setting one last time, then went back to the shop. Nessa and Allison were busy with customers, so I watched quietly for a moment—and felt lucky to have them both. Even though Allison had been working here only a short while, already I wondered how I had managed without her. The business was thriving, and I hoped it would continue to improve—if I could just stop tripping over dead bodies.

I should have known that the universe would not allow me to feel good for long. I turned to see Maddy hesitating in the doorway to the shop. As well she should: The last person I wanted to see was someone who had accused me of murder. A thick silence fell, as both Allison and Nessa joined me in glaring daggers at Maddy.

She summoned up a tremulous smile. "Em, I came to apologize. I said some things I didn't mean the other day. Can we talk?"

My first reaction was to tell her to take a very long hike, preferably straight out into the desert, and not come back. But I was a grown-up—and besides, I wanted to know what had brought her here. I could at least hear her out. "All right. Not here. I know a place around the corner. Okay?"

Maddy nodded eagerly. "Great. Thank you, Em." She glanced at Allison and Nessa, whose expressions had not changed. "Can you go now?"

"I guess." I shrugged. "Let me get a jacket."

When I came around the counter, Nessa leaned over and whispered, "Do you need backup?" in her most conspiratorial tone.

I laughed. "No, I think I can handle this. But thanks. You two okay to close?"

She nodded, and stepped back. "I think we can manage. I'll be in tomorrow."

"See you then," I said breezily, then turned to Maddy. "Let's go."

I led the way the short two blocks to a bar where I figured we would find some privacy, given the early hour. I was right: The dim interior held only a few people, mostly tourist couples looking for local color. I nodded at the bartender and made my way to a booth at the back, Maddy trailing silently. I slid in on one side, and she took a seat opposite.

A young waitress approached and looked expectantly at us. "Beer for me," I told her. "You, Maddy?"

"Oh dear, I don't know. . . . If you're having something . . . a white wine, maybe?" She was dithering.

"And some chips and salsa, please."

The waitress nodded and headed for the bar. I turned to Maddy. "Okay, you asked to talk to me. So talk."

While waiting for her to begin, which took a while, I studied her. I hadn't seen her since she had stormed into Peter's house flinging accusations, and events since had obviously taken a toll. Her blonde hair hung limply, her eyes and her nose were red, and she looked somehow shrunken. Peter's death seemed to have hit her really hard—but why?

Finally she spoke, avoiding my eyes, shredding a napkin with both hands. "Em, I wanted to say how sorry I am about accusing you of killing Peter. I didn't mean it—it just came out, in the stress of the moment."

The waitress arrived, and I framed my response while waiting for her to retreat. "Maddy, as I recall, you repeated the story to Chief Lundgren, after you'd had a chance to calm down."

"I know, I know. But I was just so upset. . . ."

As if I *wasn't* upset at finding a corpse? I have no patience for these fragile females who crumple under the least pressure, and I was in no mood to be charitable to

Maddy. She was the one who had gotten me into this in the first place, and her apology struck me as rather feeble.

"And so was I," I said tartly. "Peter Ferguson didn't deserve to die, and now his collection is who knows where, maybe gone forever. It's a lousy situation. And your accusation didn't make things any better. Come on, Maddy—I know we aren't exactly friends, but I don't think I deserved that."

"I know," she said, gulping down a sob—and the rest of her wine. "But when I saw him lying there, dead . . . We were lovers, you know."

I have to admit that stopped me in my tracks. I sat back to consider, swallowing some more of my beer, stalling for time. For a start, I didn't believe her. I had seen them together and had witnessed nothing that suggested that kind of intimacy. Talking with me, Peter had dismissed her, saying that it was an old family connection and nothing more. Him, I believed. At least his explanation had made sense. So, why was she lying to me? More of her posturing? Self-dramatizing? Did she hope to gain some small notoriety from being labeled Peter Ferguson's last . . . whatever?

Reluctantly I had to admit to myself that I was intrigued. What was Maddy's game? There was only one way to find out. I reached out a hand and laid it over one of hers. "You poor thing, you must feel awful. I didn't know. Do you want to talk about it?"

She did.

Beers and wine had somehow morphed into margaritas, against whose effects the bowls of chips had little impact, and still Maddy talked on. "He was always such a lovely boy. Quiet, shy, you know. Kept to himself. But even then I knew he was someone special. He had such a way of looking at you, like you were the only person in the world. And for the longest time he never said anything to me about the way he felt. But when he moved to Tucson, when he chose me for his special project—I knew it was to be our time, at last."

What universe was this woman living in? I searched my befuddled brain for memories of what Peter had said about Maddy. Sure, he had been an attractive man. If he had been a geeky youth, he had definitely moved past that. And yet . . . I had to admit I had wanted to believe that the appreciative gaze he had turned on me had been for me alone, that I had been special. Even though I had had no intention of acting on it, I had hoped that there really was a little spark of attraction flickering there. So how could I blame Maddy for building castles in the air?

But that was all they were—I was sure of it. Peter had been kind and patient when she was around, but I believed he had shared his true feelings toward her with me, when we had been alone.

But, hey, if Maddy was in a mood to spill her guts to me, her new best buddy . . . "You must have been upset when Peter got married," I tossed out as bait.

Maddy took it. "That bitch! All she wanted was his money."

"Hold on. Didn't they get married before he got rich and famous?"

"I never said she wasn't smart. She knew he was going places. She latched on to him like, like . . . what're those sucker fish thingies?"

"Remoras," I said absently. I am a font of useless information. "So you're saying she was a gold digger? They did have a couple of kids, didn't they?"

"Yes. They're gorgeous, and smart too. But Jennifer turned them against Peter, used them to pry more money out of him in the divorce."

"That's terrible!" If it was true. I had no way of knowing, and I didn't exactly trust Maddy's spin on it. "But they kept in touch? I mean, she's here in Tucson, isn't she?"

"She's a vampire!" I refrained from pointing out that vampires sucked blood only from living creatures, which Peter wasn't. "She had all the money she could want, but she just couldn't handle being a nobody, instead of Mrs. Peter Ferguson. And now she's going to play the grieving widow, while it's me who *really* loved him. *I'm* the one who's going to miss him more!"

Maddy threatened to dissolve into tears, but I couldn't help wondering if she wasn't as self-serving as Jennifer. And whether Maddy was just jealous that she wasn't getting the public sympathy that Jennifer was reaping.

Em, listen to yourself. You're as bad as Maddy. When had I become so cynical? *Enough.* I checked my watch: time to go home. The restaurant was full now, warm and noisy, but Maddy still looked like uncooked dough, a sodden lump of misery. It was not a pretty sight.

"Maddy?"

She brought her eyes into focus, with some effort. "Huh?"

"I think it's time to go now," I said, enunciating very clearly.

It took her a while to process the thought. "Oh. Right. It's late. Hope I didn't keep you from anything."

With Matt pursuing a killer, I probably wouldn't see him for days. "Nope, but I'm an early bird—I need my rest." I tossed some bills on the table, stood up, and waited for the floor to stop moving. "Upsy-daisy!"

It took more than one try to extricate Maddy from the depths of the booth, but we managed to make it out the front door into the crisp night air. I inhaled deeply, savoring the hint of mesquite smoke. I was very glad I had walked to the bar rather than driving, although I had no clue how Maddy planned to get home. For that matter, I had no idea where Maddy lived. But whether or not we had gone through some sisterly bonding this evening, no way was I going to offer her my couch, much less a ride home. I'd rather pay for a cab.

"Maddy? How are you getting home?"

The cool air seemed to have had an equally sobering effect on her. "My car's at my shop, but maybe I should find a cab."

"Good idea!" I agreed, a bit too heartily. "Well, it's been an interesting evening. Hope you make it home all right."

With that I turned and marched away, without looking back. Maddy was a big girl—she could find her own way home. Me, I wanted time to think about what had gone on tonight. I hadn't learned much. Maddy was deluded, apparently about a lot of things, including her relationship with Peter. But I'd already had an inkling of her limitations—and her blindness to them—when I saw her work. Maybe she didn't have many female friends in Tucson. Maybe, I added charitably, she really was grieving for Peter and just wanted someone to talk to.

Why didn't I believe that?

When I reached home, I made my way slowly up the stairs. The dogs greeted me with muted enthusiasm, which I interpreted to mean that they had already been fed and weren't desperate for a walk yet. "Cam?" I called out. No answer. When I reached the kitchen area, I saw a note on the table: "Nat asked me to dinner, back later. Love, Cam." No time mentioned. I looked at my watch: It was almost ten. Must be a good dinner. As I was standing there with the note in my hand, trying to figure out what to do next, the phone rang and I picked it up.

"Em?" Matt's voice.

"That's me," I replied cheerfully. "How are you?"

"You weren't home earlier."

Was he keeping tabs on me? It occurred to me that maybe I shouldn't mention I had been with Maddy—maybe there was some police rule that two people involved in a crime shouldn't hang out and let their hair down together. "Nope, I was out. You're a great detective, you know that?"

"Em, have you been drinking?"

"A little. After all, I've been accused of murder, so I had to drown my sorrows. I am still accused of murder, aren't I?" It might have started as an innocent question, but I found I was curious to hear what he had to say.

"Em, you know I can't talk about it."

Neither yea nor nay—that wasn't very satisfying. Well, I could play the same game. "Yup, you told me. Well, I guess I won't keep you—you have a murderer to catch. Call me when you have him." And then I hung up. Not very mature of me, I know, but it felt kind of good. For a moment. Then I felt bad—after all, he had to do his job. I debated calling him back and apologizing, but in the end I decided I could sort things out better in the morning, in a slightly more sober state.

I took the dogs out, came back and showered, and went to bed. Cam still hadn't come home by the time I fell asleep.

Chapter 15

❀

I like to sleep in on Sunday mornings, since the shop doesn't open until noon, and last night's carousing with Maddy had left me sluggish. When I woke up, I lay in bed listening for a bit and was relieved to hear the clicking of computer keys. Cam must have returned during the night, although I hadn't heard him come in. But I was curious to know what he had discovered—and what he had told Nat. Or she had told him.

Once I had dressed, I made my way toward the kitchen. "Hey, Cam. Late night, eh?"

He held up one finger, indicating he was in the middle of something, and I heard my printer whine. When it was done, he came over and sat at the table, a sheaf of papers in his hand. He looked very pleased with himself.

I poured coffee and scrounged up a stale bagel, stuffing it in the toaster. "So, you going to tell me what you've got?"

"Get some coffee into you first—I know how your mind

works. Or doesn't. And when did you get back? Allison said you disappeared with Maddy about five last night."

Dutifully I sipped coffee and waited for my head to clear. It was a slow process. "So you talked to Allison before you hit the town with Nat?"

He had the grace to look sheepish. "I told her it was business. It was. Anyway, what did Maddy want?"

"She said she wanted to apologize, which she did about six times. And then she wanted to tell me her entire life history, particularly the part where she and Peter were passionately involved." I snorted.

"You don't believe that?"

"Not for a minute. Peter tolerated her, no more. He gave her the commission as a favor to his mother, and then he called me in as backup."

"He told you that?"

"He did. I admit I wondered why he had picked such a no-talent for an important job."

Cam grinned. "Don't hold back."

"You know very well that I have never liked Maddy or respected her work, even before she accused me of murder. And now, apparently, I'm her new best friend."

"What did you two find to talk about?"

"Maddy, mostly. She is just devastated by Peter's death, because they were soulmates, blah blah blah. I get the feeling she doesn't have anyone else to talk to—not that I'm surprised. I've seldom met anyone so completely self-absorbed, with so little justification."

"That's right, Em, let it all out. So, you think she just wanted to vent, or did she want something else from you?"

"My question exactly. I think she hoped to find out how the murder investigation was going, and she was disappointed when she found out that Matt had shut me out—which was her fault in the first place. I didn't say anything about the FBI part of it—I think. Things got a little fuzzy toward the end there." I swallowed some more coffee. "So what did you come up with? Or, wait—how did you end up going out with Nat?"

"Well, she came by yesterday as promised to check on my progress. She said she didn't know much about Tucson, so I volunteered to show her a few places, and then we ate dinner."

Oh, shoot—I had completely forgotten our vague dinner plans when Maddy showed up. Poor, innocent Cam. I didn't for a moment believe that Nat was a lonely, vulnerable tourist. "What did you two talk about?"

"Let's back up a bit. Don't you want to know what's on Peter's computer?"

I sat up straighter. "Of course I do. Just explain it in English, will you?"

"I'll give you the junior version. Access wasn't hard, probably because he didn't have a whole lot of top-secret stuff on there, and not a lot from PrismCo. I don't know whether he had some other place to stash that or he really was out of the business. Still, he used reasonable protection—he didn't count on someone like me digging into them." Cam allowed himself a moment of glory, looking quite pleased with himself. Then he went on. "The files I found fall into a few main categories." He ticked them off on his fingers. "One, files pertaining to the company PrismCo—personnel, finances, reports. From what little I've read of them, everything looks kosher, but I'll let you take a look at all that—it's probably more your speed. Two, files relating to his personal finances—bank accounts, taxes, and so on. Three, items relating to his collections. Here's where it gets interesting."

"Really? How?"

Cam sat back in his chair and prepared to expound on his discovery. "There are nice tidy records of what he bought, where he bought it. Also insurance information. That should be a big help to Nat. There's a lot more stuff here, and I need some time to work through it. But I do have one observation."

"Which is?"

"There's one name that keeps popping up in the company files and also in the press: Peter's CFO, Andrew Foster, the guy who was the most outspoken about Peter's decision to dissolve the company. And he wasn't shy about talking to anyone who would listen."

"Well, if he was pretty high up the food chain, he might have felt he had a lot to gain financially if the company went public. Did Peter keep any correspondence or anything?"

Cam shook his head. "Not here. Which doesn't mean there isn't any, just that it's not on this computer. It looks like this was a secondary one—something he kept on hand at the house, with the basic files he wanted to have quick access to, but not the whole array. Or maybe he had those stored off-site. Or, heaven forbid, in hard copy."

"So you can't tell me anything about Foster?"

"Nope, just what's in the press. Although it looks like he and Peter go way back. He was with the company for quite a while." Cam handed me a printout. "Here—this pretty much summarizes the situation. If you read between the lines, Foster was mad as hell—felt that Peter had cut his legs out from under him, and gone behind his back to do it."

"Cam, you're muddling your metaphors, but I get the idea. He was not a happy camper. So here's something else that's interesting: Matt said that Foster had arrived in Tucson just before Peter died, and then he fell off the map."

"I thought Matt wasn't sharing information with you." Cam's tone was incredulous.

"Actually, he told Nat, and I happened to be in the room." I looked at the page Cam had handed me: a printout from the

Wall Street Journal with a small and grainy studio photo of Andrew Foster, looking very preppy, far more than Peter had. At least, the Peter I had seen. Maybe Peter had undergone some sort of epiphany—or a psychotic break—when he decided to dissolve the company. Maybe up until that point he had been as starchy as Andrew looked.

Maybe I was fantasizing far ahead of my sparse data. "I wonder if Matt's tracked him down yet? Not that he'd tell me. Can you tell where he lives now?"

Cam clicked a few keys. "Colorado. You want a phone number?"

"No. As Matt delights in pointing out, it's really none of my business. Let him and his crowd take care of the obvious leads. If Foster's been that vocal about his complaints, I'm sure he's high on their suspect list. Anyone else at the company have a known gripe?"

"Not that I've seen. You know, I think I had the wrong impression. It looks as if Foster was really the only one to make noise publicly. But he wouldn't let it go, and he'd talk to anyone in the press that would listen, at least until they lost interest. From what I've seen here, Peter did a decent job of shutting things down gracefully. The rest of his staff walked away in good shape, and most of them landed somewhere else pretty fast."

"So as far as you know, Peter didn't loot the coffers and sneak away, letting the whole organization self-destruct."

"No, not even close. From what I can tell, the company was in good shape—I can print out the most recent financials if you want to take a look at them. It looks as though PrismCo could have kept going fine. The story Peter gave out for public consumption was that he thought he'd taken it as far as he could. Read: He was getting bored. Sometimes computer types, even the good ones, just burn out."

I was obscurely pleased that there was no hint of illegality or bad management, although I probably shared with

Cam an unspoken question about why a vital, intelligent man like Peter would have withdrawn from the company he had founded and steered so ably, without a particularly convincing explanation. But knowing Cam as I did, I admitted freely that I didn't understand the mind of computer geniuses, and Peter obviously fell into that category.

I sighed. "We should give this to Matt."

"What do you mean?"

"I mean, you've got information on that laptop that may suggest a motive for killing Peter. Former employees—maybe Foster's not the only one who was unhappy, although he was the most vocal about it. Who holds the patents, if there is such a thing? What about the former Mrs. Ferguson—did you see anything about her? Did she think she was getting stiffed when Peter sold the company? And that's just off the top of my head. This is stuff that Matt needs to know."

"I hadn't thought of that." Poor Cam looked deflated. "But Nat's not going to like that, since the machine is her territory."

"I'm not sure it is 'her territory.'" This was really murky: Nat had appointed Cam an FBI consultant in this area, not me, so it was technically his decision what to do with whatever he found. But the information on the laptop could be important to the murder investigation, and Matt certainly wouldn't like that Cam was digging around in it. "Nat's area of expertise is art theft, not homicide."

Cam nodded.

I went on. "Maybe she didn't think it through, or maybe she didn't expect me to find anything relevant to the murder. Or maybe she *is* just trying to grab all the glory—she's the newest member of this FBI special team, and she wants to make her mark."

I sighed. Sticky situation all around. "How much of this did you share with her last night?" I asked after a moment.

"Sister of mine, I do have some decent instincts now and then. She asked about what was on there about his art collection, and I told her. I didn't mention most of the other stuff. I figured Matt should have a crack at it first."

"Good boy!" I beamed at him. "So what are we going to do about it?"

"No clue," he replied. "You're the one with the relationship with Matt. I'll let you figure that one out."

"Gee, thanks. Matt and I aren't talking, apparently, until this murder is cleared up." I didn't bother to mention I had sort of hung up on him last night. "Kind of a Catch-22, isn't it? I have evidence that might help solve this murder, but he won't let me share it with him until he solves the murder."

"Em, from what you've said, I think you have to tell him."

He was right, and I was happy that he recognized the necessity. I sighed. "I know. I just don't know how to do it. What's your schedule?"

"You mean, am I going to be around to help you explain to your boyfriend that you and I are running circles around him in the investigation he wants you to stay out of?"

"Yeah, that."

"Sorry, but I have a project at work this week that I can't blow off, so I've got to go back tonight."

"And this afternoon?"

"Allison and I have plans."

I really did want his support when I talked to Matt, particularly in explaining the technical side of things, but I knew that Cam needed to spend some quality time with Allison, if he was to depart for home on good terms with her. I would just have to bite the bullet and deal with Matt on my own. But I wasn't looking forward to it.

"Okay, baby brother, you go off and frolic with your lady love, and I'll try and patch up relations with the local constabulary. Where did you and Nat leave things?"

"She said something about getting together again today, once she'd had a chance to digest what I told her. I plan to be conveniently somewhere else, and my cell phone is about to die mysteriously."

"Then you'd better hit the road, pal. Are those printouts for me?" I pointed to the pile of papers on the table.

"Yes. I've annotated the list, so you know which ones are important."

"And where are we keeping this precious computer?"

"Nat gave it to me, and that makes it my responsibility. But I can't go wandering around Tucson with the thing in my trunk. You hang on to it for now, and I can take it with me when I leave. Or not, if you need a bargaining chip. I've got what I need from it, anyway."

I assumed he meant he'd copied the files to his own computer or stashed them somewhere in cyberspace. "Boy, we've really landed right in the thick of it, haven't we? Nat's going to be pissed if we turn the computer over to Matt; Matt's going to be pissed that we didn't tell him about the contents ASAP. A real lose-lose situation, eh?"

"That it is. But I have infinite faith in your ability to arrive at the best possible decision. Oops, gotta go!" He stood up and disappeared into the guest room, leaving me alone at the table with my quandary.

I'll admit up front that I'm a chicken, and I particularly hate personal confrontations. I persuaded myself that I really should take care of some business before devoting any more time and energy to solving Peter's murder. That meant heading for the studio and working with some glass, which always calmed me.

It took me until three o'clock in the afternoon to work up the nerve to call Matt. I made excuses to myself: The shop was busy, and I needed to make some basic trade pieces to restock my own inventory (and working in the shop where sidewalk strollers could watch was always a good draw). But I knew I couldn't put it off much longer, and finally I marched upstairs and punched in Matt's work number. I was surprised to find that he wasn't in his office. I left an innocuous message, along the lines of "we have to talk" and heaved a sigh of relief. The ball was back in his court.

Chapter 16

❧

I tried Cam on his cell phone, to let him know that I had done my duty, but true to his word, it wasn't on. I didn't leave a message. It was approaching six when I left the shop and made my way upstairs. Cam had left a note saying that he had fed and walked Fred and Gloria, and he had left the "object of interest" in my underwear drawer. Men. I wasn't sure whose property it was at this point, officially. The FBI's? Or could Matt confiscate it as evidence? I really didn't want to find myself in the middle of that argument, but I was afraid I wouldn't have a choice. In the end I stuffed it in the linen closet under my towels.

I found myself bored—and hungry. I checked my fridge, but nothing looked appealing. Heck, most of it didn't even look edible. I decided I should treat myself to a decent meal, and Sunday nights were pretty quiet in this neighborhood, so I wouldn't have to fight for a table. I gave the pups a quick turn around the block, and after I brought them back I meandered through the neighborhood, not so much reading menus as sniffing the good smells wafting from the various small restaurants that were open. Finally I stopped in front of one that smelled particularly yummy, then plunged into the dark interior, where the smells only got better. I found a table against the wall and settled in with a beer and a platter of nachos, drooling in anticipation of more food to come. So focused was I on eating that it was a couple of minutes before I sat back and checked out the room to see if I knew anyone. I wouldn't mind having someone to talk to while I ate.

There were no familiar faces, but I wasn't surprised—it was getting late, and tomorrow was a workday. My eyes lit on a guy slouched against the bar. I could see his face from the side, but he was concentrating hard on the drink in front of him. Not his first, by the looks of it.

And then I looked again. He didn't much resemble the fuzzy newspaper picture Cam had showed me—that guy had been buttoned down in a suit, his hair neatly combed. The man at the bar was a wreck—and getting more wrecked, judging from the line of glasses in front of him on the bar. Still, to my tired eyes, he looked a heck of a lot like Andrew Foster.

One way to find out. My bottle was still half full, but I stood up and made my way to the bar, signaling the bartender. "Hi, Jorge. Can I have another?"

Jorge smiled and reached for a fresh bottle. I sneaked a glance at the guy next to me, and damned if he didn't still look a lot like Andrew Foster, up close. Now what? Absurd and outdated pickup lines rambled through my head. Come here often? What's your sign? Where have you been all my life? Well, there was always the direct approach. "Aren't you Andrew Foster?"

The man responded slowly, as if he was having difficulty processing my sentence. His head turned toward me, and his eyes focused, more or less. "Yuh. Why?"

Wow. Of all the gin joints in all the towns in all the world . . . "I was a friend of Peter Ferguson's," I said quietly.

To my dismay, Andrew's eyes filled with tears. "Peter's dead."

"I know. Listen, why don't we go sit down at my table, maybe eat something, and we can talk?"

Another long pause while he processed that request. While I waited, I noticed Jorge watching us, and I nodded to him—I could handle this. Jorge shrugged and went to fill another order. Andrew managed to haul himself upright, and I took one arm and guided him to my table, where he fell heavily in the chair, sighing. I almost reeled from the blast of alcohol fumes.

"Have you had anything to eat lately?" I asked.

He shook his head. "Dunno."

"Then you need to eat something. Here." I pushed the half-finished platter of nachos toward him and watched while he stared at it for a long while before picking up a chip. Miracle of miracles, he managed to find his mouth.

When he had almost finished chewing, he mumbled, "I need a drink."

"No you don't, Andrew. You've had plenty. What are you doing here?"

He peered through the dim light, trying to find my place. "Where's here?"

I pondered how to answer that. "A bar in Tucson."

He nodded as though that meant something. "Good, that's what I thought." He took another chip and ate it. After a long pause, he said, "You knew Peter?"

I nodded, trying to gauge his tone. Was the fact that I knew Peter good or bad, in his fuzzy mind?

"Damn, he's dead. I didn't even know. I mean, I just saw him." The tears welled again.

My radar went on high alert. He had seen Peter? Of

course, the real question was, when? Followed closely by, had Peter been alive at that point? "Were you close?"

"Yes. No. Yes." Andrew looked confused. "Used to be, then I did something stupid and we weren't, but then we were again. Or coulda been, maybe."

I sat back in my chair, studying the sodden lump of a man across the table. A quirk of fate had handed me the person I most wanted to talk to at this moment—but he was almost incoherent. I contemplated my choices. A, I could take him back to wherever he was staying and let him sleep off his drunk. B, I could call Matt and tell him I had found Andrew Foster and would he please come collect him. C, I could try to wheedle Andrew's secrets out of him here in this bar, assuming he stayed conscious. D, I could take him back to my place, pour a lot of coffee down his throat, and hope he sobered up enough to be coherent, and then talk to him. Personally I liked Option D, and then I could call Matt from my place. I carefully ignored the fact that I might be inviting a killer into my home. Still, in his current state I figured I could outrun him.

"Hey, Andrew, why don't we go someplace quieter so we can talk?"

Andrew peered owlishly at me. "Talk?"

"About Peter."

"Oh. Right. Yeah. Where?"

"I live just a couple of blocks from here. We can walk. Okay?"

"Sure." I waved at the waitress, then told her to give me my food to go—not without a pang of regret, since I didn't know when I'd get to eat it.

Boy, Andrew sure was malleable. If ever he had been a titan of the computer industry, you wouldn't know it now. I had to wonder: Had he really cared that much for Peter? Was he that broken up by his death? Or was he responsible for it? Only one way to find out: Sober him up and see what he had to say.

When the waitress arrived with my dinner, carefully packaged in a paper bag, I settled up with her and then hauled Andrew out of his seat. He felt like a large wad of dough, heavy and boneless. "Up we go."

Once he found his feet again, he came along amiably enough. We made it out of the bar and halfway down the block before he started heaving. I guided him toward the curb and waited patiently while he emptied his stomach. It took a while, but when he finally straightened up he seemed more in control.

He looked at me as though he hadn't seen me before. "Where we going?"

"My home. Not far now."

We made the rest of the trip without incident, although I thought I'd lost him when he saw the stairs to my place. But he managed, and stood on the landing, swaying only slightly, as I fumbled my key into the lock. Fred and Gloria rushed to greet me, then stopped dead at the sight of Andrew. Fred emitted a low growl. Andrew stared at them and said, intelligently, "Dogs."

"Yes, dogs." I pulled him inside, shutting the door behind us. "It's okay, guys. He's with me," I said to the pups. They backed off a couple of feet but kept an eye on my visitor.

I dragged Andrew by the arm over to my table and all but shoved him into a chair. "Sit. I'm going to make some coffee." At least I could keep an eye on him while I did that. The dogs came closer and sat flanking him, watching his every move.

By the time the coffee was ready, Andrew looked markedly better. At least his eyes were focusing now. When I put a mug of coffee in front of him, he looked up at me and said, "Who are you?"

I sat down with my own mug. "I'm Emmeline Dowell. I'm a glassmaker, and my shop and studio are downstairs. I was doing some work for Peter Ferguson."

Andrew's processing time was significantly shorter now. "Okay. Why'd you bring me here?"

"Because somebody killed Peter and I want to know who. I'm the one who found his body."

Andrew stared at me, his expression clouded. If he was the killer, what would he do now? Leap across the table and strangle me? If he wasn't, I really wanted to hear when he'd last seen Peter, although in his current state I wasn't sure he could remember his own name, much less something that had happened a few days ago. When he didn't say anything at all, I prompted him. "When was the last time you saw him?"

"What's today?"

"Sunday."

"Must've been . . . Wednesday, maybe?"

The day before I found Peter. "When did you get to Tucson?"

"Wednesday." He said this with more conviction. "I got here Wednesday."

"To see Peter?"

He nodded. "Yeah. We had—I had some unfinished business with him."

Like killing and robbing him? "About the sale of the company?"

This time he really focused on me. "So you know I wasn't too happy about it."

"Yes, I do. But it was a done deal, right? What did you have to say to Peter now?"

Andrew drained his coffee mug and held it out. I took it from him and refilled it, returning it silently. Then I sat down again, waiting.

Andrew almost looked like he was smiling, and he looked

at the coffee in his mug. "Step Nine: Make amends to people you have harmed."

Some things were beginning to make sense to me, but others were getting muddier by the minute. "What did you do to Peter?" The words were out of my mouth before I recognized the worst-case double meaning.

Andrew sat back in his chair, cradling the coffee mug in his hands. "If you know about PrismCo, you know that Peter and I were partners, started it together, oh, fifteen years ago."

"Yes. Look, you hungry?" I could smell my takeout from where we sat, and I was starving.

"Huh? Oh, yeah, maybe I am." Andrew looked surprised.

"Then hang on a minute and I'll dish up." Luckily they knew me at that restaurant, and they were generous with their servings. There was enough for two of us, barely. I filled two plates and went back to the table. I allowed us both a reasonable time-out as we ate some food. "Okay. So, you were talking about PrismCo and what happened?"

The food did seem to be helping Andrew sober up. He even picked up the thread of the conversation without any more prompting from me. "PrismCo did better than we ever expected it to. I mean, we were clueless when we started—just a couple of guys who were fed up with working for other people, and we had a couple of good ideas we wanted to follow up on. So we quit our jobs and things took off from there. We were a good team—he did most of the code, and I handled the business side, marketing, that kind of thing. Ten years later we were really big, and we weren't even sure how we got there."

"So what happened? Why did Peter decide to shut things down?" For a moment I wondered if he would tell me the real story, or if he even knew it.

"My fault. I screwed up."

That wasn't what I had expected to hear. "How?"

"Like I said, we got big, and successful. And we got so wrapped up in it all that I guess our marriages kind of took a backseat, and then they fell apart. Peter has a couple of kids, but he hardly even knew them. At least I never messed up anyone else 'cept my wife. Anyway, I guess you'd say, things got kind of out of balance. And then I started drinking."

I suppose you can't rush someone's heartfelt confession, but I still didn't see how this was connected to Peter's death, and I was getting impatient. "But how did that lead to Peter dissolving the company?"

"I'm getting there." He looked down at his plate, surprised to find it empty. "Okay, my wife left, and she took a nice chunk of change with her. I was drinking, and I started doing some stupid things, like gambling. And I got in over my head, and . . . I kind of used some money that wasn't mine. Just to tide me over. I was going to pay it back. But Peter found out."

I was beginning to see some glimmerings of what had happened. "That was about the time the idea of an IPO was being tossed around?"

Andrew nodded. "Yeah. I was stupid—I didn't see the implications. But Peter did. He knew that if we were going public, there would be a lot of people trampling through our financial records, and what I had done would come out. So Peter pulled the plug."

"To cover up for you?"

"Yeah. Exactly. He said that he would see to it that nothing ever came back to me, but the only way to do it would be to shut down while we still could."

"But couldn't the company have gone on the way you had been?"

Andrew looked at me then, and the tears were back. "He said . . . he said he didn't want to work with me anymore. He said he'd bail me out this time, but that was the end of it. Of us, our friendship. And he did it—he just walked away."

We both fell silent then. At least one mystery was

solved: why Peter had quit, had turned his back on the company. For the sake of someone he had once considered a friend. And Peter had kept quiet about it and taken whatever flak had come his way.

But I was still left with a couple of big questions. "Andrew, why did you come to Tucson?"

"After Peter did what he did, I kinda got a grip on myself. I stopped drinking, joined AA. I was doing well. Almost had things back together. And by the time I got my head clear, I realized that I had to apologize to Peter and thank him for what he'd done. I mean, when he did it, I was pissed, and I said a lot of bad things, to him, and to the press. Took me a while to realize just how wrong I'd been. So I came here to tell him that."

"And you saw him Wednesday?"

"Yeah. I called when my plane got in, and I went over to his house, and we talked. Not long. It's not like we were ever going to be buddies again. Heck, he didn't even offer to have dinner with me. Maybe I didn't deserve that, but I knew there was no going back, pretending like nothing had happened. I was there for *me*, to make amends. I did that. I left. And, in case you're wondering, Peter was still very much alive when I left."

It made sense, and I believed him. But there were still several loose ends to tie up. "Did he show you his artwork?"

Andrew looked bewildered by the question. "Art? Oh, you mean his windows? He said something about them, when I asked why there wasn't any furniture in the place, but it was getting dark when I got there, so there wasn't much to see."

I took that to mean that the art was still there. There was only one more question. "Andrew, where the heck have you been since Wednesday night?"

"Huh? Oh, you mean when he . . . was killed? Do I have an alibi, that kind of thing?"

"Exactly."

"I just . . . well, I guess I just drove. I had a rental car, and I headed south, toward Mexico. Stopped someplace, paid cash. Hung out. Did anyone see me? Sure, but I don't know who. I'm not even sure where I was. I'd just said good-bye—I mean, really, finally, good-bye—to someone who was once my best friend. But I'd done the right thing, faced up to my stupid mistakes and admitted them. So I was feeling good and bad, if you know what I mean. I just wanted to get away someplace empty and think. So I did."

"And then you came back to Tucson—when?"

"This morning. And I saw something in a paper, and that's when I found out that Peter was dead, and it really hit me hard. And I went to that bar and I started drinking. It was stupid, but that's what I did. I guess I haven't come as far as I thought."

I couldn't say I blamed the poor guy. But there were still practical matters to attend to, like getting Andrew in touch with the police. Matt. "Listen, Andrew, have you talked to the police?"

He looked bewildered. "The police? Why?"

"Because it's pretty likely that you were the last person to see Peter alive. They've been looking for you anyway, because of the rather angry statements you made about Peter in the past. And they know you were in Tucson around the time of the murder."

"Oh. Right. What should I do?"

"I think I have a solution. Don't go anywhere, okay?"

When he nodded in agreement, I stood up and went into my bedroom to use my phone. I called Matt's home number, and he answered on the second ring. "Lundgren."

"Hi, Matt. Sorry to bother you so late, but I have a present for you."

"Go on," he said cautiously. Didn't he trust me?

"I've got Andrew Foster sitting at my kitchen table."

Silence. "Ferguson's ex-partner," he said, finally.

"That's the one. The guy you couldn't find, you know?" I couldn't stop myself. "You want to talk to him?"

"Bring him to the station, and I'll meet you there."

"Come here," I countered. "There's something else we have to talk about."

"Em, I thought I made it clear that it is inappropriate for us to meet while this investigation is still open."

"Matt, who found Andrew Foster?"

More silence. "I'll be there in fifteen." He hung up, but I was willing to allow him a little pique.

I went back into my living space to update Andrew. He hadn't moved from the table. "I have a friend on the police force, and he's coming over. You need more coffee?"

"I think I do. Thanks. And thanks for dragging me out of that place."

"Happy to help." He didn't have to know that my motives were purely selfish—to get this murder investigation wrapped up ASAP.

Chapter 17

❀

In fact, Matt arrived in twelve minutes. I went to let him in, but the dogs stayed behind, keeping an eye on Andrew.

Matt looked tired. "For the record, I still think this is a bad idea. Where is he?"

I was beginning to get annoyed at his sanctimonious attitude. "Matt, you've made your position clear, more than once. Point taken. What is it you think I'm trying to do? Play Mata Hari and wangle secrets out of you?"

He smiled reluctantly. "No, not really. But hold that thought for after the case is closed. It's just that I got some flack from higher up about what happened last time." When I started to protest, he held up his hand. "I know, everything turned out well, but it could just as easily have gone the other way. We were lucky. So this time I want to do it right. People are watching."

"I understand." I did, and that's why I knew he wouldn't be happy with what Nat had gone ahead and done. "Andrew's in there. And if you're interested, I don't think he killed Peter." Before he could say anything, I stopped him. "I know, you have to do what you have to do. Come on in."

I made introductions. "Andrew, this is my friend Matt Lundgren. He's with the Tucson police."

Matt didn't offer a hand. "Chief of police."

Andrew flinched. "Hey, I'm sorry I didn't come talk to you guys, but I was out in the desert somewhere. I didn't even know Peter was dead until I got back this morning."

Matt sat down. "Why don't you tell me what happened over the past few days?"

I'd heard the story before, so I sat quietly while Andrew outlined the sequence of events since his arrival in Tucson. Matt made notes, asked questions, but I thought he was remarkably un-hostile. Did my opinion about Andrew's innocence make a difference?

After a few minutes he wrapped things up and snapped his notebook shut.

"Am I in trouble here?" Andrew asked.

Matt sat back and contemplated him. "I'll want to check your alibi, and I'm asking you not to leave town, but I don't see any cause to arrest you."

"Thank you!" Andrew's relief was evident, and after coffee and food, he was beginning to look more like the guy in the picture. "I'm staying at some crappy motel near the airport, and I think I could use about twelve hours of sleep right now."

"Don't you have a car around somewhere?" I asked.

Andrew's eyes darted to Matt. "I do, near the bar, but I probably shouldn't be driving in this condition. I'll find a cab." He stood up. "Em, thank you, for everything. Chief?" He held out his hand, and this time Matt took it. "Thank you too, for believing my story. I'll do whatever I can to help you find out what happened to Peter."

"I appreciate that, Andrew. And you're right—stay away from that car."

Matt watched as I escorted Andrew to the door and watched him make his way down the stairs. Then I shut the door and turned to Matt. He still didn't look happy.

"Do you believe him?" I asked.

"I think so. But I can't talk about the investigation," he said.

I bit off a sharp response, especially because I knew he wouldn't like what I had to say next. "I know. But"—I swallowed—"Nat asked Cam to help her with something relating to it."

That confused him. "Asked Cam? About what?"

"She asked him to take a look at Peter's computer."

As I watched, Matt's complexion turned an interesting shade of red. I admired his restraint, because he didn't speak immediately. Finally he said, in a strangled voice, "Let me get this straight. She gave Peter Ferguson's computer to Cam?"

I nodded. "Well, yes, actually. She brought it to Cam so he could take a look at it, see what there was on it. About Peter's art collection, I mean."

"Did Cam find such information?"

"Yes."

He stared at me a moment before going on. "And did Cam find anything else on this computer?"

I nodded. "Yes. He identified financial information relating to both the company and to Peter's personal assets, in addition to details about the collection."

"And no doubt Cam shared this with you?" The fury in Matt's eyes was clear.

"Matt, I didn't ask for this! Nat dropped in, handed it to Cam, and asked him to help. What was I supposed to do?"

"Stay out of it, like I asked? No, that would be too much to expect, wouldn't it? Where is the damn thing now?"

I nodded toward my bedroom. "Cam left it here. He went back to San Diego this afternoon." *To avoid just this kind of unpleasantness.* Cam didn't like confrontations any more than I did. I did not mention that Cam still had all the information from the computer in his possession. Matt could figure that out for himself.

The rigidity of Matt's stance spoke volumes about how hard he was working to contain his temper. "I'm going to have to have a few words with Ms. Special Agent."

As if on cue, there was a knocking at my door. I was not surprised to see Nat on the other side of the peephole. "Looks like you're going to get your wish." I opened the door and stepped back to let her in. "Hi, Nat. Were you looking for me? Cam's not here."

Nat stalked into the room and saw Matt. She stiffened. "Chief. What are you doing here?"

"I might ask you the same question," Matt replied, steel in his voice.

Both ignored me, and I was just as happy to get out of the line of fire. I decided this would be a good time to make some more coffee. I had no idea how long it would take to clear up this mess.

Matt ignored her question. "I understand you have some property that belonged to Peter Ferguson."

"You're referring to his computer, I assume?"

Matt nodded, once. "Yes. You asked Cameron Dowell to look at it? Knowing that his sister was under suspicion in this investigation?" Matt's color was deepening again, although he held his voice level.

Nat moved into my living area. "Oh, come on, Chief, you don't really think Em killed the man, do you? That's just little Madelyn blowing smoke. And Cam's good—don't you think

I had him thoroughly checked out before I handed him that computer? But I needed someone fast, and if I went through channels this would drag on forever, and the art would be long gone."

"You could have consulted me," Matt replied.

"And what would you have done? Look, I know that maybe I could have handled this better, but I wanted to move this forward quickly." She turned to me. "Em, where is Cam?"

"He's on the road back to San Diego," I replied sweetly.

Now Nat was turning interesting colors. "He left? And he didn't answer my calls! What's his game, Em?"

I decided it was time to get back into the fray. "Nothing, Nat. You're right—he's good at what he does. And he does have a job, which he'd like to keep, so he went home. And for the record, neither of us appreciates getting stuck in a tug-of-war between the two of you. Anyway, relax, both of you. He left the computer and printouts of what he found. Why don't we all sit down and share? Play nice?"

A second passed, then another. I might have been holding my breath, waiting to see which way Matt and Nat jumped. Finally Matt made the first move. "Agent Karamanlis, I would like to request that you share whatever information you have obtained from the computer that you took possession of at the crime scene," he said formally.

Nat nodded. "Chief Lundgren, I would be happy to co-operate with you, and I'm sure that by pooling our information we will be able to proceed efficiently."

I beamed at them. "There. That wasn't too hard, was it? Now sit down, have some coffee, and we can go over what Cam found."

"We?" Matt cocked one eyebrow at me.

"Yes, we," I said firmly. "You know damn well Cam was going to let me in on whatever he found, whether you like it or not. And I'm the only one here who actually knew Peter. So get over it, and let's move on. Sit!"

They sat. I retrieved the laptop and the stack of papers Cam had left and dumped the whole pile on the table. "Okay, ground rules. You have to work together. Cam told me that there were basically three kinds of documents on that computer: corporate, personal finance, and art collection. I haven't looked at them yet, but I can help interpret the corporate and financial side of things. Nat, you should probably look at the art stuff."

"And we're all looking for a motive for killing the man," Matt added.

"Exactly." I dealt out papers around the table, then went for the coffeepot. Everyone was silent for several minutes as we reviewed the dry details of Peter Ferguson's life.

Nat riffled through the stack and pounced on some pages. Matt took the remainder from her and leafed through them more slowly. I watched their expressions. At least they didn't look as though they wanted to kill each other—or me. In fact, they were absorbed in reading, and I had the good sense to keep my mouth shut.

Since Nat had the smaller pile, she finished first. She pushed her chair back and took a long drink from her mug, which I refilled silently. She waited until Matt had turned his full attention to her before speaking.

"Okay, the lists I see here correspond to what the insurance company gave me—no surprises there. Nothing off the books, and the man used reputable dealers and kept his paperwork in order. You got anything, Matt?"

"Some ideas, I guess. Nat, who would have known about the collection, and who would have the means of disposing of it?"

"Depends on how high a profile Ferguson kept. As I said, he used top-of-the-line dealers, auction houses, so he would have been known within the collectors' community, certainly. This wasn't a secret collection, although that's where the pieces might well end up."

"What do you mean?" Matt asked. He looked honestly interested.

"A lot of the stolen art in this country ends up in the hands of passionate collectors—they want a piece and they don't care how they get it, or where it comes from. And they hoard it—they don't let anyone else see it. Twisted, isn't it? They have this weird relationship with their collection, almost sexual. Anyway, the end result is that the art disappears and is never seen again, at least not on the legitimate market. That's one of the reasons why the Art Crime Team was put together, but we haven't been around long and there aren't many of us yet, so there's a lot of ground to cover."

"So what kind of a success rate does your team have re-covering any of it?"

"Not great yet, I'm sorry to say." Nat and Matt shared a complicit look, two professionals talking to each other, and for a moment I felt shut out.

"What about his security system?" I felt the need to re-mind them that I was in the room.

Matt threw me a bone. "It was a state-of-the-art system, but it was disarmed."

Nat nodded eagerly. "In any case, this kind of thief is not a smash-and-grab type. They do their homework. They could have known exactly what system was installed, or they could have gotten to the contractor who installed it. So that doesn't really tell us much, Matt. Either Peter let the person in, or someone knew how to get around the system."

By now Matt had pulled out a notebook, and he made a note. "It could have been someone he knew and trusted. There's no sign the alarm system had been tampered with."

"There is that. But he hadn't been in Tucson long—had he, Em?"

How nice, they were going to include me in this conversation. "No. A few months. But we didn't exactly socialize, so I can't tell you who else he knew. Contractors. Maddy, me. But he must have talked to somebody, gone somewhere. That's your department, Matt." Another thought struck me. "How about this? It was clear he really cared about his collection—could someone who knew that have engineered this theft just to get back at him? If we discount Andrew Foster, what about the ex? And the murder really was just an unfortunate accident?"

Matt nodded. "We're checking her out. And I assume you are, Nat?" Now they were good buddies. "By the way, we just talked to Foster. If his story checks out, he's in the clear. He was at the house, but he claims he and Peter were on reasonably good terms. And Peter was breathing when he left. Still, he's the last person we know of who saw Peter alive, so we'll keep an eye on him."

"Thank you for filling me in on that, Matt. Saves me some time. I'll send you what we've got on the ex-wife in the morning, but it looks as though they parted amicably enough, and he was financially generous to her and the kids."

"I'd appreciate that."

The collegiality was making me gag. "Okay, what do we do now?"

Two heads turned toward me. Matt answered. "We—the police department and the FBI—continue to investigate. You do whatever you normally do."

Great, shut out again. "And Cam?"

They exchanged a glance. "Since Cam is already involved, there's no point in excluding him now. He should let one of us know if he finds anything else of value. I assume he kept copies of the material on the computer's drive?"

Busted again. "Yes, I'm sure he did." I was in no mood to mention that Cam had some ideas about the stuff there that he hadn't had time to look at yet. Let them figure that out for themselves. "Well, since you don't need me for any-thing else, I have a busy day tomorrow." I stood up and looked at them pointedly.

It took them a few seconds to get my drift, and then they stood too. "Can I offer you a lift, Nat?" Matt said courte-ously.

"No thanks, Matt, I've got a car. Why don't I swing by your office in the morning and we can compare notes?"

"An excellent idea. Say, nine thirty?"

"Great."

I felt like a kindergarten kid whose playground buddies had just abandoned her. Okay, I'd told them to make nice, but I hadn't expected them to go this far. I figured I'd better get them out of my home before I started saying stupid things to them. "Well, I wish you every success. Nat, I'll tell Cam you're looking for him, if you don't reach him first."

"Thank you, Em, I'd appreciate that. He's been a big help. Shall we?"

She and Matt left, chatting amiably. Alone, I found my-self wrestling with conflicting emotions—and annoyed at myself for having them. They were doing their jobs, and I had no role in that. Sure, I wanted to know who had killed Peter, but there was no place for me in this investigation. Except . . . I seemed to have forgotten to mention that Maddy was more than willing to talk to me, and she might know more than she had already dumped in my lap. No-body had said I couldn't talk with her, right? And Cam would share, no matter what Nat told him. No way was I going to sit back and wait for the big kids to solve this thing.

Having reached that vague but satisfying conclusion, I went to bed.

Chapter 18

❀

The next morning I was scheduled to work in the shop with Allison. Her mind was clearly somewhere else, and I wondered if there was anything I could say or do, then decided against it. I had spent a lot of years "mothering" Cam, since our own mother had fallen a bit short in that department, but there was no way I could micromanage his love life.

I looked up from sorting bills in the cash register when a customer walked in. I sized him up quickly: not local, definitely. Great suit—I might not recognize individual designers, but I knew quality when I saw it. Fortyish, tan, and fit. And he carried himself with an indefinable air of assurance. And then I realized he looked familiar—the man I had seen at Peter's house, on my first trip out there. The dealer . . . Ian Gemberling? What the heck was he doing in Shards? I put on a friendly smile and moved to intercept him.

"Is there something I can help you with?"

"You can if you're Emmeline Dowell." He smiled to reveal impossibly even teeth.

"That's me."

"I don't know if you remember, but we met very briefly at Peter Ferguson's. Ian Gemberling. I own the Gemberling Gallery in Los Angeles. Peter Ferguson spoke of you."

Interesting. And did this man know Peter was dead? "I assume you've heard . . . ?"

"About Peter's unfortunate death? Yes. A tremendous loss—he was an intriguing man."

"You knew him through the collection?"

"Oh, yes. In fact, I helped him to assemble his glass collection—I acquired two of the panels for him. That's why I'm still in Tucson. I wanted to offer my expertise in the medium to whatever law enforcement officials are working on the case."

"The FBI Art Crime Team has been called in."

"Excellent! I'm relieved to hear that."

"So how did Peter come to mention me?" I was flattered that Peter had thought enough of me to bring up my name with one of his dealers—unless, of course, he wanted this man to know that someone else might be messing with his precious works. Was Gemberling Peter's backup to my backup? No, that line of thinking was too confusing, especially for this early in the morning.

"He mentioned that he had acquired some of your glass pieces recently and thought you showed promise. He knew that I represent a select group of lesser-known artists and thought perhaps I should take a look at your work."

I was rather tickled by Gemberling's use of the term "lesser known." If I were any more lesser known I'd be invisible. "That was kind of him." And how unfortunate that my would-be benefactor was now dead.

Gemberling looked around the shop, which was, at this

early hour, still barren of customers. "Perhaps you would have some time now, to show me your portfolio?"

I glanced at Allison, and she gave me a small nod to say that she could handle the shop. "Fine, I'd be happy to. But I'd like a chance to pull together my materials." It had been a while since I had gone looking to expand my gallery exposure, and I wasn't sure which of my pieces I had pictures of, or where I'd put them.

"Not a problem. Perhaps I could offer you lunch at my hotel, and we could go over them in a more comfortable setting?"

I thought about my cramped and crowded office, and my rather chaotic living quarters. "That would be wonderful. Where are you staying?"

When he mentioned the name of La Paloma, I quickly revised my wardrobe plans. I knew the place by reputation, but I had never set foot inside its hallowed doors. "Does noon work for you?"

"Delightful. I'll look forward to it. A pleasure to meet you, Ms. Dowell." He all but bowed, then departed, leaving Allison and me staring after him.

"What was that about?" Allison breathed.

"Peter's gift from beyond the grave, I think," I answered. "Big-league gallery owner who might want to show my glass. Wow." I shook myself, returning to reality. "You okay with covering here? Because I really ought to throw together some stuff to show him. I'm kind of out of practice at pitching my work."

"Not to worry, Em. We're not exactly overwhelmed at the moment."

She had a point. Business on a weekday seldom exceeded what one person could handle. "Bless you." I looked down at my practical jeans and shirt. "I think I'll run up and change too."

"That might be wise," she replied drily. "And I expect a full report when you return."

I managed to pull together both my portfolio and my outfit in time to meet Ian Gemberling for lunch. La Paloma was nestled in the Catalina Foothills. It was perhaps the most upscale hotel Tucson had to offer, so selecting it sent a definite message about him. As I walked into the expansive lobby, I was briefly transported back to my earlier days as a stockbroker: Once I had been a regular at such posh establishments and had accepted it as my due. Now I couldn't recall the last time I had stayed in a hotel, much less a multistar luxury hotel. For a tiny moment I wavered, wondering if I missed the so-called "good life." And then I laughed to myself. I had left that lifestyle by choice to pursue a calling that I loved, and I had made a place for myself in the world that was uniquely mine. If Gemberling wanted to drive home the point that he had money to throw around, he had succeeded. I didn't need his money—but I would be happy to listen to what he had to say. And I was warmed that Peter had put in a good word with him.

After announcing myself at the concierge's desk, I tarried in the lobby, admiring the expanses of gleaming stone, until Gemberling made his appearance. "Thank you for being so prompt. Shall we move on to the restaurant?"

"Fine."

He led the way graciously, and we were escorted without delay to a table in a quiet corner. I admired the linen tablecloth and napkins, the delicate glassware, the polished silver, the hordes of hovering waiters. Maybe Matt and I could eat here someday. After taking a quick glance at the menu, I amended my plans: Maybe Matt and I could have a drink at the bar someday. One. On the way to a taqueria. I sighed.

"I brought along some pictures of my more recent pieces," I began tentatively.

Gemberling waved his hand peremptorily. "Let's not spoil our meal with business. We can look at your work later. Please, tell me more about your move to Tucson. Do I understand correctly that you're not a native?"

And we were off. Gemberling proved to be an adroit host, guiding our conversation with dexterity. I was content to let him take the lead; after all, this was his party. I didn't feel any need to suck up to him, but neither did I want to throw cold water on what was otherwise a very pleasant interchange. So it was not until the sparse remains of dessert lay before us, and our coffee cups had been refilled, that I ventured to bring up the subject of Peter.

"Had you known Peter Ferguson long?"

"A number of years. He came to me some time ago, with a list of particular pieces or examples of works that he wanted. He wasn't quite so successful in his business then, but he'd always had a good eye. Some of his early acquisitions came back to me for sale as he traded up, so to speak. In the end, what he had assembled was exquisite, no question."

"I agree. I felt privileged to have seen them, much less assembled in one place."

"Peter's death is a terrible waste." Gemberling shook his head. "I'd like to think he counted me among his friends. I know I'll miss working with him." He sat back in his chair and rubbed his hands together. "Now, what have you brought me?"

With some trepidation I brought out my binder. He cleared a space on the table, and we spent a pleasant hour or so going over the images and discussing glass art. The waitstaff left us alone, save to refill our water glasses from time to time. Gemberling proved to be well versed in contemporary glass, and a niggling little voice inside me kept wondering what I was doing in such exalted company.

I was happy with what I made, but I didn't entertain any illusions about the scope of my talents.

As I was running out of things to say, Gemberling closed the binder with a gentle hand. "Ms. Dowell," he began.

"Em, please."

He smiled. "And I'm Ian. Em, I think Peter's confidence was well placed. I see definite potential here. Certainly you have some rough edges, but there is a clear progression in your work that shows promise. I'd like you to consider putting together a show, in, say, six months' time? And perhaps I could have a hand in introducing you to a broader audience."

A show of my own? That was heady stuff. "I'd be honored. Although it would be a challenge to pull together enough pieces in that time. Let me think about it?"

"Of course, my dear. I wouldn't want to rush you." A waiter appeared with a discreet folder. Ian signed something and the waiter spirited it away. "Well, this little excursion to Tucson has been unexpectedly fruitful."

"What brought you here? Certainly not just to see me."

"You underestimate yourself. But in truth, I came initially to spend some time with Peter and see for myself what his plans were for the collection. He spoke of the house with such enthusiasm! You know, I offered him the assistance of my gallery staff for planning his display, but he seemed to have his own ideas. What can you tell me about this local person he hired?"

"Madelyn Sheffield." I managed to suppress a grimace. "I understand they have known each other for a long time."

"Ah. Well, all that is for naught now, sad to say. Have you heard how the official investigation is progressing?"

I had, of course, but I wasn't at liberty to tell anyone. "I really can't say." That was true, at least.

"I thought perhaps, since you are closer to events here . . . Well, no mind. I'm sure the local police will do their best. And you said the FBI is involved as well?"

"So I understand." Of course I understood it, since the agent in question had been sitting at my table just last night. Maybe I had already said too much. "Tell me, have you had occasion to work with the FBI art theft group before?"

Ian looked momentarily perturbed. "Certainly I am aware of their activities, as all reputable members of my profession should be. But I have had no personal interaction with them, I'm happy to say. I hope they're up to the task." He glanced quickly at his watch. "Heaven's, we've had such a delightful lunch that I completely lost track of time. I have another appointment. But may I say what a pleasure it has been to meet you and to share your work? I do hope we will be able to collaborate in the near future." He stood up, and a flunky appeared from nowhere to pull out my chair, leaving me no choice but to stand.

"I would enjoy that."

"Grand. I'll be in touch, then. May I see you out?"

He guided me out of the restaurant, and we made our farewells in the lobby. I emerged into the bright sunlight and blinked, feeling as though I had just stepped from the other side of the looking glass. What had just gone on?

I retrieved my car from the parking garage and drove back to the shop slowly. Why did I feel conflicted? Peter had told me that he had admired my work, and I had been flattered. Now Ian Gemberling was telling me that Peter had talked me up to him, a renowned gallery owner. Did that ring true? Had Peter really wanted to do me a good turn?

Or was Ian really interested in what I knew about the investigation?

Was I being paranoid, looking this gift horse in the mouth? Ian could do significant things for my artistic career. Was that what I wanted? Was I really happy with my little shop and studio, turning out modest pieces for a small audience? Was I capable of more?

I thought again of Maddy. Poor Maddy, with her piddling

talent for little pretty things. Was I really better than she was? I thought so; Peter had thought so. But how much better, and how far would that take me?

Stop it, Em! I didn't have to make a decision today. I could sleep on it. I could talk to other people about it. I could look at what I had produced over the last ten years with a critical eye, and decide if I thought my talent would carry me forward or if I had already reached my personal pinnacle. Or maybe Ian would never get in touch with me again, and I would be spared making any decision at all.

It wasn't until I pulled into my parking space behind the shop that I realized that Ian had said he had come to Tucson to see Peter—but Peter had been dead since last week. Why was Ian still here? Certainly not just to see me. Did I buy his explanation that he was eager to help track down the art? Nat hadn't mentioned any approach from him.

What was Ian Gemberling doing here?

"I guess. Give me a little time to get used to it. Did I miss anything here?"

Allison shook her head. "A few sales. Oh, I had time to go over your supply inventory, and I think you're running low on a few things."

"Thanks. You're probably right. Let me change clothes and stash my portfolio, and I'll get on it. Be right back!"

I went upstairs, greeted Fred and Gloria, who raised their heads to acknowledge my existence and went back to sleep, then slipped back into my working jeans and T-shirt. I felt like Cinderella coming back from the ball. It had been fun to meet an important gallery owner for a posh lunch, but it all seemed a little unreal. Right now I needed to get some grunt work done, to keep the day-to-day business going—while I contemplated dreams of glory in the Los Angeles art scene.

Now that Allison had reminded me, I realized that I was in fact running short of raw materials, and I had to do something about it. I didn't use standard shippers like the post office or UPS for several reasons. Cost was a big one: The supplies I ordered came in lots that weighed more than a hundred pounds. When I had started up my business a decade ago, every penny had mattered, and when one of my suppliers had suggested using his trucker, Tim Bernowski, I had jumped at the chance. That vendor had gone out of business, but Tim and I had struck up a friendship and we had worked out our own arrangement. Plus he'd always been willing to help me muscle the heavy barrels or bags of cullet into my storage area, which I'd appreciated. Unfortunately he was gone now, and I needed to find a new trucker. And while I might have a little more money to spend than I had when I started out, I had gotten spoiled working with an independent hauler, and I wasn't sure how to find a new one. Something I had to think about.

I spent some time putting together a list of what supplies I needed, then went back to the shop to spell Allison, and the rest of the day passed quickly. As we were closing up, a thought hit me. "Allison, do you have any plans for the evening?"

She looked up from the receipts she was sorting. "I've some reading I should do, but it's not urgent. Did you need something?"

"Do you want to get in some furnace time?"

"That would be grand! If it's no trouble."

"None at all. Come on through to the studio when you've closed out." I loved to teach glassblowing, and Allison was an apt pupil. Not everyone got it—they were afraid of the heat and the urgency of working the glass, or they were just klutzes and couldn't coordinate their movements. Allison was competent and efficient, and she even took criticism well and learned from it. I couldn't ask for more.

Besides which, we really hadn't had much time alone to talk lately, and I admitted—to myself, at least—a sisterly curiosity about how her relationship with Cam was going. Not that I wanted to pry, but . . . I wanted to pry. I felt responsible for them.

When she appeared, I said, "Okay, grab a pipe and we'll try a small gather." Allison knew by now just what I meant, and extracted a hot blowpipe from the pipe warmer and approached the furnace. I slid open the door so she could get at the glowing crucible inside. With an assured motion she collected a blob of glass on the end and pivoted gracefully to take a seat at the bench, keeping the pipe with its load of glass in constant motion.

"Good," I said. "Now, what's it going to be?"

"Let's keep it simple. I still mess up as many as I get right. A tumbler?"

"Fine. Using color?"

"Please. The cobalt blue frit?"

I went to the shelf to retrieve the right frit can and laid it on the marver. "Good to go." I watched as Allison manipulated the gather, shaping it, giving it a quick puff of air then watching critically for a moment, then shaping again. The glass cooled, and she returned it to the glory hole to reheat.

"You know, I think you've got the basic technique down now."

She nodded, her eyes on the piece. "I hope so. I wish I had more time to work with the glass, but between working in the shop and my classes, there just aren't enough hours in the day."

"How do you like being in school?"

"I feel like a child in a candy shop—there's so much I want to learn, although it's not easy, after so long. I spend so much time doing the reading and the rest of the work." She swung back to the bench with her glass, turning and watching. "Another gather?" She looked at me, and I nodded. "You know, the advisers there keep telling me I should choose a major or some such nonsense. They want me to have a plan."

I couldn't have asked for a better opportunity. "Do you want to go for a degree?" I asked carefully.

"I've no clue. This is all so new to me. Do I have to decide this very moment?" She went back to the glory hole. "Shall I add the frit now?"

I nodded. She heated the glass briefly, then rolled it in the crushed colored glass, then took it back to the glory hole to fuse the frit to the surface. This part was always kind of fun—you never quite knew what the end result would look like, certainly not while the glass was glowing red. She resumed shaping the piece at the bench.

"Don't let them pressure you. There's no hurry." I paused, then took the plunge. "Have you talked to Cam about this?"

I thought she smiled, although I couldn't see more than the side of her face. "He thinks whatever I do is wonderful, but he frets at the distance between us. Em, I don't mean to shilly-shally, but I'm not ready to make up my mind about him either. Is that a problem for you?"

"Hey, I'm not the person to be telling anybody else how to run their lives. My track record isn't exactly brilliant."

"You and Matt?" This time I know she smiled. "You'll work it out."

She was more confident about that than I was.

Her next question surprised me. "Em, can I ask . . . how do you know when you're good at something?"

I gave the question the consideration it deserved. Allison had been dominated by her late jerk of a husband for so long that she barely had any ego to speak of, and I wanted to encourage her. "I think that if you love what you're doing, you're likely to do it well. Are you talking about glass-making or other things?"

"I was thinking about taking an art history class, but I wondered . . . who is it that gets to decide that a work of art is good?"

Sometimes I'd wondered that myself. I'd taken the required art history classes when I went back to school for my degree in glasswork, but sometimes it did seem as though the professors kept trotting out the same old favorites, giving short shrift to new artists or movements—or female artists, for that matter. "Society, I guess. I don't think there's a simple answer, but the pieces that people love, they preserve. And those artists are encouraged. It used to be that artists—like Michelangelo or da Vinci—would find a patron. That way they knew they'd have steady work, even if they didn't get to choose their subjects. Economic reality, you know." I glanced at her piece. "You need help with the transfer?"

"One more round," she said, going back to the glory hole for another gather of clear glass. The next few minutes were devoted to the choreography of transferring her piece to a different rod, so that she could open it up and make it a vessel. Some people managed to do it solo—I'd done it plenty of times myself—but for a novice it was easier to have help, which I was happy to provide. But it took concentration, which hampered conversation

"And who gets to decide that art is art?" Allison continued, when she had a moment. "I mean, is what you do art? Or something else?"

"Got me. Oh, that's not to say there isn't a hierarchy among glassblowers, with the immortal Chihuly at the top, along with a couple of others currently—Lino Tagliapietra, William Morris—and at the bottom end, those poor people who haul minifurnaces around to Renaissance fairs and make cute little things. I'm somewhere in the middle, and that's fine with me."

In making a tumbler, it's necessary to swing the glass back and forth like a giant pendulum, which elongates it into a drinking vessel. Allison knew this, had done it before, but this time something got away from her and the poor thing crumpled into itself, beyond salvage. Allison looked sadly disappointed.

"Hey, don't sweat it," I reassured her. "Even I mess up now and then. Regularly, in fact. That's why this isn't some kind of assembly line—there's that element of risk. Makes it fun, no?"

"Maybe." She shrugged as she slid the poor deformed creature into the annealer. Even though it would never be a glass, it still had to cool gradually before we could discard it. Unfortunately there was no salvaging a piece that combined glass types such as clear and frit, and it would end up a murky mess.

"Look, you've come a long way in a short time. Don't beat yourself up because you can't do everything perfectly. Some things just don't work out, and it's not your fault."

"Like relationships?" She eyed me slyly as she cleaned up her equipment.

"Maybe. You do the best you can, but there are no guarantees."

"But once it's broken, you can't fix it. It's gone."

"Unlike relationships," I said firmly. "At least there you get more than one chance. Like Matt and me."

I had just made it upstairs when the phone rang. "Hey there, you rat," I said when I picked it up.

"Em, your cell's off." It was Cam.

"I was in the studio. You sure took off in a hurry yesterday. I didn't even get to say good-bye."

"Yeah, sorry about that. I really did need to get back here, and this is the first chance I've had to call all day."

"Your departure didn't have anything to do with avoiding Nat and Matt?"

He chuckled. "The thought had crossed my mind, but I'm sure you handled them brilliantly. Did you get any flak from them?"

I leaned against the counter and sighed. "About what you'd expect. Matt was upset that you got the computer and that Nat shared it with you. He was also annoyed that I knew anything at all about it. We all sat down and made nice, and now they're best friends. But I'm sure you'll be hearing from them again. So are you just calling to make sure that they didn't eat me alive? Oh, and we found Andrew Foster. Actually, I found him, which didn't make Matt any too happy."

"But, how . . . ? No, I'll wait for that explanation. How's he look as a suspect?"

"I'm not really sure. He spun me a good story about going off into the desert to clear his head, and he was roaring drunk when I ran into him, but he claims that he and Peter had mended their fences. Matt isn't quite convinced, so he's keeping him in Tucson for the moment."

"Huh. I guess we can't cross him off the list, then. But the reason I called—Em, I found something else interesting in Peter's computer files, but I haven't had time to really get into it. But I wanted to give you a heads-up."

"Really? What?"

"As far as I can tell, he was working on a new algorithm for identification of artworks."

"Algorithm has too many syllables. What does this mean?"

"I don't know much about tracking missing art—that's Nat's domain—but I think he was developing a program to record art in unique detail. So if it gets stolen, there'd be a definitive and widely accessible record."

"Wait a minute—doesn't this already exist? Didn't Nat tell us about that?"

"Sure, but not at this level of specificity. Nat was talking about the existing tracking and identification programs, but many of those rely on written description, which is subject to interpretation. Peter was working on a visual scanning system that would be much more accurate."

"Interesting. Was this before he shut down PrismCo?"

"No, I think this was after, something to keep his hand in. And as far as I can tell he was working pro bono. He could afford it."

"Does Nat know about this program?"

"I can't say. She didn't mention it. Maybe she figured I didn't need to know, but it's also possible that Peter hadn't shared it with anyone yet. I told you he was a perfectionist, and I'm sure he wanted to get all the bugs out first."

I turned over the implications in my head. "Nat told us that art theft is big business in this country—we're talking millions if not billions, and most of the stuff is never recovered. If Peter, who was actually a player, was coming up with a better way to track art, then the thieves might see him as a threat—but then, they didn't take his computer, did they?" I shook my head, trying to work out the implications. "Does that mean there were algorithms or whatever for his own pieces?"

Cam chuckled. "Yes, he did record his own collection. Sort of a beta test now, huh?"

"If the pieces ever resurface at all," I said glumly. "Nat says a lot of them disappear forever." I had a sudden brainstorm. "Cam, while you're snooping, could you dig a little deeper into Ian Gemberling?"

"Who?"

"That dealer who sold the glass to Peter originally. He should be in Peter's files somewhere. Remember I asked you about him a while ago? Your first search came up clean, but I don't follow the gallery scene much. Anyway, he stopped by the shop, and I had lunch with him today. He said Peter raved about me, and he might want to give me a show."

"Em, that's terrific! Why didn't you say something sooner? You must be thrilled."

"I guess." I was surprised at my own lack of enthusiasm, and tried to pump it up. "It would be a real boost for my career, and for the shop."

"But . . . ?"

"I don't know. Maybe I'm just naturally pessimistic. I don't want to get too excited."

"Em," he replied patiently, "why do you underestimate yourself? Peter saw your talent, and he happened to mention it to a dealer, who apparently agrees with Peter. What's wrong with that?"

"Nothing, I guess. Maybe I'm just surprised. After all, I've had to work for everything I've accomplished up until now, so when something just falls into my lap, I don't trust it. Look, just work your computer magic, see what you can find out about Gemberling, if only to put my mind at ease. Okay?"

"Piece of cake. Where's his gallery?"

"Los Angeles. Check Peter's files." For some reason I felt better now that I knew Cam was on the job. "By the way, Nat said she was trying to reach you. Have you talked to her? Oh, and make sure you get some sort of compensation from the FBI for the work you're doing, will you, Mr. Hotshot Consultant?"

"Yeah, she tracked me down this morning. Don't worry, I will see that I get paid. I'll call you when I have anything. Love you, sis."

"Back at you."

As I hung up, Fred and Gloria looked up at me with imploring eyes. "Yeah, yeah, walk time. And then we're all going to get a good night's sleep. Right, pals?"

They nodded. No surprise.

Chapter 20

❀

My first thought when I pried my eyes open the next morning was that I should talk to Maddy. At first I couldn't figure out why she had wormed her way into my head. I hadn't heard from her since her soggy meltdown the other night, although that didn't surprise me. But in all honesty, I had never done more than walk by her shop and peer in her window. Maybe I should take a look at what she was turning out. After all, if she had been a *total* hack, would Peter have allowed her anywhere near his art? And maybe she knew something about Peter's collection that I didn't.

Not that Maddy had the smarts to grasp the intricacies of a computer program like the one Cam had described—but then, neither did I. *No, Em, be fair. You're buying into the whole dumb blonde act.* From what little I had seen, Maddy relied on her looks and her physical charms to get ahead, rather than on her putative creative talents. But who was I to judge? She and I were peers of a sort: We both managed artisanal shops in the same neighborhood, and I knew exactly what that required. So if she had survived this far, she must have some ability—or a benefactor with deep pockets. Maybe I needed to look past Maddy's shiny surface and see if there was any substance lurking beneath. And since she had opened the door with her boozy confidences the other night, I might as well follow up.

Tuesday: no classes today, just hands-on glasswork. Nessa was opening the shop, and Allison had classes at the university. A nice, ordinary day. Hopefully one without dead bodies or interactions with law enforcement officials.

Fred and Gloria watched with eager eyes as I filled their food bowls and water dishes. When they had finished inhaling their morning ration, I asked, "Hey, kids, you want to help me?" Two tails wagged in unison. All right, then: I would combine our morning walk with a quick and unannounced visit to Maddy's shop and see how my faithful companions responded to Maddy. In the past I had found that their doggy instincts were pretty accurate, and the people they liked were invariably good people. They had even taken to Nat, although the pizza may have helped. But I had no reason to distrust Nat; she was playing things a little loose, but if she wanted to make her presence felt in her new position, solving a major, high profile theft would go a long way toward that. Solving Peter's murder would just be icing on the cake to her, though apparently Nat was smart enough to see that she'd be better off working with Matt than working around him.

I checked my watch—just enough time to go down and check in with Nessa, then arrive at Maddy's shop as she was opening. A perfect plan.

Nessa was already in the shop, dusting the shelves—a never-ending task in Tucson's dry climate—when I followed the dogs in. "Good morning, dears!" She knelt to exchange greetings with Fred and Gloria. I waited until they were done, and Nessa straightened slowly—her sixtyish knees creaking. "And how are you this lovely morning?"

"So far, so good. I had an interesting discussion yesterday." After sharing the news with Allison, I still wasn't sure how I felt about Ian Gemberling, but Nessa would be hurt if she didn't hear it from me first. "One of Peter Ferguson's art dealers took me to lunch and said he might want to give me a show in his LA gallery."

"Wouldn't that be wonderful!" Nessa beamed.

I shrugged. "Maybe. Probably. I'm still thinking about it. It would mean a lot of work, and I'd have to juggle my schedule around. And . . ."

"What?" Nessa asked.

"I don't know. Maybe I'm not sure I want to play in the big leagues. I like my life the way it is."

Nessa regarded me steadily. "Then you're a lucky woman. But you'll give it some thought?"

"Of course." I smiled at her. "What, you're angling for a raise?"

"Of course not, dear. What you pay me is more than fair. But as a single woman, and, if I may say it, not young, you do have to consider your future."

"Gee, thanks, Nessa." But she did have a point, and she was in a position to say so: When she had come to work for me, years ago, it was after a long spell during which many local employers had gently rejected her as "too old." I don't know what I would have done without her, and she could keep working with me as long as she wanted. "Yes, I'm still thinking about it. I guess I'm just surprised. We should all have such happy surprises, right?"

"And it's well deserved. You're quite talented, you know."

"I'm glad you think so. And I guess it's nice to have other people believe it too. Well, enough wallowing in my brilliance. If you can handle the shop, I thought I'd take these guys on an errand."

"You go right ahead."

I left, feeling buoyed up. Having people like Peter Ferguson and Ian Gemberling tell me I was a good artist still felt unreal, but having Nessa say the same thing meant something to me.

The pups and I walked the few blocks to Maddy's shop. I loved being out and about as the Warehouse District woke up in the morning, and I seldom had the opportunity. Since I had lived and worked here for nearly a decade, I qualified as an old-timer, and I had certainly witnessed many positive changes in the neighborhood. What had been a rather seedy industrial district had gradually transformed itself into a vibrant artists' community, without slopping over into tourist kitsch. Our reputation had spread beyond Tucson's limits, drawing in out-of-towners with disposable income, and everyone benefited.

I approached Maddy's shop slowly from the opposite side of the street, studying it. I have to admit I'm a glass snob, and I regard making pretty bits of flat glass as definitely second class compared to working in hot glass. Still, Maddy's shop window twinkled—there was no other way to put it. She had hung a variety of colorful suncatchers, some embellished with crystals, at different levels, so that they turned and sparkled in the morning light. The overall effect was quite pretty—and eye-catching. I gave her points for visual marketing as I approached the door. Peering in through the glass panel, I could see her inside behind the register. She looked up when I rapped, and came around to let me in.

"Why, good morning, Em. What brings you around so early?" She politely ignored the fact that I had never dropped in before, in the two or more years she had been here.

"I was walking the dogs"—I nodded toward my dual excuses at my feet—"and they led me in this direction, so I thought I'd stop by and say hi."

Maddy bent down and made cooing noises. "Ooh, what pretty doggies! Are you good doggies?"

To their credit, Fred and Gloria maintained a dignified demeanor as Maddy gushed over them. They allowed her to rub their heads. Based on their muted response, I thought they were reserving judgment about her. At least they hadn't condemned her outright—although I had never known them to be downright rude, except in the case of a few armed thugs, when it was more than justified.

Maddy stood up again. "You've never been here, have you?" she asked.

"I guess not. You have time to give me a quick tour?"

"Of course. This is my display area, and in the back is where I teach classes and keep my supplies." She led the way to a spacious room dominated by a couple of large tables. There were light tables at the sides for laying out the glass, and the perimeter of the room was lined with shallow cubbyholes holding vertical stacks of flat glass pieces, arranged by color and clearly labeled as to type. I was impressed—and I was always cheered by colorful displays.

"Very nice," I said. "I see you've got some Blenko . . . ." We wandered about, talking shop, and my estimation of her skills went up a notch. At least she knew her materials, and she was doing a good job of balancing her teaching and sales activities, which was never easy, as I knew well. Finally we were interrupted by chimes from the front—her first customers. I followed her out into the front room and waited while she greeted two tourists, then retreated to let them browse.

I prepared to make my escape. "Well, I'll leave you to your work—I've got to get these two back home. Oh, one more thing—who handles your shipping?"

She dragged her eyes away from the customers and back to me. "An independent trucker. Jackson? Johnson?" She wrinkled her brow. "I'd have to look up the name."

"Could you? Because I lost my last trucker, and I need to find a new one before I start running out of supplies."

"I, oh . . . well, all right. I think I have a card in the back somewhere. Let me go look." She disappeared into the back of the shop again, while I admired her window display from the reverse side. It still looked pretty good. Maybe I had underestimated Maddy.

"Here we go." Maddy emerged from the back and handed me a business card. "He's been very dependable so far."

"Thanks," I said. The name on the card was Chas Jenson. I tucked it into my jeans pocket. If this worked out, at least I'd gotten one good thing out of our collaboration. "Well, I've got work to do, and I need to get these two back first. Thanks for the tour." I gathered up the leashes and headed for the door, tossing a wave to Maddy as I left.

As the three of us made our way back toward the shop through now-busy streets, I reconsidered my original estimation of Maddy. Her shop had surprised me: It had been attractive, well laid out, with a fair sampling of pieces. Despite her come-hither demeanor, she appeared to be a fairly competent businesswoman, and I had to respect that. Maybe we had just gotten off on the wrong foot. Maybe she had seen me as a threat to her relationship with Peter, whatever that was. But Peter and his wonderful commission were gone now, and Maddy and I were back where we had started, members of the same small crafts community. We could certainly get along, couldn't we? I looked down at the dogs, and they looked back at me soberly. All right, then—back to business.

I took Fred and Gloria upstairs and settled them, then joined Nessa in the shop for a while. The crackle of the business card in my pocket reminded me that I needed to make a call. I went to my small office, pulled out the card, and punched the number into my phone. It wasn't a local prefix— a cell phone, maybe?

A male voice answered on the second ring. "Jenson Trucking."

"This is Em Dowell in Tucson. I'm a glassblower and I order a lot of supplies that are both heavy and fragile. Maddy Sheffield in town here said you do business with her, and I wondered if we could talk about your services?"

"Em, is it? Sure, I'd be happy to pick up some more business in your area. You want to get together, and you can tell me what you need? As it happens, I'm in Tucson right now. I can stop by later today."

Maybe this would be a lot easier than I had thought. "Sounds good to me. I'll be around all day." I spelled out my address and added my phone number. "See you later, then. And thanks."

"Sure thing."

When he hung up, I wondered if I even knew what questions I should ask, after using one trucker for so many years. But all I really wanted was someone reliable and affordable. At least I'd taken a step forward, and if all went well, I had solved my trucking problem with one phone call. Not bad work.

After lunch I finally ended up back in my studio, where the clear glass in the furnace called to me. It was easy to lose myself in the rhythm of glassmaking, and that was one of the things I loved about it. I'd been a good student, and a successful professional, but I'd always felt something was missing in my life—until, on a whim, I had taken a weekend glassblowing class and gotten hooked. There was something so primal and timeless about working with glass. Molten glass was like fire made solid, and what emerged from the process could outlive me. Or could turn into a shapeless mess. Even that element of uncertainty was appealing to me, since it kept me on my toes and kept challenging me.

The next time I looked at a clock it was after four, and

someone was rapping at my back door. I put the piece I had just completed in the annealer and went to open it.

"Em Dowell?" The young man standing in the alley looked barely out of high school, but the truck parked behind him was in good shape. "I'm Chas Jenson."

"Hi! Come on in."

He walked into the studio and looked around appreciatively, while I checked him out. He *was* young, but he looked strong and sturdy, and not too cocky.

"Nice place you've got here," he said.

"Thanks. I laid out the shop myself. Listen, the storeroom is over here, and I've made a list of the supplies that're running low and the vendors I use. Can you tell me a bit about how you operate? I mean, is it just you, or do you have partners, or employees?" The last was a sop to his ego, since he didn't look old enough to be the boss of anyone.

He took the list from me and smiled pleasantly. "What kind of rates were you paying?" When I mentioned a number, which I knew hadn't changed in the last five years, he said, "Might have to adjust the rates a little. But you've got pretty regular shipments, don't you? I could give you a one-year deal . . . ."

I sighed inwardly. We dickered over details for a few minutes, and I showed him the kind of items I ordered most often, and the schedule. In the end we shook hands on a new and only slightly more expensive arrangement, and I took him out through the front so he could meet Nessa.

"Chas, this is Nessa Spencer. Sometimes she puts in my orders and receives them, so you'll probably be working with her now and then. We all set?"

He tore his eyes away from the bright glass pieces arrayed around the room. "What? Oh, yeah, we're good. You'll let me know when you put in that order?"

"I'll do that." I was about to say good-bye when a

thought hit me: Whoever had stolen Peter's artworks needed
to get them out of town, and the load was large enough to
require a truck. I realized I knew very little about trucking,
but here was a real live trucker standing in front of me.
"Can I ask you something?"

"Sure," Chas replied.

"Look, I've used only one company since I arrived here,
so I never did a lot of research into shipping." When he
started to look worried, I held up a hand. "No, I'm not complaining about our deal. But I wondered . . . suppose I was a
tourist, say, and I bought this big thing, like a piece of furniture from an antique store, and wanted to ship it to Florida,
and it's too big to wrestle to the post office. So who would I
call?"

"Me." He grinned. "No, seriously, if the vendor of the
whatever-it-is didn't have any connections, and you wanted
a long-haul shipper, you could ask around or check the
phone book, or there's this website that can match you up
with truckers and where they're going. I've been thinking of
signing up with them."

I nodded, then added, "And there's word of mouth, right?
I mean, I assume you've got other regular customers in Tucson. That's how I found you, through one of them. So someone would recommend you, since you're fast, reliable, and
affordable, right?"

"Hope so!"

Since I drew the line at asking him if he knew anything
about shipping stolen goods, I guided him toward the door.
"Well, it was good to meet you, Chas, and I'm glad we can
do business. I'll be in touch."

He waved and then left by the front door.

"He seems a nice young man," Nessa said, when the door
had shut behind him.

"I think so, even if he bumped up the rate. But I guess I
have to expect that. I'll order supplies in the morning, and

then we can figure out when to expect them—and see how good Chas is. Are you ready to call it a day?"

"I think so. I'll drop off the bank deposit on my way home."

"Thanks, Nessa. Allison's in tomorrow morning, right?"

"That's right. I'll be in for the afternoon, and then she'll be back here to cover the evening."

"Good," I said, relieved. I would welcome a few months of simple work, preferably untroubled by corpses. Especially if I was going to be producing pieces for a show.

I made my way slowly up the stairs to my place and said hi to the doggies. The light on my phone was flashing, and when I checked my messages I found that Cam had called—twice. That was unusual. I checked my watch: just past five, which meant that he was most likely still at work. I pushed the button to return the call.

"Hey, baby brother, what's up?"

"Oh, Em, hi. I didn't want to bother you if you were in the studio, but I thought you should hear this."

"This about Peter's program?" That was a lot easier to say than "algorithm."

"Yes, that, and Ian Gemberling. You might as well sit down—this is going to take a little time."

Chapter 21

❀

I sat down at the table, my tummy doing belly flops.
This did not sound promising. I pulled a pad closer to me and
scrabbled through the stuff on the table for a pen. "What've
you found?"

I could hear Cam rustling papers. "I've got to say that
Peter's programming for this tracking system is gorgeous.
It manages to maximize the detailed visual information
while compressing the code. It's a beautiful balance."

"Yeah, yeah. This is me you're talking to, remember?
You're saying he did a nice job."

"Em!" Cam protested, clearly hurt. "It's more than a nice
job. It promises to be accurate enough to be useful, without
hogging computer space or crashing older machines. That
means it will probably work in the real world, assuming it
gets into the hands of the right people."

"Did Peter keep records of his glass pieces using his algorithm thingie?"

Cam's scorn was evident even over the phone. He could

never accept that I was computer impaired, even though I'd given him ample evidence. "Yes, he did. He used those as beta tests. You know, some of the panels are really intricate— lots of bits and pieces. And glass isn't easy to photograph or scan. So I think he figured if he could make it work on those, then the program would work on paintings."

"Who does it belong to, now that Peter's dead?"

Cam was silent for a moment. "I don't know. The estate? I don't think it's his old company—the dates aren't right. The files I found are dated after the company was shut down. Maybe Nat can talk to his lawyer and find out who controls them now."

Poor Cam—I'd burst his bubble. He was much more interested in the beauties of good code than in the messy realities of ownership issues. "I'm sure she'll be happy to help, and maybe she can score some points with the FBI too, if they don't know about the program already. Did you see any indication that Peter had been in touch with them?"

"Nope. I told you, he liked to polish things before he went public with them. And there are plenty of horror stories out there about new programs that just didn't work, so I can't say I blame him."

"So you're saying nobody else knew about the existence of this program?" When Cam agreed, I filed that fact away for future consideration. Right now I had other, more pressing issues. "What have you got on Ian Gemberling?"

"He seems to be the real deal. He opened up his gallery about twelve years ago, with some of his own money, plus help from a small group of investors. It's been successful— been mentioned in what I assume are all the right magazines in the art world. Not my area of expertise."

"Not mine either, really. Any mention of artists' shows that he's done?"

"A few—I can send you the websites. But mostly he trades. He's bought some stuff at auctions for pretty high dollars, and made some good sales. Short of looking at his tax returns, I'd say he's doing pretty well."

"What, you can't find his tax returns online?" I wasn't sure if I was joking.

"No, I can't. If you really want them, you'd have to talk to someone higher up. Now if he was a nonprofit, it'd be a piece of cake. But there is one thing I thought was odd."

The pups had gathered at my feet—must be dinner time. "What?"

"Peter had a lot of files of pieces that Gemberling had bought or sold over the past couple of years."

"Maybe they were collaborating? Peter was using Ian's pieces to test his system?"

"Maybe. I can't tell yet. But there are also some pieces for which I didn't find any public sale record. Not that that's conclusive, because there are a lot of art sales that don't make the news, and even if they do, there's not always a picture to go with them. So I can't tell you right now what this means. If anything. Maybe Gemberling can tell you. Will you be talking to him again any time soon?"

"I don't know. We didn't set any sort of time limit, and it takes months to plan the kind of show he was talking about, and I'm sure he's got a long forward schedule. And I don't know if he's staying in town here or if he's gone back to LA. Maybe he's hoping that Peter's panels will reappear and he'll have a crack at selling them. That'd be a nice piece of change for him, if he gets a commission on the sale." I tried to think if I had any more questions for Cam, but came up empty. "Well, my entourage is looking forward to dinner, so I'd better go. Thanks for the information, even though I'm not sure what it means."

"No problem. I'll try to reach Nat and pass this on to her. You take care."

"You too." We hung up.

As I dished out din-din for the dogs, I tried to sort out

what Cam had told me and what the implications were. Peter had plenty of high-quality images of his missing artworks: That was good news. Assuming, of course, that they ever surfaced and required identification. He also had lots of images of other works that Ian Gemberling had handled, and we didn't know why. But Ian had said that he'd known Peter for some time. In fact, he'd mentioned that he'd even resold some of Peter's early acquisitions. Maybe Peter had wanted to make sure he was getting a fair deal from Ian. Or maybe Ian had volunteered to serve as a guinea pig for Peter's project. Maybe Ian was just taking precautions, getting ahead of the curve by recording the works he bought and sold, in case Peter's program ever did go public. As for Ian's financial state, nothing had jumped out to Cam's uneducated eye, which didn't mean much one way or another. If someone was smart enough to play in the multimillion-dollar leagues, he—or she—should be smart enough to fudge a financial statement. Maybe that was why I was having such trouble dealing with Ian's offer of a show of my own: I really didn't think I was in that class, and I wasn't being humble or self-effacing, I was just stating a fact. So why had he made the offer?

I was sitting at the table staring into space, trying to fit these pieces together, when someone knocked on the door. The dogs beat me to it, but sat looking at it expectantly rather than barking furiously. Not a stranger, apparently. I checked the peephole: Nat.

I opened the door. "Hello again. Were your ears burning? I was just talking to Cam about you."

She stepped in—bearing food once again. This time it smelled like Chinese, and I started drooling like Pavlov's dog. Smart woman: She knew just how to get to me.

"I took a chance that you hadn't eaten."

"In case I didn't mention it before, I hate to cook, so I put it off as long as possible. That smells great."

"I thought so. So, you managed to have a conversation with Cam? I get the feeling he's been avoiding me."

I headed for the kitchen to round up the necessary plates and drinks, and set them on the table. I gestured toward a chair and she sat. I sat. There was something I wanted to get off my chest before things got any more complicated.

"Nat, I appreciate that you're trying to worm your way into my good graces with food. I understand that you're a single woman in a strange town and you probably don't like to eat alone. I'm flattered that you don't believe that I am either a killer or a thief. But apart from that, what the heck are you doing here?"

Nat sat back in her chair and grinned at me. "Em, I like you. You don't take any bull, and you're smart. You're right on all counts. I told you: I need your help. You know the players and the local scene, and you can tell me about them. You knew Peter, you knew his art. So, cards on the table? I appreciate anything you can give me."

"And isn't it convenient that I gave you access to both Cam and Matt," I responded drily.

She nodded. "Yup, there is that. You've been a big help with that. Oh, let's get this out of the way: Is Cam attached?"

I had to admire her forthright approach. "Definitely."

She nodded, once. "Thanks. Just checking. I don't want to make this situation any stickier than it already is. So, wanna eat? Then we can get down to the good stuff."

"Works for me," I said, reaching for the lo mein.

The next few minutes were occupied by serious eating. Finally, when I had reached a plateau, I ventured, "Cam says you're the new kid on this FBI team?" If she could be upfront, so could I.

She sucked up a noodle before answering. "Yup, although we're all pretty new to the team. But we've got some solid old-timers. I gotta tell you, this is my dream job. I started out in art history, but that was so, I don't

know—academic? Then I got into the forensic side of
things. You know, materials analysis—paint types, canvas,
wood, whatever. But I'm not real good in the lab, so when I
heard about this FBI team, I figured, what the heck? I could
combine it all. And it's been fun so far, but this is my first
solo, so I want to do it right."

She stopped and sat back in her chair, and it appeared to
me that she was trying to make up her mind about something. Then she leaned forward again and looked directly at
me. "Look, Em, maybe you're wondering why the FBI hasn't
thrown a lot more resources at this. You know, high-profile
guy, high-dollar art gone missing—why no big splash? The
thing is, there's only a handful of us for the whole country,
and there's a lot more art theft going on out there than you
probably ever hear about, and this isn't the only million-
plus case. And our federal funding sucks, but we're working on it. But I'm it on this one. So it really is important to
me to do this right, and that means using all the resources I
can scrounge, including you and your brother. And, hey, if
it works out, it'll make our unit look really good."

Not to mention making Nat look pretty good. But her
logic made sense to me. "Thanks for filling me in, even if it
doesn't make me feel much better about the glass. Look,
I'll help any way I can. And don't lose sight of the fact that
a man—a man I knew and liked—is dead. So I'm in this
for his sake too. What do you need?"

"It'd really help just to bat around some ideas here. I'm
trusting the police—and your Matt—to take care of the
murder end of things, and I'm concentrating on the art.
Frankly, there's not much of a physical trail to work with. You
say the art was there, and you saw it, over a period of time.
Andrew Foster said he saw it on Wednesday afternoon. The
art was gone when you got there Thursday afternoon.
Assuming Andrew's telling the truth, where did it go in
that twenty-four-hour period? And how?"

"What's your take?" I hadn't made up my own mind, and I was curious to find out what Nat thought.

"To be honest, I'm still not sure. Okay, we talked to Foster, and his story checks out, including the AA part. No way he could have moved the art, at least personally. And I really don't see him as an art kind of guy, you know? Heck, I think the whole idea of stealing Peter's collection just to get even with Peter is beyond his capabilities."

"I agree. What about Jennifer?"

Nat sat back in her chair and loosened her waistband. "Ah, the lovely Jennifer. No financial motive—she hasn't blown through her settlement, if you're wondering. Most of Peter's collection postdates their time together, and I doubt she had any idea how he felt about it. I think her biggest regret is that she's no longer Mrs. Famous Man, but we've found no reason to think that she'd go as far as killing Peter just for the attention. I mean, once he's dead, she's history. End of story."

"You've talked to her?"

Nat nodded. "She was quite happy to cooperate—just in time for the twelve o'clock news. But she didn't have anything to add. And I can't see her doing the deed, or even contracting for it."

This talk wasn't cheering me up at all. "Nat, you're eliminating all the suspects. Who's left?"

Nat contemplated the exposed pipes on my ceiling. "There are still people who might have had a beef with Peter Ferguson and wanted him dead. There are fewer people who understood his glass collection, and even fewer who would know what to do with it if they got their hands on it. So, was killing Peter the primary goal? I don't think so. I think the art has been at the center of this from the beginning."

I nodded. "Makes sense."

She looked pleased. "Good. Now, how about you tell me how someone got the stuff out of the house."

"You mean, the physical process of moving it? You probably know as much as I do about it."

"Maybe, but most of what I know applies to paintings or small objects. Big glass is a whole different arena. I mean, you don't just pick up a panel and toss it in the back of a pickup, do you?"

I shuddered at the thought. "Not if you want it to stay intact. Okay, let me think." Mostly I packed small individual glass items, but I knew something about the general principles. "To some extent it depends on how you're shipping the piece. If you're doing it yourself, if you've got your own truck, then it's less elaborate than if you go commercial. But in any case you've got to keep the panels vertical, and they can't be allowed to twist or torque. That usually means a crate, and that crate has to be tailored to the piece. You can't just go to a package store and buy one."

"Right. Which means somebody would have to have the measurements of each piece ahead of time."

I shook my head. "But there *were* crates—Peter was still unpacking them at the house, up until the week he died. I don't know if he'd kept the crates around, but it's possible they never left the house. That would make the thief's job a whole lot easier, if all the packing stuff was sitting right there and waiting for him."

"Interesting point, Em. Either someone knew they'd be available, or someone got very, very lucky. Anything else?"

"You've got to make sure that there is some way to stabilize the crates in the truck—they can't move around or crash into each other. That means some kind of braces, and I've heard that people also use bungee cords, which allow a little give but prevent hard bouncing. Am I telling you anything you don't know?"

Nat smiled. "Hey, you're the expert. Keep talking."

"So once you have the crate, you've got to cushion the

piece inside it—corrugated cardboard works, or high-density foam. And you need to tailor the packing if there are any irregularities in the piece."

"What, no peanuts?"

"They compress too much."

"Darn! And I thought we could just follow the trail of peanuts. Go on—I'm just having fun here."

"Really, that's about it. Protect the glass itself with some sort of covering, put it in a fitted crate, secure the crate in the truck, and away you go."

Nat leaned back and contemplated the ceiling. "Okay. Nothing exotic in there, right? Let's assume the crates were in the house. Would it take long to shift the panels into them?"

"Depends on how careful you wanted to be. You've got to remember, the oldest one of these panels is something over eight hundred years old, and it's fragile. They all are. And it would definitely take more than one person to do it."

"So someone knew the glass and knew what to do with it, and showed up with manpower and transport. How much would one of these suckers have weighed?"

"I'm just guessing, but maybe a couple of hundred pounds, even before the crating. And it would be better to have two men, to keep each one steady, maneuver it into place."

"So the thief would have to have had at least one accomplice."

"That about covers it. Does that help you any?"

Nat seemed focused on some inner voice, not me. "And it would take time, as you say. You don't just slam a valuable piece into a box and run. That means they needed to spend time at Peter's house—and they needed to know they wouldn't be disturbed."

"Yes. And for that they needed access—no alarms went

off, remember? Matt said the system wasn't on. But the question stands: Was Peter dead when the thief started, or was he killed along the way?"

"Pretty cool customers, if they stabbed the guy and watched him bleed out while they packed up the goods."

"I suppose if you find the crates and there's blood on any of them, you'll have your answer."

"Maybe."

Another thought crept into my mind. "Will Peter have a funeral?"

Nat made a sour face. "Jennifer has that covered. To be precise, she is having the body cremated, and I think she plans to spread the ashes over the Arizona desert somewhere, since this was where Peter chose to be in the end. Then she'll have some very public memorial service in someplace not quite as provincial as Tucson—starring Jennifer, of course."

"Figures. Poor Peter. I wonder if this is what he wanted."

After a moment of silence, Nat sat up straighter. "You got anything like dessert around here?"

"Ice cream."

Her eyes gleamed. "You're my kind of woman. Lead me to it."

There followed a satisfying interlude while we inhaled three different flavors of premium ice cream. We were scraping the bottom of the cartons when Nat's cell phone beeped. She turned away to answer. I busied myself with cleaning up the few dishes we had created; there were no leftovers to put away, much to Fred and Gloria's disappointment. Of course I kept one ear on Nat's end of the conversation, but it was mostly "yeahs" and "okays." Not very helpful.

After a minute she slapped the phone closed and turned to me with an air of excitement. "Looks like we've caught a break."

"You going to tell me about it?" Moment of truth: Did she trust me?

"Matt's picked up a guy who says he has info about the murder and he's willing to talk, if we cut him a deal. I'm going to head over to his office now."

And I wasn't invited. Once again I felt like the little kid left out of all the fun. But I rallied: I really didn't have any right to be there. And Nat would fill me in, if Matt wouldn't. Right?

"You'll let me know what you find out?" I said hopefully.

"I will, Em. I promise. Look, I'd better go. I'll call you later, if I get a chance. And thanks a lot—I mean it."

"Thanks for the dinner," I said as I escorted her to the door. Maybe I was easy, spilling my guts for the price of a couple of egg rolls. But I really wanted to be sure that she, with or without Matt's help, managed to get a lead on the glass before it disappeared to who-knows-where.

It was only after Nat's taillights had vanished that I realized I had never mentioned what Cam had found in Peter's files. I hoped that it was moot, that she wouldn't need Peter's algorithm to track down his own collection.

Chapter 22

❖

Nat did not call me that night. Nor did Matt. I wasn't surprised, but I certainly was frustrated. Of course, even if they had a suspect in custody, it might take a while to put a deal together, find a lawyer, and contact the Pima County District Attorney's Office and all that stuff. Or maybe the guy didn't really know anything and had just been stringing them along. Or if he did give them useful information, maybe they were busy tracking down the rest of the gang. It was clear that this heist had required more than one person to pull off, so there had to be others involved. In the end I gave up staring at the phone, willing it to ring, and went to bed. My sleep remained undisturbed by phone calls.

The next morning I was out of sorts, and even Allison noticed when I stalked into the shop. "Something wrong, Em?"

"Yes. No. I don't know. I'm just cranky. There's too much going on, and nobody will tell me anything. I'm going to try to get some work done, okay?"

"Don't forget you have a class later," she reminded me.

"I know. At least that should keep me busy. Let me know if you need me for anything."

As penance for my bad mood, I went to my so-called office next to the studio and put in the orders for the materials I needed, which involved sorting out details about my new trucker, all of which took some time. Then I called Chas and told him what I'd done, which took more time. Finally I allowed myself to go into the studio, and fired things up. Normally I could fall easily into the rhythms of working with hot glass, but today something was off, and I ended up botching more pieces than I normally would. Glass demands full attention, and unfortunately my mind was somewhere else. I was actually relieved when Allison interrupted me. "Em, there's a phone call for you."

I followed her back to the shop and picked up the phone, trying not to snarl. "Em Dowell."

It was Ian Gemberling. "Ah, Em, I'm glad I caught you. I wondered if you'd given any more thought to what we talked about the other day?"

My, he was impatient. "Of course. But I've got a lot of questions too. Where are you?"

"Still in Tucson at the moment, although I should be leaving in a day or two. Why?"

"Can we get together? Somewhere down here?" I looked at my watch. I could squeeze in lunch if he could get here quickly. *Look at you, Em—like your time is more valuable than Mr. Hotshot Gallery Owner's?* "How about lunch?"

He hesitated a moment. "That, would, ah . . . yes. Shall I meet you at your shop, say, noonish?"

"Noonish. See you then." I hung up before he could change his mind. Frankly, I wanted to see him here in the shop again, watch what pieces of mine he responded to. I wanted him to articulate what drew him to my art—if he could. Something about this still seemed off to me, and I hoped it wasn't just my lack of self-esteem talking. I looked down at myself, my usual grubby work clothes. And then I decided that I didn't care. I was doing what I loved to do, and I was comfortable, and if Ian Gemberling didn't like it, too bad. We were going to have lunch on *my* turf and talk about *my* work.

I realized that Allison was staring at me strangely. "What?" I demanded.

Poor Allison quailed at my tone. "Nothing, nothing. It's only . . . you seem a bit angry. You're having lunch with that gallery owner again?"

"I am. I don't want to have this thing hanging over my head. I want him to tell me what pieces he likes and why, and then I can decide if I want to twist my life out of shape for this show of his." And then I realized how I must sound to any rational person. "Sorry, Allison. I guess I'm on edge. A man I respected has been murdered, and I found him dead, and nobody will tell me what's happening with the investigation. And there's just so much else going on— the missing art, and now this idea of a show. But I didn't mean to take it out on you."

"Not to worry, Em. It's a lot to think about, I know. Can I do anything to help?"

"How about we go through my glass pieces and decide if we want to juggle what's on display? We've got a little time before he shows up."

In the end I did shift some of the more commercial pieces to the storeroom and brought out a couple of "artsy" pieces, but mostly we just straightened and dusted. If my pieces didn't speak for themselves, it was too late to do much about it.

Ian arrived promptly at noon, looking unruffled by our impromptu luncheon. Maybe he was used to dealing with temperamental artist types, not that I'd ever seen myself as such. I tried to be more gracious than I had been on the phone. "Welcome, Ian. I'm sorry if I've upset your plans for the day, but I thought since you were still in town, we could take a look at some of my pieces and you could tell me what you'd like to see in a show."

"Delighted, my dear. And I appreciate your candor. Most people would be blinded by the opportunity, but I think you're approaching this quite intelligently. Peter was right about you."

I tried to ignore the compliment, although I was still glad that Peter had believed in me. "Well, then, let me walk you through some of my works, and you can tell me what you think."

We spent a pleasant half hour dissecting my pieces. Not surprisingly, Ian was an informed and articulate critic, and I found myself looking at my work and how I described it in a new light. Up until now I had been proud of surviving—setting up a business and making a living doing what I loved—but Ian made me wonder if I had been underestimating myself. In any case, we both seemed very pleased with ourselves.

He checked his watch. "Shall we eat?"

"Do you like southwestern food?" When he nodded, I said, "Then follow me."

I escorted him to one of my favorite semi-upscale places—the food was reasonably authentic, but the ambience was a cut above funky. He ordered knowledgeably from the menu, and when the waiter had left, he turned to me.

"Em, from what I've seen today, I'm all the more enthusiastic about representing you. I have a time slot available in the gallery for next June. Do you think you could pull things together for a show by then?"

I took a deep breath. Did I want this? Did I *need* this? And would I regret it if I passed up this opportunity? "Ian, I'd be delighted to work with you. And June would be great."

The next half hour was filled with discussion of

minutiae—how many pieces, what types, how they would be displayed, what signage might be appropriate, how to publicize the event. I could imagine a less business-savvy artist feeling overwhelmed, but I admired Ian's business sense and could respond in kind. Our food came and disappeared without receiving its due, but by the time the plates were empty we had hammered out the details of an agreement.

"Let me work this up into a contract, after I get back to LA, and you can look it over. I take it you act as your own business manager?"

"I do. Thank you, Ian, for believing in me. I'm looking forward to this. When will you be going back to Los Angeles?"

"I was hoping that Peter's murder would be resolved soon, but that doesn't look likely, does it?"

I shook my head. "Not that I can see. It's such a waste. Do you know what will happen to his glass pieces when they're recovered?" I refused to say "if."

"I'm not sure. But I would certainly be interested in helping whomever inherits to liquidate the collection, if that's what the heirs want to do."

"What is the market for high-profile pieces like that?" I was honestly curious. "Museums? Private collections?"

Ian shrugged. "It varies. Sad though it is, there is such as thing as 'fashion' in art collecting, and much depends on market timing. As for museums, they go through fat and lean periods. Sometimes they are looking to fill in gaps in their own collections. And sometimes, if they're lucky, they find a benefactor who shares their interest. I have to say, if one is in my business, one must be prepared to invest in pieces and hold onto them until the market is right, to optimize return on investment."

"That must take a significant monetary stake."

"It does. I've been quite lucky in that sense. When I

started out, I had several friends who were willing to back my efforts, and they have been amply rewarded."

That squared with what Cam had told me. "You've certainly done well, and you have an outstanding reputation."

He smiled down at his plate. "Thank you. That's one reason I enjoy giving unknown artists such as yourself a showcase—I believe in giving something back to the artistic community." Then, as if embarrassed by his statement, he pushed his chair back and dropped his napkin on the table. He reached for the check. "Let me take care of this— after all, it's been a working lunch, hasn't it? I'm sorry I have to rush off, but I have another appointment scheduled for this afternoon and my time here is limited." He stood up, and I followed suit. "This has been delightful, and I look forward to working with you, Em." And he was gone, stopping at the desk to settle the bill.

I sat down again and tried to figure out how I felt. I was committed now; there would be a contract and dates and plans. Was I ready for this? I felt a warm glow in my stomach—and it wasn't from the chiles. Yes. I could handle this. I would do the show, and I would see what came from it. I felt good.

The glow lasted through the afternoon. I filled in Al-lison on the updated developments, and she was duly thrilled on my behalf. I walked through my afternoon class, wondering if perhaps I should raise my rates—after all, soon I would be a well-known glass artisan. Or at least, better known. When the shop closed, I went upstairs to fetch the dogs for a turn around the neighborhood. It was a cool evening, and I was grateful for a jacket, and for the brisk pace the pups set as they tugged at their leashes. I was trying to catch my breath during one of their intermittent sniff-and-pee stops and admiring the glowing windows of a restaurant when I did a double take: Ian and Maddy were sitting at a small table, heads together, deep in conversation.

Well, of course, they both knew Peter, and I recalled they'd seemed slightly acquainted when we'd all crossed paths briefly at Peter's house. But I found their intimate demeanor curious, and then troubling. Apparently they knew each other well—their little tête-à-tête suggested more than casual acquaintance. There was no reason why Ian would have mentioned a relationship with Maddy, but knowing Maddy as I did, I was surprised she had not trumpeted her friendship with a noted gallery owner to all who would listen.

At that moment Gloria saw something interesting down the street and tugged me away. I filed away my observation for further thought.

The phone was ringing as I climbed up the stairs, a dog under each arm, and fumbled with my keys. It had stopped by the time I got in, but the message showed that it was Cam, and I hit his number quickly. "Hi," I said breathlessly when he picked up on the first ring.

"Em. You okay? You sound winded."

"Fine. I was just out with the dogs, and they moved fast. Getting chilly at night, I guess. Did you talk with Nat?"

"I tried—left her a couple of messages, but she hasn't gotten back to me."

Maybe that was good news, and she and Matt were hot on the trail of . . . something they wouldn't tell me about. "I think Matt's on to something, or someone. Maybe she's tagging around with him."

"That could explain it. A break in the case?"

"Listen to you! But I really don't know. Nat said Matt had picked up somebody who knew something, and that's all I know. So why're you calling me? Not that I don't enjoy hearing your mellow baritone."

Cam snorted. "Yeah, right. Anyway, I still haven't had time to poke around Peter's program much more, but I did find one interesting item when I was looking at Gemberling." He paused, no doubt to irritate me.

"What?"

"For starters, his name's not Ian Gemberling."

"Really? So?"

"It's Morris Finkelstein."

I suppressed a snigger. "Ian Gemberling" was far more mellifluous than "Morris Finkelstein." "So he changed his name. Doesn't everyone in LA do that?"

"Probably, but that's not the most interesting part. He went to college in Kansas."

"Cam, is this going to take all night? I'd like to go to bed before midnight."

"Guess who else went to the same college in Kansas?"

There was a sinking feeling in the pit of my stomach. "Madelyn?"

"You got it."

I took a minute to digest that. So not only did Ian—or Morris—and Maddy know each other, but they had known each other for years. "I don't suppose your sources told you whether they were romantically involved?"

"Not hardly. He's gay, no question. He's got a life partner, and they attend a lot of events together, publicly—I checked the LA newspaper archives. Does it matter?"

"I don't know," I said slowly. The little scene I had witnessed earlier tonight hadn't looked to me like two old buddies catching up. "Cam, I'm going to have to think about this. But you done good. Keep digging. And if I talk to Nat, I'll see what's up and why she isn't responding to your calls. You haven't told her about Peter's program, have you? Have you seen any indication in his files that he was working with the FBI directly?"

"No, I didn't say anything, and she didn't bring it up. Nothing in the files. So let me know what's happening, will you?"

"You'll be the first to know." *If ever I know anything.* "You coming back this weekend?"

"Maybe. Can I let you know? Depends on how much I get done here."

"Okay. I should be around. And thanks, Cam. Every little bit helps."

"Later, sis." He hung up.

Leaving me more confused than ever. It could be just a common, garden-variety coincidence that Ian and Maddy had gone to the same college. But I didn't quite believe that. It could be that there had never been the right opportunity for either one to mention that curious coincidence. Nope, I wasn't buying that either. Therefore they were concealing the fact.

Was that the only thing they had to hide?

Chapter 23

❧

If it hadn't been going on in my own head, I would have been amused at the mental ping-pong match the next morning. Ian had offered me a show! *Whoopee!* No, Ian was scheming with Maddy. *Boo.* But Cam had found some interesting stuff and only I knew about it. *Hooray!* But both Matt and Nat were stonewalling me, shutting me out of Peter's murder investigation. *Bah.*

As a rational and responsible adult I understood their position—really, I did. I had no place in the middle of a criminal investigation, even though I'd been the one to find the body. But as the self-same rational, responsible adult, I liked to feel that I had some control over my life, and it galled me that they weren't sharing with me. If the universe was going to keep sending me dead bodies to stumble over, I wanted some compensation, or at least closure. I did not want Matt patting me on the head (figuratively) and telling me to let the big guys take care of things. Okay, I was being childish, but that was the way I felt.

Cam was my ace in the hole, at least until he laid things out for Nat. I enjoyed the I-know-something-you-don't-know-nyah-nyah feeling. Not very admirable, but I could live with that.

Thursday. No classes. I could work on some glass pieces, but I didn't want to do too much until I figured out if Ian's show was a reality or . . . what? Merely something to divert my attention from his other activities? Which were? As I thought about it, I realized that Ian could easily have been the mastermind behind the theft of Peter's glass. After all, he knew the collection, and he had the expertise not only to package and transport the glass but also to sell the pieces quietly, under the table. But for the life of me I couldn't see why he would need or want to do it. He was well established, respected in his field. Did he need the money? Did he have a grudge against Peter? If Cam's information was correct, it wasn't because Maddy had seduced him into doing it. Heck, for all I knew Ian had been having a torrid affair with Peter, and Peter had jilted him. No, I wasn't going to buy that either: That was not the vibe I had gotten from Peter. Unless I was totally crazy— always a possibility I acknowledged. I didn't think Peter had been gay, but then, I hadn't read Ian as gay. I had no answers. I needed more information, but apart from Cam, nobody wanted to give me any.

When I saw Fred and Gloria staring at me, I realized I had been talking out loud. Great—maybe I really was crazy. "It's okay, guys—just trying to work a few things out." Too bad I couldn't get their opinion on romantic entanglements, but I had eliminated that possibility when I got them. Sometimes I wondered if some people should consider that solution. Maybe the romantic element was clouding my judgment: If I hadn't believed I had a special relationship with Matt, would I have been more willing to accept his reticence?

The dogs cocked their heads at me sympathetically. "All right, I'll feed you. Then walkies, and I'm going to go to the shop, okay?" At the sounds of "feed" two tails wagged in unison. At least some problems were easy to solve.

I was opening up the shop this morning—Allison had a class, and Nessa was off, since she worked weekends. Thursdays were usually fairly quiet, so it wasn't a problem. I turned on the cash register and checked the phone for voice messages. All peaceful and ordinary. Throughout the morning, casual strollers wandered in and out. I answered their questions and made a few sales. Unfortunately there was not enough foot traffic to keep my mind from drifting back to the same questions: Who killed Peter, and why? Where was his collection? How long would it take to find the killer and/or the thieves? Or would they ever be found? With each day that passed, the odds declined, or so I understood. At least for the murder. Since the art objects were real and tangible, not to mention large and heavy, they wouldn't just disappear. Someone had to help them to disappear.

Just before noon I looked up to see Chas coming into the shop. "Hey there. I didn't expect to see you so soon."

"You ordered a shipment of cullet, right? I was headed this way anyway, so it worked out good. But, listen, I haven't worked with you before, so can you check the order, make sure I've got the right stuff?"

I looked around the shop: no customers. The street outside was all but empty, well before the lunch rush. "Sure. Where are you parked?"

"Around back. That's where you said you wanted deliveries, right?"

"That's right. Okay, I'll meet you in back." When Chas left, I made sure the cash drawer was locked, then cut through the studio to open the back door for him.

He was waiting beside his truck, its back doors open,

the lift gate at its raised position. I peered into the dark interior. "What did you want me to check?"

Chas looked distracted. "The stuff's at the front. Climb on in and I'll show you. Need a boost?"

"No, thanks." I hopped up onto the lift, then entered the back of the truck and spied a couple of barrels strapped against the wall nearest the cab. I heard Chas jump up behind me. "Is that what—"

I felt a tremendous blow to the back of my head and pitched forward, and then things went dark.

I woke up sometime later with a raging headache. *Shit, shit, shit, ow.* How stupid was this? How had I wandered into a bad movie? Knocked out and hauled away from my own back door? I tried to move, and things got worse. Well, duh: I was tied up. Or more precisely, bundled up. From what I could feel, I was wrapped in a padded mover's blanket, which covered me from head to toe, and which was strapped on the outside. I felt like a larva in a cocoon, or did I mean pupa? Not that it mattered, since either way I was completely helpless. Not surprisingly, there was tape over my mouth. Of course—if this was a kidnapping, they wouldn't exactly want me making noise, would they?

Who were "they"? The only person I remembered seeing was Chas, who had been behind me. I hadn't seen anyone else lurking in the van of the truck. Okay, so Chas had whacked me over the head and trussed me up like a sausage and driven off in his truck to . . . where?

I would have shaken my head to clear it, except that I couldn't move it, and from the way it was feeling, I didn't think it would improve things much. I lay still and tried to figure out where I was. In the truck, apparently, and it was moving, fairly rapidly. Highway, then—the I-10 that ran through the middle of town. And that brilliant observation exhausted what information I could collect while immobile, blind, and mute.

Well, I was just going to have to think, since there wasn't a lot else to do. Fact: Chas had kidnapped me. Why? Chas was a trucker. Someone had needed a trucker to move the stolen art. Circumstances now suggested that Chas was that man. *Very good, Em. Keep up the good work!* Fact: Chas was Maddy's trucker. Maddy was linked to both Peter and Ian. *Draw a line between the points, Em.*

But why grab me? The one nobody would tell anything? Apparently I knew something—something that someone else thought I shouldn't know, or figured could make trouble, if I ever did find someone who would listen to me. Well, they didn't know I hadn't been able to tell anyone this important something that I knew, mostly because I wasn't sure what it was, and nobody was listening to me anyway. What *did* I know?

I tried to ignore the pain in my head and the bouncing of the truck—which could really use some new shocks—and work out what I knew that might threaten anyone. Maybe there was no one event that had triggered my abduction, but somebody had put together enough pieces to believe that little Em was a threat. My seemingly innocent questions, my connection to Peter, my link with Matt, the appearance of Nat on the scene—somebody was getting panicky. But what were they going to do with me? They couldn't just make me disappear, could they? They weren't doing a very subtle job of it so far. To all appearances I had walked out of my shop today, leaving no note or message. I didn't have my wallet or my keys. How long would it take for anyone to notice I was gone? Allison would be in after lunch, and she would worry. What would she do? Check upstairs, check the phone for messages—and find nada. And then . . . would she call Cam? Matt? And what would they do?

I tried to figure out how long I had been out of it after Chas had hit me, and decided it couldn't have been very long. It would probably be two hours before Allison arrived at the shop and did anything—and I could be a long way from Tucson in two hours. Or dead. Would whoever was behind this be willing to risk killing me?

Of course they would. They had killed Peter, and Peter was a heck of a lot more important than a small-time artisan like me. There was no hard evidence to connect my disappearance to Peter's death. Had anyone seen Chas take me? Most likely not: Nobody paid any attention to the alley behind the shop, and the delivery truck would not have looked out of place. It might have been a simple plan, but the simple ones usually worked best, right?

So why wasn't I dead already? Maybe Chas was going to take me out into that very convenient desert and dump me. If he was smart and picked a good place, I might never be found. There was a lot of desert, and people—mostly illegal immigrants—disappeared there all the time. Even if my corpse was found, how would the authorities identify me? The desert wasn't exactly kind to bodies, and I had no ID on me. No, wait, my fingerprints would be on file with the police—they had taken them to eliminate me as a suspect in a previous investigation. *Take that, Evil Mastermind—you didn't count on that, did you?* Still, neither option was particularly appealing. I forced my mind away from all the unlovely ways that Chas could kill me, none of which required technology or even a lot of force. I was alive right now, and I'd just have to take things one step at a time.

The truck turned off the highway, then turned again. I strained to hear anything. The traffic sounds faded, so we had to be on a secondary road. And a bumpy one at that, I noted, as the truck bounced roughly, bouncing me with it. It stopped, and I heard the cab door open, followed by the creak of a gate or fence being opened. After a moment, the truck began to move again, slowly. Another stop, only this time I heard a metal door go up, then Chas drove through it. The door was rolled down behind the truck, with a definitive clang. We were in a building, one that echoed. Large. A warehouse?

The cab door opened again and the driver climbed out and slammed it. Footsteps: Someone was approaching.

"You got her?" *Damn, damn, damn: Ian Gemberling. The rat.* My instincts had been right. He'd been stringing me along all the time, trying to figure out if I knew anything. Dangling dreams of glory in front of me in the hope that I wouldn't look too hard at the theft, the murder—which plainly he had been involved in. And I had almost fallen for it. Almost. Great—I'd been right, but now I might end up dead.

Right now I had to be content just to listen. Not that I had a lot of choice. I didn't have a handy penknife in my pocket, and my cell phone was sitting at home, doing me no good at all. I couldn't exactly chew my way through the duct tape and padded stuff that covered me. On the other hand, if they'd wanted me dead, I probably would be already, so either they wanted something from me—like how much I had told anyone else—or they were squeamish. Practically speaking, if they just left me somewhere long enough and did nothing, I'd end up dead eventually. How long was it a person could go without water?

I was jerked from my cheerful thoughts by the arrival of someone else at the warehouse. A door opened, shut. The click of heels: female.

"Ian, what is going on?"

Of course: Maddy.

Chapter 24

❀

I lay very still, trying to hush my breathing, and strained to catch what might prove to be an interesting conversation.

"You call me, tell me to drop everything and rush over here. I'm missing the lunchtime shoppers. What's so important—"

Ian cut her off. "Madelyn, shut up. We have a situation here."

Ooh, Ian was getting testy!

"What? I thought everything was on track. Nobody's talked to me about Peter's death in days. The papers have forgotten it. You worked out what to do with his collection. What's the problem?"

"Your friend Em has been doing a little too much snooping. She's been asking about shipping."

"Well, of course she has. She lost her previous trucker recently and needed a replacement. We used the same guy, remember? I found Chas to replace him—that's how I knew him. I couldn't very well lie to Em and say I didn't have anyone, so I gave her Chas's number."

Ian didn't answer for a moment, and when he spoke, his tone was icy. "That is information you might have shared with me earlier." Ian apparently was one of those annoying types who got cold and sarcastic when he was angry. He sounded angry now, which did not bode well. "That puts things in a different light."

"Well, you didn't ask," Maddy protested. "You said, 'Find me a trucker.' I did. What's the problem?"

More silence from Ian. I could only imagine what was going through his head as he tried to rearrange the pieces. Finally he said, "I found it . . . desirable to extricate Ms. Dowell from the situation, and I asked Chas to assist me again."

"What do you mean, 'extricate'? You didn't . . . I mean, you haven't . . ."

"She's in the truck," Ian said, his tone flat.

"Is she . . . ?" I had to strain to hear Maddy's response.

"Not yet. But it may become necessary."

"You can't!" Maddy's voice rose to a near shriek. "Good God, Ian, she's dating the police chief! You think he's not going to notice if she turns up dead?"

If I hadn't been the potential victim here, I would truly have enjoyed Ian's misery right now. Obviously he had thought I was expendable—he hadn't counted on my link to Matt. Although it was a little unsettling to know that our semiromantic relationship—or was it a romantic semirelationship?—was common knowledge, except to out-of-towners like Ian. The question remained, what impact did this turn of events have on Ian's plans?

In the interim, Maddy was working herself up into a nice hysterical snit. "Ian, what are we going to do? I never thought something like this would happen. What are you doing, kidnapping people? What are you going to do with her? You can't just kill her! It's bad enough that Peter died, but that was an accident. This is different. Ian, you . . ." The rest of whatever she had been going to say was muffled, apparently by someone's hand. Ian had had enough, and I couldn't say I blamed him. If I was planning a crime, Maddy would not be my first choice of accomplice. She was rapidly becoming a liability.

"Madelyn," Ian said, his voice tightly controlled, "your caterwauling makes it impossible for me to think. It might be best if you calmed down before we discuss this any further. Chas—would you open the back of the truck for me? I seem to have my hands full."

Chas was still here? He'd been awfully quiet. But the truck doors opened and what I presumed was Maddy landed with a heavy thud in the truck. The doors slammed behind her, and when silence fell I could hear her sniveling. I contemplated my options: Let her know I was awake, or lay low and see what happened next?

Then I heard Ian say, "Chas, come with me. I want to discuss something with you." Ian wasn't stupid: He knew Maddy could still hear him, and he didn't want to let her in on his nefarious plans, whatever they were. I wondered just how fed up he was with Maddy's whining, and what he would do about it. Poor Ian: He now had *two* inconvenient females on his hands.

But right now I was in no mood to do nothing. "Maddy!" I tried to say, except that it came out "Mmp-pheee." Still, I made enough noise to attract Maddy's attention, if she could just stop feeling sorry for herself for a moment. To drive my point home, I wriggled as hard as I could.

Maddy's mewling stopped, thank goodness. "Em?" she whispered.

"Mmphh!" I said as forcefully as possible. "Ubbeee!" I hoped she could translate that to "untie me."

For several seconds she did nothing. Did she really believe that if she just calmed down and played nice, Ian would let things go on as before? I didn't for a moment believe that. Maddy now officially knew too much, and she was definitely a weak link. I'd have to ask her about that Peter dying part when I got a chance. *If* I got a chance. I breathed a sigh of relief, as far as the musty wrapping would allow, when she crawled over to me and started tugging at whatever held the wrapping in place. It took a damnably long time for her to make any headway, during which time I contemplated methods for strangling her.

Finally she managed to unwrap the bulky padded blanket, then peeled the tape off my mouth. "Are you all right, Em?"

I swallowed my first response—how stupid a question was that?—as I stretched the kinks out of my cramped muscles. I stood up quietly and brushed myself off, then sat down again and leaned toward Maddy. "Keep your voice down! Ian and Chas haven't gone far, and I'd rather they didn't know I'm awake. I'd like to retain some element of surprise here."

Maddy nodded and whispered, "Oh, right, of course. So, what do we do now?"

I listened for a moment, but whatever plans Ian and Chas were hatching, it was taking time, and they were doing it out of earshot. "Figure out how to get out of this." I refrained from asking her if she had any ideas, since clearly she didn't.

What she did have was a severe case of self-pity. She wrapped her arms around herself and rocked back and forth. "This is all my fault. Ian knew he could talk me into anything, and I just went along, like always. Except when I killed Peter. He hadn't planned on that, and he was so angry at me! But he said he'd take care of it, and he did—at least, I thought so. But then you started poking around, and look what happened. Why did you have to stick your nose into this, Em? Were you sleeping with Peter?"

The twists and turns of this woman's logic continued to amaze me. Was I sleeping with him? Was she? What did it matter? Whoa, wait a minute: She had said she had killed Peter. I'd save that bit for future examination. Right now, Peter was dead and we weren't—yet. But we were likely to be shortly if somebody didn't do something practical now, and I nominated myself as that somebody. It was a short election and I won. I hoped Maddy would be as biddable for me as she had been for Ian.

"For the record, no. Never mind that for now, Maddy. Did Ian steal the glass pieces?"

She nodded.

"What's he done with them?"

She gulped down a sob. "When Peter . . . died, the schedule got screwed up and he had to hurry things up. I think he's still waiting for the truck to move them to LA."

My brain was working overtime trying to process new information. She had said there was a schedule? "Hang on—you mean you and Ian had planned the theft?"

She nodded. "Yes. I know it was wrong, but Ian—"

"Never mind. Are you telling me that the glass panels haven't left Tucson? They're here?" Wherever the heck "here" was.

"Maybe. Probably. Oh, I don't know!"

I fought the temptation to shake some sense into her. "Maddy, focus. You set Peter up for the theft?"

"Ian made me. He wanted me to use my ties with Peter to get access to the house."

"But his death wasn't part of the plan?"

She wouldn't meet my eyes, at least as far as I could tell in the dim interior of the truck. "No. Em, I've loved Peter almost my whole life. But he never paid me any attention. Then when he moved here, and he got in touch with me, I thought, 'Finally!' But it turned out that our mothers sweet-talked him into doing me a favor and letting me work with his collection. Em, don't look at me like that! I know I don't have a whole lot of talent, but I needed the money, and it meant I'd get to spend time with Peter, so I just kept my mouth shut and took his charity. I didn't even mind when he wanted to bring you in. I just thought that at last I'd have a chance to be alone with him, and maybe he'd see the real me and come to care for me." She sniffed. "But then you came in and the two of you hit it off, always talking about the art—all that highbrow stuff. And he ate it up! I saw the way he looked at you. I knew you were going out to the house when I wasn't there."

More sobs threatened. I was torn in about six different directions. My head hurt, I was straining to hear if our captors were coming back, I couldn't believe what I was hearing from Maddy, and I was trying to figure out what to do next. And I didn't think we had a lot of time before Ian hatched a new plan. "Maddy, what the hell are you talking about? Sure, we talked about the art—that's why he hired me. I'm with Matt, remember? I don't sleep around, and I wasn't interested in Peter."

This statement threatened to set off a new storm of tears. "That's what he said, but I didn't believe him! All these years, and then I thought it was all happening at last, and then he starts paying attention to you. We had this huge fight, and he threatened to fire me, no matter what his mother said, and I just got so mad . . . ."

"That you stabbed him with the first thing that you could grab." At least that made sense, in a strange way.

She nodded vigorously. "Yes. I'd been showing him some glass samples, for color. And then we got to arguing,

and he said awful things to me, called me a hack, and . . .
the next thing I knew, I had stabbed him, and then he fell
down and he wasn't moving, and there was blood, and I got
all panicky, and I called Ian on his cell phone and he said
he'd be right over, and I shouldn't touch anything, or do
anything." Her words tumbled out, faster and faster.

I had to stop the flood. "Breathe, Maddy. So Ian came
over to Peter's house then?"

"Yes, and he told me to leave and he'd take care of
everything."

"You mean the art, right? Because he left Peter lying
right there, bleeding to death."

"What do you mean? Peter was dead."

Aha—I recognized one small fact I hadn't known I
knew. "I don't think so. Not right away, anyway. There was
too much blood on the floor around him. If his heart had
stopped when you stabbed him, there wouldn't have been
that much blood."

I should have kept my mouth shut. Clearly Maddy was
having trouble grasping all this. Her renewed sobs threatened to grow into full-blown hysterics. I decided I would
welcome the opportunity to slug the idiot woman, if that
would shut her up. *No, Em, that wouldn't be constructive.*
Right now I needed whatever feeble help she could provide
to save both our lives, retrieve the art, and save the day.
Yeah, right. Em Dowell, superwoman.

I could hear Ian and Chas heading our way, and they
were arguing. "Put a cork in it, Maddy," I hissed, trying to
listen. Mostly it was Ian talking, with Chas protesting.

"No, Chas, we don't have a choice. We have to eliminate them, and we have to make it look accidental."

"Damn it, I didn't sign on for this! You said I just had to
make a shipment and I could go. You never said anything
about killing people."

"Well, it's a bit late to worry about that now, because you're right in the middle of it. All I'm asking is that you keep an eye on things here for a bit longer. I have to go meet with my people, and I'll take a look at Madelyn's shop. I don't think it should be too difficult to stage an unfortunate incident there, and it's already established that Madelyn and Em have been working together. It would be perfectly reasonable to assume Em had gone to see Madelyn and something tragic occurred. Madelyn was always flighty, probably left a soldering iron on and forgot about it, that kind of thing, and they were both overcome. But we have to move quickly—Em has already been absent from her own shop for an hour or more, and someone will be bound to send up the alarm."

"I don't have to hurt anyone? Just keep an eye on things here?" Chas was clutching at straws.

"Yes, Chas," Ian replied with remarkable patience. "You stay with the truck, and I'll be back as quickly as I can. Under an hour." Footsteps, a slamming door, and Ian was gone—for now.

My mind began to race. So Ian was planning to stage an accident at Maddy's shop, and Maddy and I would be found dead. *Not if I could help it.* Now I also knew that we weren't very far from downtown, if Ian could make the round-trip in less than an hour. The downside was, that didn't give us much time to overpower Chas and call the Mounties: Matt.

Maddy was sniveling again. I let her go ahead, since it was in character. In fact, I decided that she should ramp up the noise. That would annoy Chas—and would give me cover to get ready . . . to do what? I scanned the interior of the truck. There was my cullet, as Chas had said, but I couldn't see any way to use that as a weapon. Throwing handfuls of glass chunks at him would annoy him but

Chapter 25

❖

"What?" Maddy sniffled.

At least I had her attention. "Look, we don't have much time before Ian comes back, probably with reinforcements. You heard what he said—whatever is going to happen has to happen quickly, or someone will notice that I'm missing." At least, I hoped someone would. "So our best bet right now is to overpower Chas and make a run for it."

Maddy snorted. It was an unbecoming sound. "And how do you intend to do that? He's a lot stronger than we are."

"Maybe than you are, lady, but I sling hot glass, remember? Anyway, if we surprise him, I'm betting that we can get him under control quickly. And there are two of us. What've we got to lose? If we don't do anything, Ian's going to kill us."

"Maybe you're right. So what do we do?"

I explained.

Maddy turned out to be a better actress than I expected. She gave a very convincing performance, cranking up her wails until Chas pounded on the side of the truck and yelled, "You in there, shut up!"

At my prompting, Maddy wailed louder. The noise gave me plenty of cover to rip the cartons open and arm myself. Then I went back to Maddy. "Okay," I whispered, "quiet down a bit, and then ask to use the bathroom."

"This is so undignified." She sniffed.

"Hey, you want to come out of this alive?"

Maddy nodded, pouting. She subsided into whimpers punctuated with occasional sobs. I retreated to the back of the truck and nodded to Maddy. "You're on!" I hissed.

She nodded back, then got up and went to the doors and pounded on them. "Chas? Chas, where are you?"

Nothing. For a brief moment I panicked—if he was out of range, we were screwed.

"Chas?" Maddy said again, more loudly, with a convincing note of hysteria in her voice. Of course it was convincing—it was real.

Finally I heard footsteps approaching. "What?"

In a small voice Maddy replied, "I have to use the bathroom."

Silence. Obviously Chas hadn't considered this possibility. "You can't."

"Chas, I have to go! Really badly! Do you want me to pee in your truck?"

More silence as Chas worked through the implications of that. Presumably he hoped to return to a normal life after he got out of this mess, and a truck that stank of urine was not good advertising for his business. At least, I hoped his mind would work that way.

"She still out?"

"You mean Em? Yes, she hasn't moved. Oh, God, Chas, maybe she's dead! Maybe I'm locked in here with a dead person! You've got to get me out!" I was beginning to think that Maddy had a future in the theater.

I held my breath as I heard Chas unlocking the truck doors. We would have a brief window of opportunity before Chas's eyes adjusted to the dark interior. As instructed, Maddy moved front and center, blocking his view of me, as I rose up from my crouch and started lobbing . . . salsa.

Those other boxes had been loaded with a shipment of Tucson's finest, and I knew just what to do with it. As Maddy stepped clear, I dashed the contents of an open jar of extra spicy straight into Chas's face, and the chiles did their work. He clawed at his eyes and spat. But I didn't stop with one jar. I'd opened several, just to be prepared, and I let loose with all of them. Then I followed up with unopened jars, which must have weighed two pounds each. After all my glass work, I had a strong arm, and what I lacked in accuracy (I never was much into baseball) I made up for in power and enthusiasm. Even Maddy got into the act and tossed a few jars, although several of them fell short of the target, smashing on the floor and adding to the mess.

Chas fell down, blinded, and curled up into a ball, protecting his head. "Maddy, the bungee cords!" I yelled.

She tossed me the cords, and I wrapped them around any moving parts of Chas that I could grab. I had neglected to take into account the fact that the salsa would make him slippery, but I managed. "Duct tape—now!" I ordered, and Maddy scrounged around the truck until she found a roll and tossed it to me. I reinforced the bungee cord bonds, then stepped back to admire my handiwork. "That should hold him."

Maddy stepped delicately down from the truck and joined me in contemplation of our captive. "Good job, Em. I don't think he's going anywhere soon." She poked him, not gently, with her foot. "Now what?"

I hadn't thought much beyond this first stage of my

plan, but I knew that we had little time before Ian returned. "You—find a phone and call the police. I'm going to see if the glass pieces are here."

Chas moaned. "My eyes! I'm going to go blind! Do something!"

I looked down at him, lying in a colorful pool of condiment. I couldn't muster up a lot of sympathy for him. "Why should I help you? You kidnapped me, and if I'm not mistaken, you were going to let Ian kill me."

"It hurts!" he protested.

"I think being dead might hurt too. Okay, hotshot, where did Gemberling go, and what's he bringing back?"

"He was going to go set up an accident at Maddy's shop, and then he was going to meet the guys with the truck."

I knew the first part, but I was more curious about the second. "What guys? He wasn't going to use you to ship the goods?"

"No. He didn't think my truck was good enough for his precious artworks. He called some guys he's used before. They've got a fancier truck. The only reason I got into this at all was because he needed somebody in a hurry."

"Not to mention somebody who would be willing to bend the law. More than once."

"Hey," he said, "I didn't know the stuff was stolen. All he said was he needed some stuff moved fast, and he offered good money."

"Pal, first you conveniently ignored the dead body on the floor when you picked up your shipment. Then you grabbed me right out of my own shop. You're just an innocent bystander, right?"

"I was never in the house! He hired these guys who carried the stuff out, and I just stowed the crates in the back of the truck. I didn't know anything about a murder until I came back to collect what he owed me. And then I put two and two together and I figured out it was Ferguson's house."

And Gemberling said he couldn't pay me until I helped him get you out of the way."

My kidnapping could wait; I wanted to hear more about the theft. I was surprised that Ian had trusted outside labor to do his dirty work, but he clearly wasn't strong enough to wrestle with the heavy crates by himself. And Maddy's impetuous act had forced his hand, and he had had to improvise. It must have been one of those "guys" that Matt had picked up, the one who said he wanted to make a deal. "Didn't you wonder why he had you drive the glass here? And by the way, where are we?"

"He lied to me, said he had to hide the crates—something about a nasty divorce, and he didn't want his wife to know where to find them. And we're somewhere just outside of town—he'd checked out this place ahead of time. Look, what about my eyes? They hurt!"

"I'll see if I can find some water." I stalked off, looking for running water. I didn't have much luck. From what I could see, this warehouse hadn't been used for a while, at least, not for any legitimate purpose. When I tried a light switch, nothing happened, so the electricity was off. Then Maddy emerged from what looked like an office. "The phone's dead," she said.

"I'm not surprised. This place must be off the radar, which is what Ian wanted. Did you find a bathroom?"

She looked blankly at me. "But that was just a story!"

I sighed. "I was going to try to find some water to wash the salsa out of Chas's eyes. I guess he's out of luck, huh?"

Maddy started whimpering again. "Oh, Em, what do we do now? Ian's going to be back any minute. Should we make a run for it? Take the truck? What?"

"You have your cell phone?"

Maddy looked surprised, then baffled, then disappointed. "No, it's back at the shop."

"Chas? What about you? Cell phone?"

"In the truck," he said in a sulky voice.

Ah, yes, we did have Chas's truck, and that could get us out of here. I crossed the echoing expanse of floor and checked the big metal door at the warehouse entrance—which wouldn't budge. Damn! Ian must have locked it. He was definitely not a trusting soul. I rattled the thing, and it seemed pretty sturdy. Maybe I could ram the truck through it—or maybe not.

But what about the art? Where was it? Ian and his helpers would be back soon, but I needed to be sure it was here. I reversed course and loped toward the dim recesses of the back of the warehouse.

"Em, what are you doing? We have to get out of here!" Maddy tottered along after me, her heels clacking.

"Not until I find Peter's collection," I said grimly.

"But Ian is going to kill us!" She was having trouble keeping up with me. There was a good reason why I didn't wear heels to work in—not that I'd ever expected to have to flee murderous art thieves. But it paid to be prepared.

"Then go and find Chas's phone and call the cops. I'm going to find the glass."

Maddy turned and headed back toward the truck, while I continued toward the back of the warehouse. There was a lot of leftover crap, long abandoned, but luckily I knew what I was looking for. When I reached the back end, I was relieved to find a stack of tall crates. I recognized them from Peter's house. I managed to shift one slightly: Yes, the glass had to be inside, because the crate was seriously heavy. No way we could move the crates to Chas's truck, even if we did have time. Which we didn't.

Time to vamoose. Maybe we could ram the truck through the door, and I was getting desperate enough to give it a try. But what should we do about Chas, still writhing on the floor outside the truck? At the very least we'd have to move him out of the way, to turn the truck around. It might be a good idea to take him along and hand him over to the authorities, but I doubted that Maddy and I could lift him into the truck, with or without the coating of salsa that made him slippery as a fish. He'd have to stay where he was for now and take his lumps from Ian and his thugs. I jogged back toward the truck, gauging angles, looking for alternatives. The side door? We could walk out, no problem, but I still had no idea where we were, and I didn't want to risk running into Ian in a deserted industrial park. He'd just grab us all over again. I didn't think Maddy with her silly shoes would be very good at running and hiding. I'd rather take the truck and take my chances on the road.

I'd reached the side door while working this out in my head. It wasn't locked, to my relief. I opened it a crack, slowly—and closed it much more quickly. We were out of time: There was a truck approaching. It had stopped at the exterior gate, and I recognized Ian as he rolled the gate back for the truck to pass. Ian was certainly a cautious type, taking no chances. Well, with a multimillion-dollar art collection sitting here, I probably would have been careful too. I turned to Maddy, who had slid down from the front seat of the truck, Chas's phone in her hand. "Too late—Ian's back, and it looks like he's brought some friends along. Did you get through to the police?"

Maddy whimpered. For a brief moment I was tempted to throw her to the wolves and make a run for it—that was the kind of feeling she inspired in me. Luckily for her that wasn't possible. The nearly empty warehouse offered few places to hide: The largest contents at the moment were the crated glassworks, and that was the first place these guys would look, once they saw salsa-covered Chas tied up on the floor. "Yes, they're coming," she said in a dramatic whisper.

Great: Help was on the way. Unfortunately Ian was closer. Maybe we could reenact our assault on Chas? But somehow I doubted that we had enough salsa left to take on

Ian and friends, and we were outnumbered. And we certainly didn't have time to wrestle Chas out of sight.

"Maddy!" I said urgently. "Slap some tape over Chas's mouth to shut him up. I'm going to get into the truck cab and make sure the keys are there." I hoped. If they weren't . . . well, I didn't have any other ideas lined up. "Then get in with me. When Ian and his pals open the doors to bring in their truck, I'm going to make a break for it. If we're lucky they won't notice anything's wrong until we clear the building." I figured the truck could handle an old chain link fence outside, as long as we were through the warehouse door. I just prayed the other truck didn't block our exit route completely.

For once Maddy acted quickly. I dashed to the truck door and climbed in. *Damn!* No keys—which meant . . .

Maddy climbed in on the other side. "Looking for these?" She held up a ring of keys. "They were in Chas's pocket."

"Terrific! Now duck down so they don't see us."

I could hear the other truck idling outside the warehouse as Ian worked the padlock for the outer door. I stuck the likeliest-looking key into the ignition and prayed the truck would start quickly. We would have a few seconds at most before Ian and crew figured out what had happened, and I didn't want to waste time—not that we had any time to waste. Either this worked, or we might well be dead in minutes. I looked at Maddy, crouched opposite me in the cramped cab, phone at her ear. "Ready?"

She nodded silently. The outer door rolled up, and the other truck rolled into the warehouse.

Chapter 26

❖

"Hang on," I said grimly to Maddy, who shrank into her seat. I sat up, jammed my feet on the clutch and the gas, and sent up a prayer to any gods who might be listening. The engine turned over on the first try—*thank you, Chas, or whoever had kept this truck running smoothly*—and I fumbled for a moment with the unfamiliar gear shift. Ian and his buddies had turned toward our truck when the engine roared to life, immobilized for a moment, but now they were moving toward us. I shifted into what I hoped was first gear and gunned the engine, heading straight for the door. If the men got in the way, too bad. Yet a small part of me was relieved when they jumped clear as I wove around their truck and raced toward daylight.

I was not surprised to hear a faint pop of gunfire. I couldn't tell if they hit anything important, but I wasn't going to stay around to check. Once outside the building I made a beeline for the outer fence, where punctilious Ian had indeed closed the gate again. I will admit to closing my eyes as the front end of the truck rammed into the chain link—and kept right on going.

When I opened my eyes there were police cars in front of me. I slammed on my brakes in time to avoid hitting the nearest one. The officers in the car had jumped out and were pointing guns at me. I took a quick peek at Maddy, who was bolt upright and white as a sheet. "You okay?"

She nodded.

"Then we'd better start explaining." I opened the truck door slowly and stepped out, my hands high. "Boy, am I glad to see you guys! You sure got here fast."

"On the ground." One officer advanced cautiously, gun still drawn. He gestured toward me, then down.

Who, me? But who was I to argue? "Yes, sir," I said as I laid myself facedown on the cracked asphalt. "But you might want to check out what's going on in the warehouse. I think the guys in there have guns."

The officer made no reply as he frisked me efficiently, then pulled me to my feet. "What's going on?"

I was debating about how to answer that when I saw another car pull up behind the two, no, three squad cars, and Matt climbed out. I felt a surge of relief, and for a brief moment contemplated throwing myself into his arms and bawling. I controlled myself. After all, we had an audience—and an art collection to rescue.

Matt strode up to me. "Em, what the hell is going on?"

I tried to make my answer succinct. "Ian Gemberling had a trucker named Chas Jenson kidnap me from the shop and bring me here so he could kill me. He called Maddy and she came and he was going to kill her too—she's in the truck. Peter's art collection is in the warehouse there. So is Ian, and he's got a couple of friends with guns. And Chas is in the warehouse too, but he was tied up when we left. This is his truck." Looking a little the worse for wear after its encounter with the fence. Too bad. I was not disposed to feel charitably toward Chas at the moment.

Matt gave me a long look, as if he didn't quite believe me. I couldn't blame him—I wasn't sure I would have believed me either.

I kept talking. "No, seriously. Ian planned to steal Peter's collection, probably been planning it for a while, and Maddy says she accidentally killed Peter. She stabbed him and then called Ian, and he came and got the stuff out of there as fast as he could and stashed the art here to wait until things settled down and he could get his own people here to move it. But I guess I made too much of a stink, because he figured he'd better get me out of the way so he could leave town. He was planning to kill me and Maddy and try to make it look like an accident at Maddy's shop."

Matt was still staring at me, but more in horror now than in disbelief. "Em, slow down and breathe. You just figured this out?"

"Yup, in the last hour or so. By the way, how'd you get here so fast?"

Another officer approached, a firm hand on a squirming Maddy's arm. "What do I do with her, Chief?"

Matt gestured him away. "Hang on to her for a minute." For once Maddy kept her mouth shut. Matt turned back to me. "When you were nowhere to be found, Allison called Cam, who called me. But we would have found the place anyway. One of the guys Gemberling hired to move the stuff out of Peter's house ratted him out, and he remembered the trucker's name. Chas has a GPS tracker in the truck." He hesitated. "You sure you're okay? I got a little worried."

We could congratulate each other later. Right now Ian and his merry men were guarding the fortress, and we needed to apprehend him and save the fair maiden . . . er, the glass. "I'm fine. Never better. What now?"

"We arrest Gemberling. How many are there?"

"I think I saw two men, in addition to Ian. But I was a little busy trying to get the truck moving, so there might be more. Oh, and Chas, except we left him tied up. I'm not sure Ian will untie him, under the circumstances."

"Right. Stay here." Matt strode off and conferred with his men. There was much nodding and pointing as they worked out an assault plan.

It was then that another horrible possibility hit me. "Wait, Matt!" I joined the party. "You can't fire."

"What?"

"I mean, if there's any shooting, you can't fire back, because you might hit the glassworks." I ignored the irony that I really didn't care if they hit human being Ian Gemberling or any of his friends, as long as Tiffany, Chagall, and Morris survived unscathed.

"I'd prefer that there was no shooting. We thought we'd try talking to Gemberling first."

"Oh." I subsided, feeling a little silly, as another officer handed a bullhorn to Matt.

He took it and switched it on. "Ian Gemberling," his voice—tinny, electronic—boomed. "Throw out your weapons and come out with your hands up."

So they actually said that in the real world, not just on cop shows. I held my breath. No matter how many dollars were at stake in this heist, I had trouble believing that Ian would choose to shoot it out with the police. He should know that the game was over now. But then, I hadn't thought he'd try to kill me, either. I didn't really understand the criminal mind—thank goodness.

After what seemed like forever but was probably no more than five seconds, a voice called out, "We're coming out."

"Throw out your weapons first, and keep your hands where we can see them."

Another pause. Then two pistols came skittering out across the pavement. Matt looked at me. "How many guns?"

I shrugged. "I don't know. All I know is, I heard a shot, maybe more than one."

He nodded to two of his men, arrayed in bulletproof vests, who approached the doorway cautiously, one on either side. They flattened themselves against the wall near the door as Ian and two men came out, hands in the air. Ian and friends were quickly swarmed by more police and hustled toward waiting police cars. Ian gave me an evil glare as he passed, which cheered me no end. "I guess this means the show is off?" I said sweetly. He didn't answer.

Matt issued more instructions, and his men loaded Ian and the goons into police cars. Then he came back to me. "Show me what's inside."

"What about Maddy?" She was still in the firm grasp of the other officer, and she looked like a rag doll.

"Bring her along."

We made our way to the door of the warehouse. Matt peered in, and in a moment he spied Chas, still trussed, lying on the ground.

"Good God, Em, what did they do to him?"

I followed his gaze and started laughing. "They didn't do it, I did. Relax, Chief—it's salsa. I was improvising."

Matt's mouth twitched. He nodded to another officer to check out Chas. The officer untangled the bungee cords and the duct tape and hauled Chas to his feet, soaked in salsa but unharmed.

Chas peeled off the last of the tape. "What'd you do with my truck?" he demanded.

"Son, I think that's the least of your problems," Matt replied. "Ortega, read him his rights and take him to the station with the rest of them. But keep them all separate. I want to hear their stories one at a time."

"Right, Chief." The officer led Chas out to another

squad car, leaving me and Maddy and guard with Matt in the cavernous warehouse.

"Okay, where's this art collection I keep hearing about?"

I pointed toward the back corner. "Over there." I led the way, until we all stood in front of the stack of crates.

Matt sighed. "Guess we can't just leave it sitting here, can we? How much is it worth?"

Maddy spoke up for the first time. "Ian said three million."

"Were you going to receive a percentage from the deal?"

Maddy looked at Matt, then her eyes shifted to me. "I think maybe I should talk to a lawyer before I say anything else."

"That's your right, Ms. Sheffield. But you're not under arrest at the moment."

Before he could issue any orders, I stepped up. "Matt, can you post a man or two here, to watch the collection? I don't think it's good for the pieces to be shuttled around by unskilled handlers. Art shipping is pretty specialized, and these babies have been through a lot already."

"You may have a point. I'll have to call in some more guys. Are all the pieces here?"

I made a quick count. "I think so, but don't hold me to it. I don't think Ian's had time to move any."

"Let's hope not. This whole thing is complicated enough already." He turned away to make a call. I looked at Maddy, drooping in the relentless grasp of the young officer, and I almost felt sorry for her. I stopped myself, though—she had almost gotten me killed, and for the flimsiest of reasons. No, she had made her own bed and she could wallow in it.

Matt returned. "We'll wait until the others show up—shouldn't be long. Em, can I talk to you?"

I assumed he meant without the eager ears of Maddy and her police escort. "Sure." I followed him until we were standing in the middle of the warehouse, out of earshot.

"Em, I warned you to stay out of this," he began.

I didn't let him continue. "Matt Lundgren, it is *not* my fault that I got dragged into this. Maddy asked me to help her, and that was Peter's idea. It was a good business opportunity for me. Was that wrong?" He shook his head and started to speak, but I cut him off. "Then Peter was killed, and I found him; that was also *not* my fault. Maddy, based on whatever twisted fantasy was going on in her head at the time, accused me of killing him. Okay, I can see why you wanted to keep me out of things from that point on, even though I can't believe you ever thought I might have killed him. But all I did after that was a little Internet surfing."

"You enlisted the help of your brother."

"I did not! That was Nat's doing, and she didn't exactly ask me first. So he shared what he found with me—what did any of you expect? And look what he found!"

"What did he find?" Matt asked.

Oh, right. I hadn't exactly filled him in on what Cam had unearthed on the computer. Well, he hadn't asked. "Cam found a software package for tracking stolen artwork that Peter was working on. And he found a bunch of files about transactions of Ian Gemberling's. Peter must have figured that something fishy was going on, and that made me suspicious about Ian. Apparently I was right. And I bet that you'll find that Ian had a finger in a lot more than this theft."

"That remains to be seen. Why, then, knowing what you knew, did you associate with Gemberling at all?"

"But I didn't know! I knew Peter had been looking at his transactions, but I didn't know why. See? It was *not* knowing that got me in trouble, not *knowing*." This was not coming out right. And I was frustrated, and feeling the aftereffects of the adrenaline rush. Heck, I'd just been kidnapped, found millions of dollars' worth of art the FBI was looking for, overpowered one man, stolen a truck, and made a dramatic getaway, so I figured I had every right to feel a bit frazzled. And why was the man who was supposed to care about me yelling at me now? I was an innocent bystander. And one who was getting pretty close to tears, and I hated that.

Thank goodness Matt knew me well enough to back off. "I'm sorry, Em," he said, his voice gentle. "The last week or two must have been hard on you."

"Damn it, don't be nice to me or I'll lose it," I said in a strangled voice.

He smiled. "Then why don't we wait until we get back to the police station to sort all this out? It's going to take a while."

And then in full view of his junior officer and Maddy, he pulled me close. I leaned against him, and his arms tightened around me.

"Better?" he said, into my hair.

"Definitely."

Chapter 27

❀

Matt drove back to the station with me sitting in the front seat in bemused silence. I was trying to sort out what had just happened, but I was still missing a lot of the pieces. Okay, maybe I dozed a bit too—being kidnapped can be wearying.

I could now recognize where the warehouse was. Ian had chosen well. It was inconspicuous, in a lightly traveled area, with convenient access to highways. Just what he needed to hide a multimillion-dollar cache of stolen artwork. Which meant he had scouted the area and made his arrangements well before the event. Had Maddy helped him? I still wasn't sure about her role. I had trouble seeing her running around the outskirts of town looking at drafty old buildings—not her style.

I finally roused myself to say something, since Matt wasn't volunteering anything. "What happens next?"

"A lot of paperwork," he replied.

Big help. "No, I mean, how do you sort out the crimes

and the criminals? You've got a murder, a major art theft, a kidnapping. I could probably come up with more if I tried."

"The murder is where I came in, so that's where I'm going to start."

I waited for him to add more, but he didn't. "Have you told Nat?"

"I called her. She's on her way to the station."

If anyone was going to come out of this happy, it would be Nat. She would recover the missing art and nab the culprit, and no doubt send her FBI career soaring.

We pulled into the parking lot at the station, and Matt turned off the engine. Before we could get out, I laid a hand on his arm. "Matt, are you going to let me sit in on this?"

He turned to look at me. "If you keep your mouth shut."

Same old line. "Matt, if I have something to add I'm going to say it. I've been involved with this from the beginning, if you recall."

"And look what happened," he said flatly.

"Well, excuse me for getting kidnapped. And don't be so high and mighty—I managed to get us out of the warehouse, didn't I? I was doing fine without you."

He grunted something inarticulate and climbed out of the car. I followed suit. So he was pissed at me—so what? If I hadn't poked around, Ian Gemberling would have made off with Peter's collection and most likely no one would ever have traced it.

Inside, the desk sergeant Mariana looked up at me and smiled. "Hi, Em!" Then catching the scowl on Matt's face, she quickly turned back to the stack of papers on her desk. I followed Matt down a corridor to an interrogation room. Matt pointed to a chair; I sat. After all, I didn't want to be petty.

Matt disappeared and a couple of minutes later returned with Maddy in tow. She was looking the worse for wear: Her blonde hair hung in greasy strings around her face; her clothes were grimy and rumpled. I assumed I didn't look much better. She took the chair Matt pointed to and sat, wringing her hands. She looked at me, then looked away.

Matt began. "Ms. Sheffield, at the moment you haven't been charged with any crimes. I would very much appreciate it if you could provide information that would help us to sort things out, and I assure you that your cooperation will be taken into account if charges are filed."

Maddy was having a hard time processing what Matt had just said, and I didn't feel like translating cop speak for her. "Wait a minute—you're *not* charging me with murder?" she bleated.

"No. You didn't kill Peter Ferguson."

"What?" This time Maddy and I were in synch. "But I stabbed him!" Maddy protested.

To my surprise, Matt ignored that statement. "Can you run through what happened on the day Peter died?"

Maddy seemed to have forgotten about having a lawyer, and I wasn't about to remind her. Of course, if she wasn't under arrest, then this was just a request for information, right? And I wanted to hear this.

"I went to Peter's house, to ask him about something." Her eyes glanced at me furtively. "Well, I wanted to know what was going on with Em. I knew she'd been to the house, alone, and I didn't see any need for that. It was my project, after all. I was in charge."

I held my tongue. I knew that Maddy was far more concerned with Peter's personal interest in me than in the pecking order for the project, although I'd never given her any reason to worry. Apparently she hadn't needed one.

"And we got into an argument. He laughed at me, told me I had no right to tell him what to do or who to see. I was angry, and I guess . . . I just lost it. I mean, I'd waited so long, and I hoped . . . Anyway, I was holding a piece of glass—I'd brought it along to check the color—and I just stabbed him. In the chest. And he stumbled backward and fell over, and then he didn't move."

"Go on," Matt urged, in a neutral tone.

"I . . . I panicked. I didn't know what to do. So I got out of the room and I called Ian."

Matt interrupted. "Hold on. What is your relationship with Ian Gemberling?"

"I've known him for years. Since college."

"And you knew he was in Tucson?"

"Of course. Peter bought his art from Ian, and Ian was here to see the house. We met to discuss . . . things."

"And I saw them together, last night," I added. "That's one thing that got me thinking. I could tell they knew each other pretty well."

Matt glared at me, and I sat back in my chair, silent once more.

"And he was the only person you could think of to call when you thought you had killed someone? Not 911?"

Maddy tried her helpless damsel look on Matt, but he wasn't buying it. Finally she shrugged. "I thought he would take care of it."

I fought back a scathing retort. Pretty little Maddy, so sure that a smart man would come along and make things right for her. But then, Ian had proved a bad choice, so maybe there was some justice.

Matt sighed, almost imperceptibly. "Then what?"

"Ian came to the house, and he brought a truck along with him, and a couple of guys. I thought . . . they were go- ing to take Peter's body away somewhere. Anyway, Ian came into the house, and he went into the big room where Peter was lying, and then he came out and told me to go home. So I did."

"But you came back!" I couldn't keep my mouth shut, apparently. "That's when you accused me of killing Peter."

"I couldn't stand not knowing. I thought if I just stopped

by, like it was any other day . . . Oh, I don't know what I was thinking, all right? Maybe it wasn't true. Maybe I'd imagined the whole thing. But then the police were there, and you were there, and Peter's body was still there, and I just said what came into my head."

Never mind that she had accused me of murder and messed up my life. I tried to feel some sympathy, for about two seconds. "But the art was gone," I said flatly.

"Well, I didn't know that then, did I?"

Huh? Did this woman never think things through?

Matt intervened. "Ian Gemberling took the art with him, in that truck you mentioned. We have a witness."

Maddy didn't look very surprised. "But what about Peter?"

"Ah, yes," Matt said. "The autopsy results show that you did stab him, and that he hit his head when he fell, knocking him out."

Realization flashed over Maddy's face, making her look ten years older. "You mean, he wasn't dead? I was sure . . . ."

"No, just unconscious. And in case you're wondering, the blow to the head wouldn't have killed him either. There were, in fact, two stab wounds. The first one wasn't very deep, but then he fell and was knocked out. It was the second, deeper stab wound that killed him. He would have bled to death in minutes after that."

"Ian," Maddy whispered. "That bastard!" she said in a much stronger voice. "He used me! He let me go on thinking that I'd killed Peter, just so I'd keep quiet, when all the time it was him. And after everything I did for him!"

Matt interrupted. "Before you say anything else, you might want to see about that lawyer."

Maddy was angry now. "I don't care! I'll waive whatever you want, and I'll tell you what you want to know, just as long as Ian doesn't get away with this."

I had to say that this was interesting to watch. Maddy

had morphed before our very eyes from a frail damsel to a virago, and she was about to throw Ian Gemberling to the wolves.

"You waive the right to have an attorney present?" Matt said carefully.

"Yes. Whatever. Look, here's the story. I told you, I've known Ian since college. My mother helped him get started in his business—she thinks she's a real patroness of the arts. Then she steered Peter to Ian when Peter started collecting. Ian and I, we've kept in touch. He's done very well for himself, hasn't he?"

"A bit too well, maybe?" I just had to add something here.

Maddy looked at me when she answered. "I began to think that too, after a while. But it really wasn't my business—I mean, he'd paid my mother back years ago. And then I moved to Tucson, and Peter moved here too, and then Ian contacted me, and Peter got in touch with me. Oh, I know it was just our mothers trying to help, but I didn't care if it meant I could see Peter."

"Go on," Matt said, not unkindly.

I was busy rearranging the puzzle pieces in my head. Maddy's mother . . . Ian . . . Peter and his mother. It took me a moment to work through it. Ian knew Maddy's mother knew Peter's mother, so Ian planted the seed that got Maddy into Peter's house here in Tucson. "So I bet it was Ian's idea to get your mother to ask Peter's mother to do a big favor for you. Just being a good friend and all."

Maddy was still talking. "Something like that. Oh, I know my limitations—I knew I'd never get a commission like that without some help, but I wasn't about to look a gift horse in the mouth."

Matt and I exchanged a glance at that, but there didn't seem to be any reason to elaborate. I knew Maddy had wanted Peter; Peter had not wanted Maddy. He'd gone along with hiring Maddy to make their mothers happy, but he'd made sure she had backup for the artistic side—me. It galled Maddy, but she wasn't going to blow the deal just because I was part of it.

Unfortunately Peter had shown an interest in me, even if it was no more than intellectual, which must have been salt in the wound to Maddy.

And Ian Gemberling had set up the whole thing. I had to admire his planning, his foresight—and his ruthlessness. "He wanted access to the house, wanted you to get around the security system, which he knew would be first-rate," I said.

"I guess so. We hadn't worked all that out yet. I know he met with Peter at the house—after all, he had sold works to Peter, so that would have seemed normal. You saw him there too."

But something about her logic didn't seem right to me. "Maddy, you said you loved Peter. Why on earth did you go along with Ian to rip Peter off?"

Anger flared in her eyes. "Because Peter cared more about those stupid glass panels than about me. He was just being kind to me, I could tell. And then Ian came along and started hinting about taking the glass, and I thought maybe if the glass was stolen I could be there for Peter."

How stupid could this woman be? No doubt Ian had been manipulating her from the start, for his own ends, but did she really think she could comfort Peter for the loss of his magnificent collection?

Matt interrupted. "Can we please get back to the theft? Why couldn't Ian take care of the security system himself?"

"I don't know. We didn't discuss all the details about whatever he was planning, believe me. We thought we had plenty of time. Although he did ask me about finding a trucker."

I hate it when anyone says "believe me"—it usually

meant they're lying. So that was how Chas had come into the picture. Poor Chas, trying to get his business off the ground, and probably willing to look the other way about his cargo if the price was right. But he hadn't counted on getting mixed up with murder and kidnapping. He'd just been in the wrong place at the wrong time.

"But if Ian had something planned, the whole thing fell apart when I . . . stabbed Peter."

"Of course! He had to move fast, and that's why he brought in the local talent—he couldn't wait." I looked at Matt to see if he agreed. He was looking at me with a mixture of frustration and amusement on his face.

"Do go on, Em. You seem to have things under control."

Sarcasm didn't sit well on him—that was my territory. I decided to ignore it. "Matt, you have Ian Gemberling in custody?"

"Yes, of course."

"You going to talk to him?"

"Would you prefer I deputize you and let you do it?"

"What? Oh, you're kidding. But I do want to hear his story."

The door to the hall opened, and Nat appeared in time to hear that. "So do I. I gather you've had a busy day or two, Chief."

If she said anything else, I missed it, because Cam had followed her into the room. Him I could throw myself on, so I did. "Cam! What are you doing here?"

He was prevented from answering because I had plastered myself to him. He hugged me hard then backed off. "Allison called me when you went missing, so I called Matt, and then I hopped on a plane. I ran into Nat in the lobby here. But I think I've got some information that will help."

I beamed at Matt. "Then let's go talk to Ian, shall we? If that's all right with you, Chief."

Matt had risen when Nat and Cam appeared, and now he

held up his hand. "Slow down, all of you. There are proce-
dures to be followed here, if you want this case to hold up in
court. Ian Gemberling has not yet made any statement, nor
has he asked for an attorney. But he is still a suspect, and as
such it is entirely inappropriate for all of you to participate
in interviewing him. That includes Ms. Sheffield here. So
here's what we're going to do. Ms. Sheffield, I'm going to
have to ask you to wait here. Nat, you'll come with me. Em,
Cam, you can observe, but I don't want you in the room.
Everybody got it?"

I didn't like being shut out, but I could see his point. Ian
was smart, and given half a chance he would weasel out of
any involvement here, protesting his innocence. I was surprised when Cam spoke up.

"Matt, I think I need to be there. I've been working on
something with Nat, and I think it has direct relevance to
this case."

Matt gave him a long look before nodding. "All right.
But stick to the point. Em, I guess that means you're going
to be all by yourself."

And didn't he just love that? Still, at least I'd get to hear
the story. "That will be just fine, Chief," I said demurely.
He could pay for it later.

"Then let's go talk to Ian."

Chapter 28

❧

Matt stuck me in a small room with a couple of uncomfortable-looking chairs and a television monitor. I was so dazed that it took me a moment to realize that it was one of those places I had seen in movies, and that the main on-screen attraction would be Ian Gemberling. That was cool, for about twelve seconds. I sat and watched as Matt, Nat, and Cam filed into the interrogation room, and then a few moments later, Ian Gemberling was ushered in by another officer. He didn't look particularly rattled by the adventures of the day. But then, he'd been handling millions of dollars of stolen art, so he must think that this little arrest problem in backwater Tucson was small potatoes. I settled in to watch the show.

Matt began the process. "Ian Gemberling? Or should I say, Morris Finkelstein?"

A brief flash of distaste crossed Ian's face. "Gemberling. I made the change legally."

"Thank you." Matt made a note on a piece of paper. "Are you acquainted with Natalie Karamanlis?"

"I don't believe I've had the privilege," Ian said calmly.

Nat was looking at him as though he were a particularly yummy piece of pastry and she hadn't had dessert. "I'm with the FBI's Art Crime Team, Mr. Gemberling."

Ian nodded in apparent approval. "How interesting. I've heard about your unit—an excellent idea. It's disgraceful how poorly the investigation of art thefts has been managed until now. I hope your group will rectify that."

"Oh, I think I can promise that." Nat smiled, showing a lot of teeth.

Ian sat relaxed in his chair, looking from Matt to Nat, seated at opposite ends of the table. Cam had pulled up a chair next to Nat, but apparently he didn't merit Ian's attention. "What can I help you with?" Ian said calmly.

Matt took his time in responding. "Mr. Gemberling, you are under arrest for the murder of Peter Ferguson. I'm sure Agent Karamanlis will have additional charges regarding the theft of Ferguson's art collection. I need to advise you of your rights," and he launched into the official warning that we've all heard on television a million times.

Ian's reaction surprised me. "Chief Lundgren, I will waive my right to have an attorney present. I have nothing to hide, and I am eager to help you clear up this tragic situation." He adjusted his expression to reflect the seriousness of the moment. "Peter's death is a great loss. He was a fine man, and a connoisseur. Of course, you are aware that he purchased several items from me over the course of the past few years."

Funny, I noticed he had completely ignored the murder accusation. Matt glanced once at Nat, who shrugged. My impression was that they were quite happy to let Ian hang himself.

"Yes, we're aware of that. You don't seem troubled by the murder charge." Good, Matt had noticed it too.

"Because it's patently ridiculous. Why would I kill the man? It would be like killing the goose that lays the golden eggs. Peter was amassing an outstanding collection of glass pieces, and it was a privilege to assist him. On what evidence do you make this absurd accusation?"

"And you have no knowledge of how Peter Ferguson died?"

"None whatsoever."

The arrogance of the man was astonishing. Did he really think he could talk his way out of a murder charge?

"Are you sure you don't want a lawyer, Mr. Gemberling?" Matt pressed.

"I really don't see the need. I'm sure there's a reasonable explanation for what you've been told."

Matt said, "Madelyn Sheffield has stated that you asked her to help you gain access to Ferguson's home in order to steal his art objects."

Ian gave a short laugh. "Maddy. Well, that explains it. I've known Madelyn for years, as no doubt she has told you. She has always been . . . imaginative, shall we say? And a touch self-aggrandizing. I think her own life has disappointed her, so she feels compelled to embellish it, to inject some drama. What does she claim I have done?"

The man was smooth; I had to give him credit for that. He sounded so convincing. If I hadn't known what I did, I might have bought his line. As it was, I was in a position to watch Nat's face, and her eyes gleamed with almost feral intensity. She was clearly enjoying the moment.

Matt had assumed the role of straight man, sticking to the standard script. "Mr. Gemberling, you've been inside Peter Ferguson's house?"

"Of course I have. He showed me what he was planning for the installation of his glass pieces, and I offered a few suggestions. It really was an outstanding setting for what he had in mind. So if you're wondering how my fingerprints came to be there, there's a perfectly innocent explanation."

Matt made another note. Matt was not generally a note taker, and I wondered if he was making meaningless doodles just to draw out the interrogation. If he was hoping to make Ian Gemberling sweat, so far he hadn't succeeded. "Do you know how Madelyn Sheffield came to be chosen to assist Ferguson with his installation?"

Ian crossed one leg over the other. "Ah. Well, sir, I confess that I had a small hand in that—my good deed. I knew that Maddy was struggling with her business here, and I thought that a commission like this would be a real boost. But, to be frank, I also knew that her talents were—how shall I put it?—insufficient for the scope of the project, so I did a little research and suggested to Peter that another local artisan be called in to help her."

"Emmeline Dowell," Matt said.

"Yes, that's the name. Very talented, in a minor way. Certainly more so than Maddy. And, of course, Peter knew he could call on me if things went awry."

Talented in a minor way? I didn't harbor any illusions about my abilities, but I didn't like hearing them dissed in such a contemptuous tone. Patronizing creep!

Matt looked down at his pad. "So let me summarize. You contend that you had no involvement in Peter Ferguson's death?"

Ian sat up straight again and placed his hands flat on the table in front of him. "Exactly. If Maddy says otherwise, I'm afraid she's deluded."

"She claims that she called you, and you arrived at Peter Ferguson's house after she had stabbed him."

"Pure fiction, I assure you."

Matt almost smiled. "Mr. Gemberling, we have a witness who states that you hired him to help remove Ferguson's artworks from the house and transfer them to a truck owned by Chas Jenson. Let me remind you that Chas Jenson is also in our custody."

Was Ian looking a little paler? But his tone was as smooth as ever. "I'm sorry, Officer, but I have no idea what you're talking about."

Matt studied the man in front of him. "Let's take another tack. How do you explain the events of this afternoon?"

This time Ian was not so quick to answer. "You mean, at the warehouse?"

"Yes. Ms. Dowell claims that she was forcibly seized by Chas Jenson, whom you hired, and brought to the warehouse against her will. While she was there, Madelyn Sheffield arrived, the two of you argued, and you threw Ms. Sheffield into the truck. You were overheard making plans with the trucker to dispose of both of them."

Ian sat back in his chair once again, and I could swear that his expression held pity. I was beginning to wonder if he and Maddy had taken acting classes together at that small college in Kansas. "Officer, why would I do such a thing? I have an extremely successful business in Los Angeles. I came to Tucson to visit a client—one whom I regarded as a friend—and to touch base with a college classmate. And now you're telling me that I'm a suspect in the murder of the first, and that the second is one of my accusers. I suggest that perhaps you should take Maddy's accusations with a grain of salt."

"And Ms. Dowell's?" Matt said with great calm.

"Ms. Dowell is no doubt angry at me because I suggested that I might be able to open a few doors for her, assist her in distributing her wares, and then I withdrew my offer. As I became more familiar with the scope of her work, I came to find it rather pedestrian."

Matt had been smart to stick me in here. If I had been in the room I would have been tempted to hit Ian.

"She said you offered her a show in Los Angeles."

"Oh, come now, do you find that credible? I've exhib-ited some of the major names in the contemporary arts, and I'm afraid she is simply not in their league."

"So you're saying that both women are lying because they are trying to get back at you for dismissing them as second-rate talents?"

"It appears so."

"Let me get this straight. You're telling me that your old friend Madelyn Sheffield, the trucker Chas Jenson, the Tucson thug we arrested the other day, and Emmeline Dowell are *all* lying about your activities?"

Ian sat up straighter in his chair and assumed a sincere expression. "I have no idea what they have been telling you, but I assure you I am in no way involved in either the death of Peter Ferguson or the theft of his artworks."

Matt didn't respond to Ian's implied question. "Then tell me, Mr. Gemberling, if this is all a fabrication, what were you doing at that warehouse this afternoon?"

I could almost see the gears turning in Ian's head. He'd done a good job so far, cobbling together a story or evading the questions. And I had to admit, knowing Maddy as I did, I could have bought what Ian said about her. But Ian was beginning to sense undercurrents in the room. I leaned for-ward to see what his next move would be.

"You spoke of a trucker. Maddy uses him, and after Pe-ter's death he came to me and said he had some information about the missing pieces of art, and was I interested? For a price, of course. I played along, because I was concerned for the safety of the glass pieces."

"It didn't occur to you to contact the police or the FBI?"

"Frankly, Officer, I didn't think you'd react quickly enough. By the time I had finished laying out my bona fides and explaining the situation, they could have been on a boat to Hong Kong. And the FBI's track record in recovering stolen art items is less than stellar."

I glanced quickly at Nat's face on the screen: She looked positively gleeful.

"And the other men with you?" Matt went on. "The ones with guns?"

"I thought it prudent to enlist some colleagues. They've worked for me before, and they are expert shippers of art objects. There are times when that job requires them to carry weapons, which are, I might add, fully licensed."

Matt sat back as well and looked at Ian for several seconds. "I'm impressed, Mr. Gemberling. You have an explanation for everything. Madelyn Sheffield is unstable, Em Dowell is trying to get back at you for dismissing her as second-rate, the trucker was looking to sell you information about the theft, and you're the hero in this little farce, sweeping in with your hired guns and saving the day—or at least the art. Have I got that right?"

Ian's face hardened. "Officer, I resent your insinuations. You have not presented any hard evidence of my involvement in either the murder or the theft, relying instead on the wild accusations of questionable individuals. I am a legitimate art dealer, and I have no need to engage in such illegal activities. Peter was my friend, and I thought Madelyn was. If you have any substantial evidence, I'd like to hear it before I call my lawyer."

"Mr. Gemberling," Nat purred, "it might interest you to know that your 'friend' Peter had serious doubts about your honesty."

"Excuse me?" Ian favored her with an icy glance.

Nat smiled sweetly. "Oh, you're very good. Very smart, very careful. But so was Peter. Tell me, did he discuss with you the software he was working on at the time of his death?"

The blank expression on Ian's face was answer enough.

"Well, then, let me fill you in," Nat continued. "All of your transactions with Peter were completely aboveboard and legitimate. But let me suggest that perhaps you had a longer-range goal in dealing with Peter. You might have thought that he was a man with a lot of money on his hands, one who was willing to pour it into a nice trophy art collection. You might even have credited him with some taste— no doubt shaped and guided by you. You helped Peter Ferguson assemble a world-class collection of glass pieces, and he paid well for it, and you received nice fees. But I think you may have had a second motive: You planned to steal it from the beginning."

"That's preposterous!" Ian sputtered. "You have no right to make such an accusation."

"Oh, I think I do, Mr. Gemberling." Nat's voice was growing steely. "You made one mistake in your planning, although I think that can be excused since Maddy forced your hand by stabbing Peter, and you had to accelerate your schedule. But if you'd just thought to take his computer with you, you might have gotten away with it."

Ian said nothing but raised one eyebrow, questioning.

"Unfortunately for you, you left it behind, and I gave it to a consultant to look at. Oh, I'm sorry, I haven't introduced my consultant." Nat nodded toward Cam. "This is Cameron Dowell. He's a software designer and a long-term admirer of Peter Ferguson's work. By the way, he's also Em's brother."

Was it my imagination, or had Ian grown a shade paler?

"Cam took a look at the contents of the laptop, at my request, and he found some very interesting things. Perhaps the most interesting was a computer program that Peter had been working on for some time. It was intended to provide a means of identifying and tracking stolen artworks, and from what we've seen, it's far superior to anything that the government law enforcement agencies are currently using."

Ian swallowed. "I'm happy to hear that. I respected Peter's abilities, and I'm sure this will be a valuable tool. But what relevance does that have here?"

"Peter was almost finished with his programming, and he wanted to test it. He chose items from your gallery—I assume with your permission? We found the files on his computer. Did his interest make you nervous, Mr. Gemberling?"

Yes, Ian was definitely paler now.

Nat went on, savoring every moment. "And then he started looking a little further. It seems that a surprising number of works that passed through your hands have subsequently been stolen. Maybe not immediately, or from the person to whom you sold it, but eventually. And many of those items have never resurfaced in the art market. Would you care to comment, Mr. Gemberling?"

"I think I'd like to call my lawyer now."

"I think that would be advisable, Mr. Gemberling."

Matt and Nat smiled at each other across the expanse of table. Ian looked miserable.

I felt great.

Chapter 29

❧

The "great" part lasted for a little while but was soon swamped by exhaustion and boredom. When you watch cop shows on TV, you get to see the high points: the action, the drama. In the real world there's a heck of a lot of paperwork, and that takes time. I was kind of at loose ends: Matt had brought me here, and I had no transport. I wanted to wait for Cam and see what his story was, but he was still tied up with Nat. Matt and Nat obviously had to confer about charges and then determine what to do with their prisoners. Me—I had nothing to do but wait. I settled myself in a chair and dozed intermittently. I figured I was allowed. After all, it had been a rather harrowing day.

I was awakened some time later by a hand on my shoulder, and looked up to see Cam. "Hey, Em, want to go home?"

"About time," I grumbled. "Everything wrapped up? What time is it?"

"For now. And it's after five. You look beat."

I stood up, not very gracefully, and stretched to work

the kinks out of my joints. "Good, because I am. It's been a long day. Have you got a ride?"

"Nat'll drop us off. Then she's coming back to talk to Matt."

As if on cue, Nat appeared. She looked very pleased with herself. "You two ready?"

"Definitely. You look happy. Did either of our friends say anything else?"

Nat shook her head. "Not yet, but it doesn't matter. They are so busted! And I'll let Cam fill you in on the rest of it. Looks like our Ian has been a busy boy."

I knew Ian was too good to be true. But since he'd called me second-rate to my face—well, not exactly, since I'd been watching it on-screen, but close enough—I was going to relish his downfall. "Let's go before I fall asleep again."

Riding home through the busy early evening streets, I felt as though I had been gone for a week, not just hours. Maybe I was getting old, but it was hard to keep adjusting my concept of reality where all this was concerned. Maddy was a flake; Maddy was an accomplice to murder and larceny. Ian was a respected member of his profession; Ian was a thieving scumbag who had been systematically exploiting his clients for years. I was a genius; I was a hack. Too much to handle. I took another short nap.

I woke up again when we reached my building. Cam helped me out of the car, then waved to Nat as she pulled away. I looked up my stairs, which seemed to go on for miles, but somehow we arrived at the top. Before Cam could pull out his key, the door opened and I had a second to take in the fact that Allison was standing there before I was mobbed by two enthusiastic dogs. We did a silly dance, trying to get two humans through the door while two dogs insisted on wrapping themselves around our legs. It took a few moments for the excitement to subside. Well, the doggy excitement anyway: When they released me, Allison took over, hugging me hard.

"Oh, Em, I didn't know what to do. You weren't there, and you'd left no message, and then I found your bag so I knew you didn't have your keys. All I could think of was to call Cam, and he said to call Matt, so I did."

I hugged her back. "You did good. And thank you. I wondered when somebody would notice I was missing. And thanks for looking after the pups."

"Well, I knew they'd be alone, and I couldn't just go home and worry myself sick about you, now could I? I was glad that Cam got here so quickly."

Cam was still holding my arm, as though I was about to fall over. I laid my hand over his, then pushed him gently away. "Hey, guys, what I need right now is a shower and some food. And then I'll try to fill you in on my side, and maybe Cam can tell us what he's been up to." I looked at him. "I gather the FBI has been keeping him busy."

He laughed. "I think we can cobble a meal together from what you've got. You staying, Allison?"

"If you want. I don't want to be in the way."

"Nonsense," I said firmly. "You're family, and you deserve to hear the story. Work it out, you two, because I'm headed for the shower." I did, with Fred and Gloria hard on my heels. I had the feeling they knew something had happened, and they weren't about to let me out of their sight any time soon.

I spent a glorious time washing away the events of the day. Being wrapped in that cruddy blanket and tossed around in the truck had not been much fun, but hot water put that right. And I was ravenous; I couldn't even remember my last meal. I emerged from the bathroom wrapped in a huge towel, but as I darted toward my bedroom I caught a glimpse of Cam and Allison, and there wasn't any light showing between them. I guessed there was no reason to get dressed in a hurry—dinner might be a bit delayed.

But by the time I dressed and ambled back to the living area, there were pots rattling on the stove with good smells emerging from them. I took a seat at the table to watch, and Cam handed me a cold beer without asking. I accepted it gratefully.

I couldn't have named what they set in front of me, but it was delicious. Of course, under the circumstances, stewed tire might have been delicious. I filled them in on what had happened to me, and Allison made all the appropriate horrified noises. I even included Ian's unkind remarks about my skills, which still rankled.

"Oh, Em, I'm so sorry," Allison said. "That show would have been a wonderful opportunity for you."

I snorted. "That show was never anything more than a smoke screen. Ian just wanted to distract me from thinking about what else was going on. Face it, he was right. I'm just not a top-tier talent." When Allison started to protest, I held up my hand. "No, I'm not being modest, just honest with myself. Look, I like what I do. I'm a competent craftsperson, but I don't delude myself that I'm going to step into Dale Chihuly's shoes. I'm happy, and I make a fair living doing what I like to do. What more could I want?"

"Hear, hear!" Cam raised his bottle of beer to me. "Well, if nothing else has come of this, you've made Nat very happy. Looks like the FBI is going to have a new toy to play with, if they can get the rights to it, and Nat gets the privilege of taking it home to them."

I peeked at Allison, but she didn't twitch when Cam mentioned Nat. All must be right in their little world. I smiled at him, because he understood what I had been trying to say: I had made the effort to please our parents, following a path I thought they would approve of, but it just hadn't worked. So then I had done what I wanted, and it had brought me to this place, this moment. And I was content with that.

I hadn't expected to hear from Matt, knowing he would be caught up with administrative necessities. And he knew I had Cam to hold my hand, should I have nightmares. Ha! I slept like a log and woke up ready to face bears. Even so, Cam was already up when I came out of my bedroom. I threw myself in a chair, and he presented me with a cup of hot coffee.

"So, baby brother, what news? You seem to have enjoyed unraveling Peter's computer."

He smiled, more to himself than to me. "Let me tell you, it was a privilege to go through his code. Peter Ferguson was a genius. And there is such an elegant simplicity to what he's done with the program . . . ." I tuned out when Cam lapsed into computerese, but I got the picture. The program was solid and simple enough for anyone to use. And it was clear that Cam had enjoyed his assignment. Eventually he ran out of steam. "Anyway, Nat's over the moon about it."

"That's great—at least something positive has come out of all this. Too bad Peter won't be around to enjoy it." We both fell silent for a moment in honor of the late, great Peter Ferguson. "I wonder who ends up with the glass collection?"

Cam shrugged. "Probably the kids, but who knows if they'll want it. Nat's going to look into all that, since she wants clear title to the software."

"Ah." I chewed pensively on my English muffin. "Cam, about you and Allison . . ."

"We're fine."

I looked at him squarely. "I know, it's not my business, but you've been a bit, I don't know, at cross-purposes lately?"

He nodded, staring at his coffee. "You're right. I guess I wanted too much, too fast, and I didn't want to give Allison time to sort things out. But we're good. How about you and Matt?"

I sighed. Cam had every right to turn the tables, since I'd been poking into his love life, but I still wasn't comfortable answering. "I . . . don't know. I'm kind of pissed at him at the moment, because he tried to keep me on the sidelines, and look what happened."

"Em, he's just trying to do his job, and like it or not, you're a civilian."

"Well, so are you, pal, and *you* got to play with the big boys. Girls. Whatever. And I understand his position, really, I do. But this involved me—my life, my work. He shouldn't have shut me out."

Cam stood up and started collecting the dishes. "In the words of a wise woman, that's something you two have to work out."

"Gee, thanks. Listen, you going to hang around for a while?"

"The weekend, at least."

I stood up too. "Good. Because I'd better get down to the shop and see what I've missed."

Nessa was in this morning, and looked up and beamed when I walked into the shop. "My, you seem to have had some excitement."

"Tell me about it." I sighed. "I could do without it. But at least things should calm down now. Good thing—I'm way behind, and I really need to make some glass pieces."

"You go right ahead, dear. I'm sure I can handle things out here."

"You're a pal. Look, how about lunch? I can give you all the gory details then. Allison will be in later, won't she?"

"Yes, and lunch would be lovely."

I went to the studio and immersed myself in what I liked to do best, interrupted only by a phone call from Matt. "Em, will you have dinner with me? We need to talk."

Well, duh. "All right," I said neutrally.

"Great. I'll pick you up around seven, if that works for you." Was that relief I heard in his voice?

"Fine. See you then."

And I went back to work. I wasn't going to stew over what Matt might or might not say. I was just going to wait and see what unfolded. In the meantime, I had hot glass to work with.

Matt arrived promptly at seven. I was ready, after an agonizing internal debate about whether I should dress up or not. Was this an important dinner? A special dinner? Was he going to lecture me or apologize? I had no idea. I opted for dressy, at least by my standards—heck, Tucson didn't care.

He wasn't providing any clues. "Shall we go?"

"Let me get my coat." If he was going to play it formal, so was I.

We made meaningless chitchat as we drove to the restaurant. We were shown to a quiet table, and after Matt ordered a bottle of wine, the waiter retreated discreetly. Matt snagged the conversational ball then. "Em, I'm sorry. And I know you're upset, and you probably have a right to be. But please look at it from my side: I'm the chief of police here. I have to set a standard for the department, and everyone was watching."

The waiter appeared with a chilled bottle, Matt tasted, nodded, and the waiter filled our glasses. I waited silently until he withdrew.

So far the script held no surprises. Now it was my turn. "I do understand, Matt. And I certainly didn't want to find myself in the middle of another murder—the last one was plenty. But the fact remains that I *was* in it, in more ways than one. And the fact that you were trying to protect me, or protect your professional integrity, nearly got me killed."

"I know." He really did look miserable. "But I had no way of knowing that would happen. Look, I appreciate what you did. If you hadn't had your suspicions about Maddy and Ian, I can't say what would have happened. And to tell you the truth, you scared me to death when you disappeared."

I took a deep breath. What did I want? I wasn't planning to join the police force or set up shop as a PI. So what was my problem? That Matt found it so easy to shut me out of the professional side of his life? That he had treated me as though the expertise I possessed was insignificant and ir- relevant, when I knew and had told him it wasn't? And was this an argument that I could win, or that was even worth fighting?

"Matt, I appreciate that you need to keep your job and . . . us separate. That's fine. I guess I'm angry that you dismissed me, when I did have information that you could have used. You shut me out, and that was your loss. Maybe it's policy not to involve outsiders, but you could have used my intelligence to your own advantage. And we both would have benefited."

To his credit, Matt did not become defensive; he actually took time to think about what I had said. Maybe that was progress. "Em, I see that now, even if it's a little late. Look, my ex never wanted to hear about my job. Maybe that was one of the problems with our marriage. But that was the rou- tine we fell into. I know you're different, and you were right about this case. How many more times do I have to apolo- gize?"

I could be magnanimous in victory. "I think we're square. Look, I promise to try to avoid any further murders, as long as you promise to share as much as you can if, heaven forbid, this happens again. Good enough?"

He grinned then. "Okay." Then his eyes gleamed. "By the way, Nat passed on to me a little piece of information that might interest you."

I took a sip of wine. "What?"

"As you can guess, she's tracked down Peter's will, and she's been consulting various lawyers about who now owns the rights to Peter's software, because her unit really, really wants it. Luckily Peter's will is up-to-date. And he did make provisions for this software."

"That's good, isn't it?"

"Yes. He made it clear that he wanted this program to be put to the broadest possible use, so it looks like the FBI will get it. But there's one more really interesting provision in Ferguson's will."

Matt was having far too much fun with this, and he had certainly piqued my curiosity. "Okay, pal, spit it out."

"He established and endowed a fund to provide what you might call a finder's fee—a reward for people who provide material assistance or information in recovering stolen artworks. It will be administered by an independent board of directors, not the FBI. There's a good chance that you might qualify."

"That sounds nice. What does that mean, out here in the real world?"

"Peter specified that the fee should be a percentage of the fair market value of the recovered property—a flat ten percent." He sat back and waited for me to work this out.

This was a simple calculation. If Peter's collection was worth, conservatively, $3 million, then 10 percent would be . . . $300,000. Even net of taxes and such, that was a nice piece of change. *Oh, wow.*

A Brief History of Stained Glass

❈

The techniques of medieval stained glass were described around 1125 by the German monk Theophilus, who set forth both the philosophy underlying the use of glass and the technology that fascinated him. He laid out the steps for constructing a window: Mark the dimensions, select the colors, cut the pieces and fit them together, enclose the pieces with lead cames, and solder them together before setting into a wooden frame. Relatively few changes have occurred since.

The glass itself was colored by the addition of metallic oxides, creating intense blues, greens, and reds. In some cases the color became too dark to permit light to pass, so an alternate technique of "flashing" a thin layer of color over clear glass emerged. The glass was blown and shaped into sheets that were then cut into smaller pieces. Details such as faces, drapery folds, or inscriptions could be added with paint, after which the pieces would be baked in a kiln to make the paint fuse with the glass.

MEDIEVAL GLASS

Stained glass was used for windows as early as the first century AD; examples have been found in the ruins of Roman villas in Pompeii. But stained glass took on new importance with the surge of church construction in the Middle Ages, especially the tenth through twelfth centuries, when glass was used as pictorial shorthand to illustrate scenes and stories from the Bible for a largely illiterate population.

This form of glass art reached its peak with the Gothic cathedrals of the eleventh and twelfth centuries, when a better understanding of architectural structure allowed the walls to be opened up and filled with radiant glass panels.

THE NINETEENTH-CENTURY REVIVAL

A revived version of Gothic architecture became the dominant style in the middle and later nineteenth century, accompanied by a resurgence of the use of stained glass. This movement inspired the Englishman William Morris, who created his own firm in 1861 to provide home decoration. Stained glass was prominent in his workshop from the beginning.

At a time when mass-production techniques made glass available to a much wider market, Morris and his colleagues of the era believed that machine production was degrading and resulted in mass quantities of inferior goods. As a result, he became obsessed with craftsmanship and detail, as seen in many of the windows of his time. His example inspired a number of American craftsmen as well.

ART NOUVEAU

Art Nouveau, or "new art," emerged from Europe and America at the end of the nineteenth century, a lingering reaction to the mass-produced designs of the Industrial Revolution as well as to Victorian traditions. The style, inspired by natural forms, emphasized sensuous curves and iridescent colors.

John La Farge and Louis Comfort Tiffany vie for credit for the invention of opalescent glass in the 1880s. Tiffany was one of the leading proponents of the new style, but he was also an innovator in glassmaking. He founded the Tiffany Glass Company in 1885 to complement his interior decorating company, and patented a new type of colored, opalescent glass known as "favrile."

Tiffany is perhaps best known today for his glass lampshades, in which he combined the rich colors of his glass with intricate cutting and often layered glass to achieve varied effects. He developed a technique of using copper foil to hold the glass pieces together, rather than the traditional, heavier lead cames, which enabled him to take advantage of the new electric lighting.

GLASS IN THE TWENTIETH CENTURY

William Morris's ideas reached the United States through the Greene brothers on the West Coast, Gustav Stickley on the East Coast, and Frank Lloyd Wright in the Midwest. Wright popularized the Prairie Style and brought about a new integration of buildings with their landscape and furnishings. His open interiors were a perfect setting for glass doors and windows.

Wright emphasized simple, geometric patterns—parallel lines and smaller squares or circles, set with minimal leading. At least one of the houses he designed has over 100 leaded windows, and over the course of his career he designed more than 4,500 windows for 160 buildings, both private and public.

Recipes

❊

Em's Foolproof Slow-Cooker Chicken Chili

3 boneless, skinless chicken breasts
1 large white onion, chopped
3 ancho chiles with seeds and veins removed, cut into
    strips or pieces
2 teaspoons oregano
2 large cloves garlic (you may leave them whole or chop
    them)
salt and black pepper to taste
4 cups chicken broth
1 15-ounce can beans (you may use black, white, or what-
    ever you have)
Fresh cilantro, chopped

In a slow cooker, put the chicken, chopped onion, ancho
chiles, oregano, garlic, and salt and pepper. Pour in the

chicken broth to cover. Cook at low heat for 4 hours (more or less).

Remove the chicken breasts, shred them (when they're cool enough to handle), and return them to the cooker. Add the beans and continue cooking for another hour (more or less).

Just before serving, add the cilantro and stir.

Serve over cooked rice. Serves 4.

The beauty of this dish is its flexibility. You can use pork instead of chicken, or increase the proportion of meat or beans. If you want more heat, add more dried chiles or a different kind of chile, or throw in a dash of Tabasco sauce. You can stir in heavy cream or sour cream at the end. It's very hard to mess up!

Stained-Glass Cookies

For the dough:

½ cup (¼ pound) butter
½ cup solid vegetable shortening
1½ cups sugar
½ cup sour cream
1 teaspoon vanilla
1 egg
3¾ cups all-purpose flour
½ teaspoon baking soda
½ teaspoon salt

For the "glass" centers:

**30 to 40 hard candies in different flavors and colors
(LifeSavers will work)**

Preheat oven to 350 degrees.

In the large bowl of an electric mixer, beat butter, shortening, and sugar until creamy. Beat in the sour cream, vanilla, and egg.

In another bowl, sift together flour, baking soda, and salt. Add gradually to butter mixture and blend thoroughly.

Cover dough tightly with plastic wrap and refrigerate overnight.

Divide the dough into quarters. Working with one portion at a time (keep the others refrigerated), roll out on a floured board to about ¼-inch thick. Cut out with a large cookie cutter (round is easiest, but you may use other ornamental forms). Transfer cut cookies to a greased baking sheet, leaving about 1 inch between them. Cut out the centers with a smaller cutter (again, any shape you like, but leave at least half an inch around the outside of the cookie).

If you wish to hang these cookies, make a small hole in the cookie through which you can thread a ribbon later.

Place the hard candies, by color, in small plastic bags. Place a towel over the bags and crush the candy by hitting it with a mallet or rolling pin.

Fill the holes in the cookies with the crushed candy, then bake in preheated oven for 10 to 15 minutes, or until the cookies are lightly browned and the candy has melted.

Let the cookies cool completely, then twist gently to loosen from the cookie sheet and slide off.

Store in a single layer in an airtight container.

Makes about 2½ dozen, depending on size.